THE
WITCHES
AT THE
END
OF THE
WORLD

THE
WITCHES
AT THE
END
OF THE
WORLD

CHELSEA IVERSEN

Copyright © 2023 by Chelsea Iversen
Cover and internal design © 2023 by Sourcebooks
Cover design by Lisa Marie Pompilio
Internal design by Laura Boren/Sourcebooks
Internal images © LisaAlisa_ill/istock

Published by Sourcebooks Landmark, an imprint of Sourcebooks
P.O. Box 4410, Naperville, Illinois 60567-4410
(630) 961-3900
sourcebooks.com

Cataloging-in-Publication Data is on file with the Library of Congress.

Printed and bound in the United States of America.
VP 10 9 8 7 6 5 4 3 2 1

For sisters everywhere, especially mine.

FINNMARK, NORWAY
AUTUMN, 1677

Minna

For the living, death is a scar.

It's always there, a raised bump just above the surface of your skin. You run your finger over it once in a while, when you're not thinking, and the pain of how it got there comes searing back. When the person you loved died a cold, normal death, I guess the scar is a sad reminder.

But when the person you love burned at the stake, that scar is something much more powerful.

That's why Mormor's death surprises me so much. Until now, I thought dying was all torture and fire and screams. At least I thought that was how it was for witches. It never occurred to me that a witch could die peacefully in her sleep.

But overnight, death came tiptoeing into our little hut hidden away in the birchwood—a neighbor we didn't invite but who arrived anyway, even through all our protections and enchantments.

There was no fire. There were no bone-shattering screams, no eyes like ice against the flames. Death came quietly, with no pain. Kaija and I made sure of that.

When death comes for me eventually, I know I won't be so lucky. It will come for me the way it did for Mamma.

The clouds are gray, and the sun is hiding, maybe out of respect. Maybe out of fear. Mormor will soon be on her way up there, and she can be wild when she wants to be. The birch trees around us flicker a burning orange. We bury her with her head facing north, and I do most of the work, though Kaija makes it look like she's helping.

She's lost in thought as I finish covering the grave and then kneel on the soft scrub, wipe my hands on my skirt, and pull what we need from my belt: the knife, the jet-black feather, and the rune stone. I'm sure she's sad, but there is magic to do, a soul to take care of.

My skin lights up with the itch now. The witch inside knows what's coming, and she's delighted. But this little bit of soul magic is nothing compared to what I need her for later. I scratch at my wrist to keep her quiet for now.

Kaija stands next to me, and I get the sense she doesn't know what to do. I glare up at her until she notices I'm on the ground, ready to do the ritual. She blinks, then pulls out her own rune stone and her own raven feather.

I finally catch her eye and try to hand her the knife. She shakes her head, something pleading on her face. Of course, she doesn't want to do it. I knew she wouldn't, but I thought maybe because it was Mormor, she might find the strength in her somewhere.

I palm the hilt of the knife. It's warm from my body, and I know the shape of it as well as I know the shape of anything. I press the sharp end to my left shoulder.

Taking your own blood should happen in one swift motion—a dig and swipe—if you do it right.

Right away, I feel the liquid trickling down my arm. We must work quickly now. I made the cut, but I won't be putting it onto Kaija's rune stone. She can do that herself. Really, she should put her own blood on there—the more witch blood, the better is what I think—but we only need mine.

We smear our stones, and the shapes carved on them soak up the blood. Both are the same: a straight line scratched down the center, a point like a thorn out to the right, and a line shooting out from where they meet. Kneeling beside me, Kaija closes her eyes and lays the feather next to the stones. Then she takes a dried and crumbling flower from her hair and puts that down, too.

I close my eyes because I know it's time for the galdr.

Sometimes the galdr comes out as a scream, sometimes as a song. When Kaija says it now, it's a whisper. "Rise now and fly, soul to meet sky." The words soothe the witch in me. She's happy, as always, to be steeped in magic. "Ride Odin's flight in spellfire light."

But the way Kaija says the galdr, so quiet and sad, irritates me. It's not right for Mormor, who was tough and short-tempered and pushy. She was everything. Our teacher. Our savior. Our captor. And now she's gone. Not *gone*, gone. Her soul is on its way up to dance and sing. On some bone-chilling night, she'll light the sky with an acrid green, a blood red, or a wild blue just when we think the dark is going to swallow us whole. So, yes, she deserves more than my sister's tempered magic. Mormor always was more witch than whisper.

I think Kaija will say more, but she doesn't. There's a moment of quiet, and again, I get the sense that she doesn't know what to do now. My sister may be hesitant, but I am not.

I know exactly what I'm going to do once the sun goes down and the shadows come out. It's all I can think about now that the ritual is done and Mormor's soul is journeying to where it needs to be. It feels like the next step, and I don't know if it's because this ritual just feels so small, too small for a powerful witch like Mormor, or if it's the fire that's been burning inside me for as long as I can remember, finally about to be freed.

After darkness falls, I won't wait around to let death take everything. Not again. I plan to make it come.

The itch is already scratching against the inside of my fingers. The witch in me is clawing at my skin. She wants freedom, and I'm prepared to give it to her because I want revenge. It's the kind of revenge Mormor wanted but never let herself have. Her death leaves a bitter taste on my tongue. Despite all this time, she was never the same. Nothing could ever be the same. They took her spirit—our world—and burned it all to the ground.

It's why I still have a scar. It's why the witch inside me is always near the surface of my skin. Scalding. A reminder of what must be done. And now that Mormor is gone, I can finally do this. I can do it for her.

Beneath my knees, the earth crunches from the lack of rain. The clouds darken and twist anyway, as if preparing. Snow will come soon, and then it won't leave for a long time.

Kaija looks into the distance, and I follow her gaze to see two reindeer grazing, antlers dark against the gray sky beyond. They move together without acknowledging each other, soundless and unconcerned. I wonder if Mormor brought them here for us, her last dying spell.

Kaija watches the animals for too long, then wanders back toward the hut. I seethe. I keep still, to try and contain my magic just a little longer.

Before turning away from the grave, I look one last time at the magic that will send our grandmother's soul to dance in the sky with her ancestors. I notice that my rune stone looks upside down at this angle: its thorn facing left, and its straight line facing right.

The rune positioned like that is not a good sign at all, but I don't bother to fix it. There's a hare to butcher, and it's time to light the fire.

"What do we do now?" I ask the question later, with the flames crackling between us. I only ask because Kaija's been wearing that helpless expression all day, and it's really getting under my skin. It's also a perfectly practical question. We're just two now, not three anymore. What will happen tomorrow and the next day and the next? Everything will be different.

It's hard to look at the fire and not see Mormor. My sister and I would have been cinders if not for her. Mormor did what she could to make sure Kaija and I survived. She taught us the runes, the spells, the galdr, the hunting. Living out here in these woods, it was freedom, but a kind of hidden freedom. Mormor taught us how to stay both free and safe.

It was just like her to bring us here. She found the wildest place she could find—an isolated birchwood on a fell where the villagers would never seek us out. Not even the local Sami people passed through here on their way to the lake lands for the winter.

For so long, this little fell, with its twisted trees, scarred from wind and rain, has been for us alone. My sister, Mormor, and me.

But I'm not one for sentimental thoughts.

As I wait for Kaija to respond to my question, I shove meat into my mouth and chew loudly.

I see Mamma in the fire, too. Not that I can remember her face. I have only snippets of that day and really nothing before. But I stare into the fire anyway, watching it whip around in the mounting wind, thinking about flames and all they can destroy in the hands of humans.

I bite down hard and catch my tongue. I taste the hot blood swelling in my mouth and gasp instinctively. When the villagers burned Mamma, most of what I felt was senseless pain, which doesn't leave room for much else. But it's been thirteen years since then, and now Mormor is gone, too, and there's just a blistering hole where she should be. That faraway village along the coast can keep its laughter, its tørrfisk suppers, its soft linen beds. Kaija and I have power. We are witches. Their fire can't reach us here.

But ours can reach them.

I swallow the chewed meat, taking my own blood down with it.

"I'm going to live in the village." Kaija says it so quietly that I barely hear her over my own chewing. All is silent for a few moments except the flames in the wind. "The village," she says again, and now I know I'm not imagining things. "I have to go."

I can't move. Can't think. Can't even breathe. A hunk of meat falls out of my fingers and onto the ground. The fire snaps.

"Will you come?"

I can't see anything in the darkness beyond our small ring of light. But it's all there. Our home, built with earth and birch and bare hands, cobbled-together wood for a door. Our hares from yesterday with their eyes black and lifeless, swaying in the night air between two spindly trees. Our herbs and stones and staves for witching.

As I look out toward the darkness, I feel it in my bones. It's desperate and cold, but it's ours.

In the village, they gather and gossip. They go to kirke; they pray. They don't do anything to change the world. They just accept it as it is. That's what Mormor used to tell us about the villagers. And it was exactly what they can't understand about witching, she said.

Witching means harnessing something they don't think can be harnessed. Only their god can do that. But Mormor never accepted their god into her heart, not really. Nor did her mother, nor her mother before that. I come from a long line of resolute witches, and our powers stretch back to before memory itself, so I know where I stand. But I guess Kaija doesn't care about that.

She's always been too delicate for life in the wild anyway.

My sister doesn't know how much Mormor used to bury her rage for Kaija's sake. They seemed to focus on protections and healing when they were together, nothing more powerful than that. But when Mormor and I were alone under the silver moon, I got to see the wild witch. I watched as she screamed, tore at her white hair, and cast spells worse than those Mamma had been accused of. She never wanted Kaija to see any of that, but she didn't mind if I did. Maybe she recognized the wildness inside me, too.

She knew what kind of witch I was, even then.

But on the days after Mormor cast her hexes, we would catch Kaija weaving snow-white poppies into crowns to guard against hunger or charming petals to bury under west-leaning birch trees for protection. That's when Mormor would suddenly break. She would see my sister's hands doing that tender kind of magic and sob later as she reversed her dark spells, begging for forgiveness—forgiveness from whom, she never said.

I could never understand why she would reverse a spell that would satiate her deepest desires. If a curse could make the witch inside happy, why deny her? But Mormor never let a single curse last for more than a few hours. Her tenderness held her back. A tenderness she shared with Kaija. But tenderness never helped anyone survive, did it? It was Mormor's fierceness that kept us alive. I know that now.

Kaija is looking at me over the fire. Her eyes are pleading. I know what she wants me to say, and I'm so disgusted, I could laugh.

After everything, I could never imagine wanting to return to the village. I can't imagine seeing their pale, sunken faces or looking into the eyes of the murderers who burned mothers just so they could sleep more soundly. What about the sleeps of daughters? Do they ever think of that? Of course they don't. That is why we are here and they are there.

The heat inside me has been simmering for years. It was stoked whenever Mormor spoke of Mamma. I felt it burn hot every time Mormor flinched from a fire, even if its flames were the small tame, everyday kind, meant only for cooking.

When I look across at my sister, I can tell she's starting to lose hope in me. I can imagine the people of the village—their faces twisted, voices terrifying and shrill—and I can't believe she doesn't imagine them, too. I don't remember what happened that day, but I have the proof burned into my hand.

I know what it feels like to hate people so much, all you want is to watch them burn until they're no more than a pile of black ash at your feet. And I'm no fool. I know this makes me like them. But there's one distinct difference between us. They don't know I still exist and that I hold a torch for the life they wrenched from us. They don't know my true power.

I swallow a final time. Without giving Kaija the satisfaction of a response, I stand and walk into the darkness.

Kaija

I catch myself sighing again. It's only because as soon as Minna disappears beyond the fire's glow, I realize what she's going to do.

She's going to do magic, of course. I could see it written on her face. I'd seen it all day, in fact, but when she looked at me across those flames as I broke the news to her, something seemed to go wild inside her. I could see the magic already edging its way to the surface of her skin. It was obvious from the tiny white scratches on her hands this afternoon. She was doing her best to control it, and so I suppose I was the one who pushed her over. She was not happy to hear the news. Nothing could have been plainer than that. And I truly am sorry for it, but I had to tell her. She thinks I don't know my own mind, but I do. This is how it must be.

My own magic is minimal these days, and I think Minna has noticed. The truth is I've been so focused on figuring out how to reach the village, I haven't wanted to do much else. I knew I was meant to leave when the rune stones divined it weeks ago, but I have felt it in my heart for as long as I can remember. Seeing it in the stones made it real, and that's when I began to prepare.

Over these past weeks, I've kept this all to myself, of course. Mormor was sick with the slow, blameless illness of old age, which meant we had many tasks to ensure she was comfortable and at peace, and Minna and I still had to live. There isn't much rest out here in the wild. Despite all that, I think I've kept this decision so close to my heart most of all because I knew how Minna would react. Well, at least I knew her response wouldn't be pleasant, that she wouldn't make it easy. In truth, I understand her frustration. We've been together all these years, hiding away from the village we fled. But it has been too long—two sisters and their mormor, shutting out the world, strapped to this isolated place, hiding from dark memories and even darker futures.

I stand and leave the flames, just as Minna did, but I go in the opposite direction. I clutch the folds of my skirt and duck into our little hut. I don't need to use magic in here. Besides, I can't rely on magic anymore. If I'm to stay safe where I'm going, there will be none of that. I'll have to erase it from my very heart. I will pack and go over my route out of these woods using only my wit. That and the map I created from what Mormor has told me about the Sami settlement, which I know is only a couple of days' walk away, down along the coast. All in all, it should get me far enough. Mormor taught us how to be savvy, how to stay hidden and only leave this birchwood when we desperately needed supplies. I don't know if she'd think this was desperate enough, but I suppose she might understand. Because I had to, I learned how to trap a rabbit and skin it. Because it was necessary, I learned how to stalk an elk. But this knife-wielding life doesn't fit me, not really. I have hated every hunt, every splatter of blood, every second of ravenous hunger that's had me diving into my food like an animal. Being alone out here, fending for ourselves like this—I can't imagine doing it one more day.

I take out a small basket I made of birch bark and hope it's not too rough-looking for where I'm going, but I know it is. Inside it, I place a large handful of dried bilberries, making sure to leave most of them for

Minna. She will need them. I know her fury will be insatiable once she discovers me gone in the morning. I plan to wait until she falls asleep and then creep out as quietly as I can. I just hope she doesn't wake up. I won't be able to handle a long stormy goodbye, which is the only reason I've decided to leave tonight. Besides, I know she'll eventually understand why I've left, and I hope—I pray—she decides to follow.

Mamma used to tell me she knew the difference between Minna and me right away. *You both made trouble for me.* She would laugh as she mindlessly ran her fingers over my hair. I was born more than four weeks late, growing at a leisurely pace that worried my parents, but my sister sprang into the world two months early and as stubborn as they come. My heart breaks when I think of my little sister and how she'll be without me, pacing around our small hut, brewing pain in her heart, and stoking the fires of her rage. It's true—she'll be devastated to be left on her own, but she won't sulk about it. She'll get on with things, her anger at me fueling her daily activities. The thought of it makes me lean up against the wall for a moment. She and I have been out here together through thirteen icy winters. Through Mormor's stories and our own stumbles, we learned to sing the galdr correctly and carve our runes just right. This will be the end of all that, and I don't know how she'll cope without me. I hope she won't let the hate and darkness burn straight through her. But I can't stay here one more moment, or I may die from the loneliness.

I say I haven't been doing much magic lately, but in a sense, I suppose that's not true. I divined all this from the runes. I spilled the small carved stones twice to make sure I was reading them right, and each time they foretold a journey toward comfort, toward community, toward the sea. Although, even without the runes, I still would have known. I've felt a strong pull toward the village since the day we left. I missed my friends. I missed the smell of the sea, the squawk of the gulls. I missed the simple comfort of a solid roof and a family underneath it. Mamma would have wanted this for me—and for Minna, too, I suspect—though the thought of us splitting up would surely not have been her preference. She would have wanted us to be protected, certainly, and I know that's why Mormor brought us out here all those years ago. But Mamma would have wanted us to be a part of something, too. A life in the village was the life she chose for herself, after all, even though she was full of magic she couldn't use. And that is the life I want for myself, too. I want what she nearly had. And now that Mormor is gone, I finally feel like I have a choice. She would have never allowed me to go back while she was alive. Her rage burned as hot as Minna's sometimes, and though neither of them suspected it, I followed them out into the night to watch the curses Mormor spit at the sky. That was when I would do the gentle protective spells most of all. It was to remind myself there was another way, to remind Mormor that there was safety in goodness, too.

I flatten a piece of birch bark against my knee and scribble out a note for my sister. I desperately wanted Minna to say yes when I asked her to come. I thought about that moment many times. She could find a life in the village, too. We could be the long-lost nieces of Mormor's cousin Tilde, escape this ruggedness, and finally find some ease. We've put in our fair share of hard years out here alone, and I'm already twenty-three; Minna, nineteen. It's past time. But even before I asked my sister, I could see her ice-blue eyes swimming with magic, and I already knew what she'd say. I sigh again. I know where her hatred has grown from. That day was probably one of her first memories. If I remembered the village like that, I would be swimming in my own confused emotions, too. It's no wonder pain and fear burn so violently in her heart. I would say I should have realized it about her before, but I know who she is and how she feels. I have always known. Perhaps that's why I kept my desire to leave a secret from her and Mormor. But I finally feel free to follow my heart. I cannot wait around for Minna because I know she won't listen to my pleading. She will only dig her heels in deeper if I ask her again. And yet I must go back. I have never wanted anything more.

I smooth the front of my skirt. If telling her was a knife in my dear sister's hide, following through will be a deep butcher's cut. When she discovers me gone, Minna will doubtless be hurt and scared, caught in the snare but not yet dead, and so will I, if I'm honest with myself. I am well aware of the pain I am inflicting on us both. But I'm not an animal, and there is no trap here. I am a woman, and so is my sister. Which means we will recover. Which means no one will make a meal of us. We will be wounded, maybe, but weren't we already?

There are more pelts outside, hidden under a leafy pile, ready for me to take them. I have been collecting them without her noticing, which has been difficult. I have also been drying bilberries and herbs for her, enough to last her a few months if she's frugal, and I have tied sixteen new snares—twelve for her, four for me—and hidden them underneath my sleeping pelt.

I prepare everything as quickly as I can, and then I grab Mamma's shoes. I've not kept them a secret, but I have kept them for thirteen years, never far from where I sleep, so I could wear them for this exact occasion. I slip them on. They fit perfectly, but I knew they would since I've tried them on about a thousand times, always imagining Mamma walking down village lanes. I can't recall her ever actually wearing them, but I know she kept them just outside the door to the house in the summer and just inside it during the winter. These are the little things I can remember, and they're the kinds of things my heart aches to have for itself.

I can hear a storm brewing outside the hut's brittle walls. I hope it won't be too bad. Minna still hasn't come back. I don't always understand her desire to change things with magic. Sometimes I want to shake her and tell her to just let some things be. But maybe magic is just deeper in her than it is in me. Maybe I'm not cut out to be a witch, not a real one, with all that wild power. My skin tingles when magic is around, just as Mormor said it should, but I don't always like the tingle. It reminds me of Mamma so much, it burns sometimes.

I love my sister dearly, I think as I sit and wait, pretending to ready myself for sleep. She and Mormor have been everything to me these past thirteen years. Minna and I have grown up together in this quiet, lonely birchwood, and that kind of survival forges a bond that can't be easily broken by something as weak as distance. And, of course, she and I are sisters, which is the strongest bond of all. Mormor reminded us of that every day.

And yet. There's the look of Minna when she's got magic rising inside her and even when she doesn't. The anger is always bubbling right up near the surface. When she lets it out, it sears, even cuts sometimes. I know she doesn't mean it, but she's difficult to be around for too long.

So, as much as I yearn for a new life in the village, a less proud part of me simply wants to be free of this, I suppose. To be free of her.

I check outside once more and am rewarded with a wild gust of wind that sends my hair spiraling up. No sign of Minna, and it's getting late. Rain will be here soon, but it doesn't matter. The pull is strong, and it's calling me away. How can I wait for Minna to fall asleep if Minna doesn't come back? I realize now that I cannot.

I truly do hope she will join me one day. I wish I could say goodbye, but I know it would only make things worse. After making a loose braid of my hair, I leave the note, along with a little crown adorned with dried white flowers, on Minna's pelt. Then I grab my bag and basket, leave as much shame and sorrow inside the hut as I can, and disappear into the night.

Minna

The wind tugs at the loose strands of my hair. I push them tightly back, securing it all with a braid like a head vise.

Cold rain splatters on my hands, and the resolve inside me hardens. I have a small pouch cinched to my thigh, underneath my skirt, and it slaps against me as I walk.

The ritual actually begins much earlier than Mormor said it does. She said it starts when you kneel, when you close your eyes and call the spell to you, once you start the galdr, the incantation, but I can already feel it.

I've been feeling it all day.

It started inside me, and now it's trying to get out. I pick up my pace, finding myself running in a crooked line between the birches, which are slick and glowing with rain. The trees here claw up from the ground in unpredictable patterns. Some grow out more than up, with three or four different trunks clustered together, bending to capture the thick stormy air like fingers.

When I pass too close or move by too fast, these gnarled birchwoods bite at me, leaving fresh pink scrapes along any skin that dares remain exposed. They grab at my skirts and tear holes in the wool.

Above me, thunder rolls, and I run even faster, twisting my ankles over sharp-sided rocks that hide beneath moss and grass. I need to expel this feeling, this tingling that's burning the inside layers of my skin.

I think of Kaija, wonder if she ever feels this way. I know she's stopped witching almost completely, even though she never told me outright. Discovering that made something harden inside me, mostly because we're meant to be in this together. But no, she decided to believe what they believe—that being a witch is evil, that we are to be feared and hated for who we are and what we do.

We were bonded in our magic before, but not now.

Lately, I've been witching alone. Not even Mormor had the strength for it.

Strangely, the love I have for my sister stings the way witching does in some ways, and it comes and goes the way witching does, too. For instance, I felt it dim earlier, at the fire, when she told me she wanted to leave me here alone for a life in the village.

The thought of the village boils my blood, and my feet can barely keep up with my rage.

I know my face is twisted strangely. I must look like those witches they hate so much, the ones they fear. And I hear myself laugh. How can Kaija love the village so much when I can do nothing but hate it? My cackle scares me a little, I must admit, but I can't fully control it.

This power in me is very close to what they imagine a witch's power to be. It's worse than that, I realize, because they can do nothing to stop me.

Finally, I can make out the clearing just ahead. The birch trees stop abruptly here, as if they all at once decided they'd gone too far. I can't see the moon through the clouds, but I know it's there, sending me power and light.

It's just like Mormor to die on the full moon. She was all witch, except the parts of her that were sad. Those parts were human. There was nothing she could do about that.

Mormor used to tell us that witching is as unique to each of us as our blood, as the color of our eyes. I wonder now if Kaija ever really cared what Mormor had to say about magic. It was like my sister shut out all the wildness.

But not me. I've always been fascinated with it.

Maybe it's because Kaija was older when it all happened with Mamma and just saw more than I did. But I think it's really because she's soft.

Me, I'm a stone, hard enough to crack a skull if thrown in the right direction.

I stare out into the clearing before leaving the safety of the wood, understanding that once I cross the threshold, I'll be at the storm's full mercy. It's picked up now, bending branches this way and that, sending leaves swirling upward.

A flash interrupts my thoughts, followed by a cracking of the sky— one I feel deep inside my body. Out in the clearing, if lightning wants me, it will have me.

But that's what's so delicious about the clearing. It's where I like to come to do my most powerful spells, the spells that need to be exposed so they can rise and expand. It's where Mormor taught me the rituals, too. *The ritual is the most important part,* she would say just before she closed her eyes and brought the magic to the surface. It's where she showed me how to heal the lung-squeezing coughs that spring up in winter. It's where she used witching to call the reindeer to our fell all those times.

A candle, cloths of different colors, rune stones, feathers, her own breath. The tools varied, and the words she used changed. But it was the ritual—the doing—that turned her witching into reality.

This clearing has a lot of magic, and I can feel my skin dance with it.

I can almost see Mormor shaking her head, though. She would not be happy with me doing this now. It would be better if it were not storming, even I can admit that. A storm like this, Mormor would tell me, which has come on so quickly and with such fierceness, will make a spell potent, but it could make it just as easily go awry. *The less control you have over your ritual, the less control you have over its consequences.* My fingers hover near my belt as I weigh the options.

My hesitation only lasts until the next flash of lightning and the soul-stirring tremble of thunder that follows.

I'll take potency, I decide, and dig underneath my woolen skirt for the pouch. This will have to be quick.

The candle is made of hare tallow and dyed with charcoal, which will make the smoke black as night, if only I can get the damn thing lit.

I flip my hood onto my head, blowing rain off the tip of my nose. I lean forward, hands over the candle. If there's one thing every witch can do, it's light a witching candle without even striking a flint.

But the water is on my hands and in the air—the goddess Jörð's earth magic tampering with mine.

I kneel, and when I do, I know what I have to do. I've been so consumed by the fury searing in my heart that I've forgotten to embrace my connection to this place. Mormor taught us the old magic, the stories of giants and gods who created our world and shaped it. Witching lives within me, but it only comes alive when it touches the old magic that lives in the earth, the sky, and the wind.

Forging this relationship takes grit. But it also takes patience.

I'm aware enough to know I possess the former but severely lack the latter.

Right now, I concentrate. I know I must feel the power of Jörð beneath my feet, to place myself in the here and now, to ground my witching. I concentrate, feeling it creep up through my knees, into my stomach, and through my heart. Using the heat burning inside me and the strength and persistence that belongs to Jörð, I manage to light the black candle. The flame grows tall and lean at first, then fat, spitting out a protective circle that blocks out the rain and keeps it lit.

"Like magic," I say, resting back on my feet.

But my relief doesn't last long. The witch inside knows it's her moment. As my blood runs thick and hot and my fingers pulse and the sound of the thunder is drowned out by my own heartbeat, I grab the rest of what I need.

Crushed bloodroot. Heart of hare. Thorns. A square of cloth.

I lay them all next to the black candle before unwrapping the heart tenderly, carefully, as if it were my own. Once I get the cloth off, the wind wrenches the linen from my hand.

I chase it, but it's too late. It's gone, tumbling up toward the sky.

Maybe it's a sign from Mormor. She's telling me she's here, watching to make sure I do it right. I hesitate again—why do I keep doing that?—but it's the thought of Mormor that gives me pause.

I can almost hear her. *When you cast a spell with hesitation, you must be prepared for what you do not expect.* My anger flares at the memory of her words. I know exactly what to expect, and they deserve everything that's coming to them. They never thought about the consequences, did they?

You can't cook mothers alive and not expect their daughters to make you pay.

They took Mamma in their evil flames, burning half Mormor's heart with it. And soon they'll take my sister.

I double over suddenly, bracing my hands on the ground, clutching gravel and crusted heather in my fists, as I think back to Kaija's announcement. When she said it, I let myself believe she was just testing me to see what I would say. But I know now—in the way sisters know—that she meant it. At least she's not gone yet. There will still be time to talk some sense into her.

Another blaze of lightning.

I tear a small square of wool from the edge of my skirt, lay it gently over the wet brown heart. This will have to do. I shake the rain from my hood and point my face to the sky.

"Revenge is sweet and like no other." The words come out slick and garbled as rain slides into my mouth. The wind picks up the sounds and carries them off with urgency. I stab the first thorn into the wool until I feel the squelch of flesh beneath it. I leave the thorn there, letting it stand on its own.

"Cast to those who burned my mother."

The next thorn goes in even deeper.

"May you writhe and feel my pain."

I stab two more through the dampening wool. My breath is fast now, rage boiling inside me, surging through my body, igniting my fingertips. "Till only ash and souls remain."

There's a long silence smattered with wind and wet. I stare hard into the candlelight, which stands stalwart against the storm. Then I stand, letting my feet sink into the mud. I look up at the sky again, but the water stings at my eyes, and I'm forced to shut them.

With nothing left to do, I leave my rage there, letting it simmer in the flame rather than in my blood, and I turn around and walk back into the forest.

Behind me, the black candle will burn well into the night before melting into the earth as if nothing has happened at all.

Kaija

I should have waited for the storm to pass. I've been living long enough in the wild that I should know when to venture out and when not to. It was so fierce, I had to take shelter almost as soon as I left and start fresh this morning. I considered turning back as the rain smattered mud onto my legs and the lighting cracked open the night sky. But turning back seemed worse somehow. Instead, I just let myself cry for most of the night, regret tearing at my heart as wind tried to tear the trees up by the roots.

I don't know why it hurts so much. I know I am doing the right thing. I know I am doing what is best for me, and yet I can't help but think I'm evil. I'm certain that's what Minna thinks now that she has discovered I'm gone.

I know I'm not evil, but she will never see the truth. She chooses to live behind a stubborn, stony exterior. At least that's how she is now. My sister wasn't always so hard or so angry. She was once a little girl, one hand gripping mine, the other limp and swollen as Mormor rubbed a poultice on it and muttered a spell. Tears once traced Minna's pain, which was perhaps frightening to her because she was so young.

I sometimes wonder if the burn she sustained that day was a gift in a way, that perhaps her physical pain eclipsed the deep thundering help-lessness of seeing Mamma like that. The memory haunts me, even still: my sister wriggling free from Mormor's grasp, her little feet kicking up dirt and skirts, how she reached into that fire, as if all Mamma needed was a hand to hold. My sister's sweet red cheeks, hair stuck to the tears she wiped with her sleeve as Mormor and I pulled her toward the birch-wood and away from our lives, from everything we had ever known. Minna wasn't always so hard, I suppose, but she has always been brave.

Last night, as my tears seeped into my skirt, blending with the rain-drops, I thought Minna might have caused the storm. It's not beyond her to curse my travels and make me turn back. Even as I sat there miserable and cold, I knew I would have to live with the guilt of leaving her behind.

But my memories and the shame that accompanied them ended with the storm last night. I know they cannot come with me to the village, and so I must will them away as much as I can. It's easier today, now that the sky is a bright, inviting blue, though the wind from the previous night remains, blowing the last of the birch leaves reluctantly from their branches. I still step carefully, almost certain I'll walk straight into another one of Minna's storms or come across an angry swarm of wasps that forces me back the way I came. I'm on edge because I know what my sister is capable of. She can reach me even when I'm not there—though none of her spells will save her from the hurt I caused her. I hope she doesn't dwell on that fact for too long. *Not even magic can temper pain in our hearts*, Mormor said over and over in the months after we arrived in the birchwood. We can control what happens to us. We can control what happens to other people. We can even change how others feel. But to cast a spell to change your own mind or your own heart's desire? No witch is that powerful.

Now that I'm awake and the storm has left valleys of rainwater at my feet, I see that I've already walked farther than I realized. But daylight seems to have fortified my resolve because my steps are sure, if a little slow. I shake off the remorse that tore at me as the storm raged. It was only fleeting, and I know Minna will eventually be fine without me. Time is something witches often forget about, but it can be more powerful than a spell. In any case, if anyone can handle herself in the birchwood alone, it is my sister. She has the fortitude of someone who has had to survive in the wilderness for far too long.

It isn't quite the same for me. I found my first-ever roots in the village by the sea. I had friends. I wonder about them now—about Ingebor and Maren and the others—whether they will recognize me, though I will make sure I'm unrecognizable when I arrive. I wonder, too, about the boys. Will they be as scrawny as they were when they were ten, or did they grow up to have necks as wide as their heads, just like their fathers? Men who fish have a strong and quiet presence, I remember. It's probably from years of waiting patiently for a good catch and only letting out bursts of strength to haul in nets or sail through sudden mast-snapping kuling out at sea.

I stop and set my basket near a creek. It's about midday, and I've been walking for a few hours, but I'm not clear of the birch forest yet. Soon, I know, the tree line will end, and the heath will begin. Fells and valleys of autumn reds and browns will lie before me, showing me the way to the sea. I consult my makeshift map. It's only a few more hours to the Sami settlement, where I can trade for more supplies. I'll need to look like a woman who hasn't spent the past decade weaving her own baskets out of the bark from dead trees. I'll need a proper skirt with an apron and a bonnet. These are the clothes I remember Mamma wearing. I slip off one of her shoes and examine my foot. I can feel a stubborn blister forming, the skin around it already red and raw and starting to peel. In my bag, I find Mamma's spinning stave. If it was ever carved with runes, they're long gone by now, smoothed over to look like it was never used for magic. This tool will be useful to spin linen so I can fit in with the other women. I can't use magic but will need to work all the same, and this stave is a good reminder of that.

I dip my hands and feet in the cool water that tumbles over the rocks at my feet, and I take a drink. My mind meanders back to the boys I knew—those who will be men now. I try to remember them. I know there were some blond ones and some with freckles on their cheeks, some well tanned and others with jet-black hair. Names come to me—Marcus, Anders, Nils, Jonny—but the faces and the names don't match. They're all twisted into a single image of a man who doesn't look far from my memories of Pappa. I suppose he is one of the only men I've ever really known. He's the only man I've ever properly gotten a good look at anyway, but even he was mostly beard and cap.

Once my hands are dry and my shoes are laced, I search for the box I have stuffed my flowers into. They're thin and delicate, and a few flutter onto the ground as I lift the lid. This box is another one of Mamma's possessions. I kept the silver coins in there all this time, saved from when Pappa used to trade with the Pomors from Russia, but there was extra room, so I used it for my flowers. There are so many beautiful spells that involve flowers. Those are my favorite: purple petals that darken as they dry in the sun, white petals that stay as vibrant as ever, and yellow petals that turn a golden brown, aged and powerful with magic when the ritual is done right. I'm not planning on doing magic when I get there, but I couldn't part with the box of flowers. The box was special to Mamma, I remember, which is why I couldn't part with the runes etched under the lid either. Two runes, side by side, making one unbreakable bindrune that ties the souls of our family together with its powerful magic. I trace the faded runes with my finger, wondering why they weren't strong enough to keep Pappa from dying, Mamma from burning, Mormor from wilting away, and Minna from planting roots as if she were a birch tree herself. I suppose I am the only one left.

I close the box with care and place it into my bag. I am journeying back to the place where we all came from, am I not? I suppose it's up to me to continue the strong bonds of family by creating a family of my own. This is a sacred wish I've held for some time, of course, though it's just one more thing I never told Minna. Change doesn't come easily to her—certainly not change like this. She has a way of choosing the hard path when given the choice between that and comfort. Nothing is worth having if it isn't gained with blood. That's what my sister would say if she were here now.

꒐꒑꒒꒓

I speed up so I can make it to the Sami settlement quickly. The area is bustling and busy. A few fishing boats dot the calm fjord waters, while a group of men sits along the shore hammering and repairing more boats. A cluster of children greets me, and I'm led by a small warm hand toward the settlement. There I find Riiga, whose name I only know from Mormor's stories of trading trips that took her alone to this crook of the fjord while Minna and I stayed safely hidden in our fell. She looks up from her task of milking an untroubled reindeer and nods as if she knows who I am already. Riiga requires me to stay and help mend the skirt and shirt I want to purchase. She assists me more than I deserve when I'm fastening the buttons, but I suspect she and Mormor had an understanding I cannot comprehend. I'm grateful for her help. I say my goodbyes in haste after asking one more thing of her. She nods at me warmly as she takes my silver and points me in the right direction. I all but run along the coast, not even stopping to admire the jagged purple rocks lined like teeth down toward the sea or the way the water slides in like a serpent's tail. When I come to another village—there are a few along the way—I give it a wide berth. Even though I am wearing my new clothes, I don't want to be seen yet.

Only a handful of shriveled bilberries remain by the time I smell the familiar smoke and sea of the village. The journey has taken eighteen days in total, and that number is a good omen. The night is thick by now, but I can see hearths and candles lighting up the insides of gray-sided houses. One deep breath and a tightening of my shoes. Then I do a last little spell to make sure I choose the right house and don't so much as look behind me as I leave the wilderness for good.

Minna

I squeeze the rune stones in my hand. The weight of them feels light, like the group is lacking half of itself. We used some in Mormor's burial one week ago. Those will stay at her grave, and I'll need to carve more to make the set whole again. But not now because I don't want to remember my sister's absence. I refuse to think of Kaija today.

The witch under my skin gives an anticipatory sting, hoping the feel of the runes means I'll be letting her out to do a spell, but I nearly tear a hole in my skin with my fingernail to get her to quiet down. I've already had enough of her today, and it's only morning. She does eventually leave me be—but only once I leave the rune stones on a flat rock near the fire pit outside.

───

The clouds dim the morning light, and with the barren birch trees standing like skeletons against it, it looks like there's no color left in the world.

I'm dressed practically from the waist up, although I wish I didn't have to wear this damn skirt. I make a mental note to fashion it into breeches somehow. I may look like a man, but I am the only one here, so it doesn't really matter much what I look like anymore. I wonder if it ever really did. It's just that the skirt I wear now keeps getting snagged on low-slung branches that have been snapped free from their bodies.

There was so much damage after the storm, which surprises me since these twisted trees usually laugh in the face of strong winds. But the force of this one must have been something else. Twigs scatter the ground like the bones of birds. The branches that managed to hang on look stranded and lonely, as if they were stripped naked before they were ready. Fiery-orange birch leaves stick sharply out of the browning scrub.

No matter what they look like, downed branches this time of year are good. They're easy firewood for me.

With my breath gathering in pools of fog in front of me, I start with twigs and kindling.

There's so much of it that I fill the hide I brought within just a few minutes, and I venture back to drop them at the hut before heading out again. I do this a dozen or so times, until I have a pile decent enough to last several fires. Once I drop the last bundle, I stop to drink some water. It's cold and soothing on my throat.

It's been seven nights since Kaija left. When I saw she'd gone, I spent the night screaming after her, and then, when she didn't come back, I screamed into the sky, cursing that damn village until my throat was raw and I couldn't speak.

That restriction felt good for a few days. My anger manifested into something I could feel, and it was satisfying.

But it kept me from doing what I should have done the moment I discovered her gone, which was to send her another rainstorm or maybe some hail. Maybe I could have pointed the wind southward, pushing her back up the hill. I could have brought her back here, apologizing and asking for my forgiveness. By the time I recovered my voice, I knew she was too far to turn back because of a storm.

She was out of my reach. She'll be out of my reach from now on, I know, softened even more by the villagers' promises of warm fish cakes and beds stuffed with hay. All of it poison. Those people know nothing about what it means to survive. Even Kaija will soon forget.

The rawness in my throat has calmed enough for me to speak now, even though I don't have much reason to do it. I stopped wanting to scream at the sky eventually. I could have wished for the burning of a thousand villages, I was so mad. But now, even if Kaija turns around and comes tiptoeing back home, I won't care.

She was the one who decided to leave me. It was altogether pathetic.

If she does turn up again eventually, I probably won't even speak to her.

I curse myself. I said I would not think of her. Not today.

The water cools something deep within me, and I'm ready to get back to my task. Collecting kindling has taken me twice as long as I thought it would, and the day won't last forever.

Dragging my feet, I get back to picking up branches. I come across a tree pulled up by the roots. The horizontal carcass of the would-be birch tree doesn't look too different from its family members who made it through the storm, except that it's young and small. It wouldn't have made it too long anyway. Too weak to survive. I add it to my collection to feed a future fire.

Once all my branches and sticks are piled high, my arms are whining at me to take a break, but I don't. The sun is already eyeing me from the horizon, and great shadows are starting to form. I want to get at least some of this bark off and hack up the rest. My breathing is heavy. It feels good to let the cool air fill my chest. The birchwood is still and dead silent as I take in the long view in front of me. Nothing out there moves. This is what it's like to be alone.

I've brought my knife, which is nestled in the sheath that lives at my side, and an axe. I examine the axe blade with my scarred hand. It isn't too sharp but has the strength to chop wood if I put enough of my back into it. I notice the witch's tingle simmering at my wrist.

She's not sated. She's antsy. I can tell by the way the feeling changes to a stinging as I give it attention. I want her to leave me for now, so I start chopping to forget about it.

I only have time to hack up one tree, which ends up in four different pieces before I decide it's time to get what I have back to the hut. By the time I'm done, the shadows have melted into a pool of darkness.

Back at the hut, I start a small fire with some of my new kindling and some brown leaves. It's modest, but it's enough to see by. I eat a few strips of dried meat and examine my birch logs. I chopped them into equal lengths for the most part, which I hope will give me enough bark for four large bowls I can melt snow in throughout the winter.

I take another bite of meat and stare at my scarred hand in the firelight. I remember a similar night, years ago, when I asked Mormor why it can't be summer all the time. We're witches—it didn't make sense to me why we couldn't just change the seasons to create a perpetual summer, and then we wouldn't have to worry about the snowy season or prepare so much in advance or go without fresh berries for half the year.

I remember she stared at me for a while before speaking. Her answer was careful and sure. *If you take away winter, then you take away summer, too, since one cannot exist without the other. And then you'll be left with nothing.* There are no spells to change the seasons. The magic of Jörð is even more powerful than the magic of witches.

The witch inside me seems to spark to life at the memory, and I remind myself to keep my hands moving. Too much stillness means too much time to think. I must stay busy. I grunt as I put aside my meat and begin my new task.

To start, I slide the knife out of its sheath, and I examine the blade.

It catches the flicker of the flames, glowing cold in my hand. It's too damn dull to make neat work of this. I wish I had checked that yesterday.

I consider waiting, but I know I need to shape this bark into bowls tomorrow. I realize, too, that if this knife needs sharpening, I can probably assume the same for my arrows. Those, I'll need soon.

I use the dull knife, and it takes more energy than it should to cut down the length of each log, but I manage to slice them all and peel back the bark I need. And the inner witch stays quiet. It's not the same satisfaction as doing magic, but it still works. I get four almost-equal sheets and move them away from the flames so I can work with them tomorrow.

Finally, I lean back on my hands, which are swollen from the day's work, and look around. The place looks so empty and dark beyond the ring of light that warms my face. The side of the hut looks like it could use a fresh coat of peat to fill in a small hole I can make out from here, and I spot a crack in the drying rack.

I know I'll need to mend that rack before the next hunt, and the thought of it makes my eyelids feel heavy.

Before I can convince myself to get up and go into the hut for the night, there's a muffled crunch of leaves behind me.

I can't see anything when I look back. I stare out into the darkness, trying to catch a glimpse of whatever it is, wondering if maybe I'll see the pale face and witchy black braids of my sister, but there are no more sounds. It's probably just weasels, but for some reason—I'm probably overtired—I let myself think of Kaija.

I wish I could remember the protective enchantments she did for the winter, but I can't for the life of me think of one. I toss a lazy handful of leaves into the fire and watch them singe at the sides and burst into flame, then curl like an old woman's hands before turning black and fading into the coals.

Kaija can't do a protective spell for the winter because she's not here. She's not here to help me patch up the hut before the snow. She's not here to help me sharpen the tools, to make these birch-bark sheets into bowls, to bend them around rocks and cool them in a row like a family. She's not here to talk to either, I realize, and I hadn't thought about it before, but I do wish there were someone to say something to. Not the witch inside me—someone who would say something back.

I wish I didn't want it to be Kaija.

I wish for Mormor, but even when she was well, she liked to tell stories, not to exchange them. She was a wise and enchanting witch in her own right, but she also liked to go to bed early and sleep in.

I suddenly remember the rune stones from this morning and make my way around the fire to find them. They're perched on the same rock I set them down on earlier, waiting patiently for me to carve more of them and make up for those lost to Mormor's grave, to make the set whole again. But stepping away from the fire has made me cold, and I can't imagine carving a single thing tonight.

If my sister were here, she would have carved these and then protected the hut for the season, all while I gathered the kindling. It's not like her to leave things unprotected, and for a moment, I'm lost in the idea that she will come back.

My inner witch is always good about telling me when she wants to do magic. Kaija could always tell when the itch became too strong, which I hated. My sister would offer to do a spell with me or just massage my wrists. I didn't want her calming ways to work, but the witch would respond to her touch obediently in a way she didn't to mine.

When it was just me, I'd scratch her clean out if she didn't leave me alone. But Kaija would never let me get that far.

I stare at the runes and their etched surfaces. The river stones are all shapes and colors, and on them are carefully carved symbols that represent different possibilities. Cast them, and you will see your future spelled out—the near and the distant, the happy and the bleak. Mormor always admitted that living out here in the birchwood gave her the freedom to practice witching like never before.

She taught us to carve the runes until they were smooth and sharp on both staves made of birch and stones collected from the river. Staves emitted power when used as part of a witching ritual. Rune stones were cast to show a witch her future. We spent long afternoons memorizing and repeating the meanings of all twenty-four runes. Then we would practice casting them on flat rocks during the full moon, interpreting each other's futures.

The runes that landed in the center were always the most potent, but any that fell off and landed close to our feet would signify our nearest futures.

The sheer torture of learning rune stone meanings was one of the few things that bonded Kaija and me together.

I flinch. I promised I would not think of her, and this is why.

Now, in the dark, I can't help but notice something about the runes as they lie. I move closer to see properly, but I look at them through the eyes of a witch for the first time all day.

The rune at the center glows brightest in the low red light of the coals. I can see the symbol on it—two parallel lines down, their tops connected by a bent line—symbolizing a coming together of opposites. Another rune, which sits just next to it, tells me there will be a journey. A journey and a joining in harmony.

My breath catches for a small moment. They're telling me that Kaija is coming home.

And soon I'm frowning deeply, hating that I allowed myself to feel happy at the thought of my sister. She left, and I don't want to care, even if she does come back.

Before I become too sentimental, my body reminds me that I'm bone weary. Sleep will set me straight again. I step over the stones toward the hut, allowing my eyes to leave the center runes. But as I do, I catch sight of one that fell to the ground.

I bend down and take it in my fingers. It's one of the norn runes, marked by a diagonal line slashing through the center of a line that stands tall and straight. I know this rune signifies pain and struggle, and it's not a good omen.

For a moment, I remember the curse I cast the night Kaija left, and I think the rune stone is telling me about the fate of the villagers, that they're beginning to feel the pain of my curse. Good. Long may they suffer.

But I soon realize that can't be. This rune stone is in my hand. It's meant for me, of course. My eyes grow wide, and the stone suddenly feels hot. I throw it to the ground before grabbing my skirt with the hand that touched it. Then I use my foot to shove the rune stone into the fire. I kick the top log over it, and what's left of the fire smokes at me in protest.

I only release my fist after I turn my back on it, when its flames are again reduced to spots of red, and I know the norn rune is buried somewhere deep underneath.

Kaija

It seems that everything in the world has shifted. I am sitting in a quiet house in front of a hearth that lets off enough heat to calm my nerves and warm my bones. My little spell helped me find the house I wanted to without any trouble. Now Tante Tilde, a woman I have wondered about for years, sits across from me, eyeing me from head to foot and back again. She's been staring more than talking, which is making me a little uncomfortable, but her fire is alight with seemingly endless orange flames, and it's the warmest I've felt since I left the birchwood. I welcome her stare if it means I can stay here longer.

She is just as Mormor described her: sturdy, with deep wrinkles and large hands that rest gently on the cream apron she wears over her gray skirt. She hands me another strip of cod atop a square of gjetost, a creamy goat's cheese, and a warm piece of flat, crispy bread. Lefse. I immediately remember the taste.

"You know, you will have to change your name."

Her face is kind, but her command is stern, as if this is the final word on the matter. I wonder if all women of a certain age have the same grandmotherly tone, if they learn it somewhere along the way.

I look around the small home for anything familiar, some token or symbol from Mormor that I've chosen right, but Tante Tilde's lean— which is ever-so-slightly away from the flicker of the fire—and the understanding in her eyes is enough.

The truth is I know I will have to change my name. And not just my name. I've already made small adjustments to my appearance. My hair was black before I arrived, but it's almost as blond as Minna's now. It wasn't any kind of special magic, exactly, but I did tap into an old coloration spell Mormor used to stay her gray hairs. It was just the one spell. Well, if you include the second time I did it, on my eyes, then that makes two spells. Coming to the village was an easy choice, but that doesn't mean I can be careless about my own survival. These people knew Mamma. I am—was—her spitting image. I'm realizing quickly that if I am going to be here, I must hide in plain sight, and that may mean using magic, as it so often does.

"Kirsti," I say. I have had the name for weeks. It sounds innocent enough for a young woman who says she's from a village out west and plain enough not to draw too much attention. It's also a name I've dreamed of since I was a girl when I imagined myself grown, with a husband and children.

Tante Tilde nods approvingly, hands me another strip of cod. The fish is salty and packed with the flavor of the sea. I haven't tasted anything like it in a long time. It reminds me so much of home, and it takes me a moment to remember that's exactly where I am.

She continues to feed me like that, piece by piece, until I'm not hungry anymore and we've worked out our full story. The firelight dances across our faces as we talk. She tells me how she discussed the possibility of this day many years ago with Mormor, but she didn't believe it would happen. She thought we were all dead. I am listening, though I'm quiet, mostly because I'm amazed at Mormor's forethought. She always suggested to me that coming back could be a possibility if I was extremely careful. But I didn't realize she'd make it so easy for me. I am glad she let me follow that thread of curiosity that brought me here, even after her death. When Minna wasn't around, Mormor would often tell me stories about Mamma and Pappa. I think she understood how unfair it was to ask a young woman to stay hidden away from the opportunities of community life forever, especially when it was never the life she chose for herself. I think—though I know my sister would disagree with me completely—that Mormor intended for us to make our way back here one day. She couldn't have wanted us to live out in the wilderness by ourselves and not have husbands, families, lives like everyone else.

Soon, Tante Tilde and I move to lighter subjects and lean back in our chairs. We are getting used to each other's presence as the hours pass. And maybe it's the warmth from the flames, but it's so nice to have a woman to talk to about everyday village things—more than just the sharpness of knives, the direction of the wind, and the coming snow.

"Ah, Inge." She sighs, her heavy bosom moving up and down. "She was my cousin on my mother's side." Then she whispers, "Spellfire take her soul."

She's so devoted to Mormor's memory, so loyal. I can tell this from her stories and her aged smile when she speaks of her. Tante Tilde is old, and she hasn't seen her dearest friend in over a decade, but she hasn't abandoned her feelings. I push aside a twinge of guilt. I left my own sister alone in the woods a three weeks' walk from here. But there is hardly a comparison between a pair of cousins strolling the lanes of their village and a couple of sisters surviving the wild fells of the birchwood.

She doesn't ask me how Mormor died, though I suppose she assumes it was from age, and she is right. I ask her about the village again, and she offers me a small cup of beer. I really love hearing about it. I want to know who is who and maybe catch a name or two I recognize. I shift in my seat.

"Ah, well, the village is the village." I think she's going to leave it at that since she pours a cup for herself and takes a long sip. But she continues, a carefulness spreading over her. "They don't look so hard for witches anymore—"

"Oh, I didn't—"

"But they still keep their eye on anyone with Sami blood, that's for certain. Things are better for our women now, but we are always on our guard, especially those of us who truly have witching blood. We keep our magic to a minimum and never perform it in front of anyone, not even a neighbor. The days of that are long past."

I don't say anything, but witching is the last thing I want to talk about. My skin itches with memories of it. I push down the feeling, take another sip of beer. It tastes sour but bubbles delicately in my mouth, which seems to only remember stream water.

Tante Tilde sighs. "Let's see. My neighbor Erich Pedersen, his mother, Frida, and I used to be friends, but she is gone now, too. And Erich is married, of course. I will admit, I'm not too fond of Mari, though that fact should remain between us. She always has her pointy nose stuck up in the air, sniffing for something, like she's waiting for someone to do her wrong. She and Erich, though—they have lovely children. Their young men are the reason we have this tørrfisk. They never forget about me, no matter how old I get. But other than Erich's family and another nosy neighbor I've not been able to shake for fifty years—even your mormor would remember Astrid—not too many people pay an old woman like me much mind. People won't ask too many questions about you. I've talked here and there about my husband's great-nieces, just like Inge said I should do, so I hope there won't be any suspicions. I don't expect there to be."

I look down at my cup, knowing what is coming next. She's giving me a look, trying to see inside my mind, to understand where the other half of me is. If she only knew how much I don't want to hear it.

"You have a sister, no?"

It breaks my heart afresh, thinking about Minna, but I nod, still not looking up.

"And she's…" Tante Tilde looks around, as if Minna could be in the room, hiding behind the table. Then she peers at me again, trying to meet my eyes. I glance up and then away just as quickly. She sits back in her chair with a knowing sigh. "Ah, well, we should get some sleep now. We'll have to introduce you to everyone tomorrow. Brace yourself. They can be a tough bunch, but if you can get through kirke without too many whispers, you'll be all right."

⇥⋈⋐

The bed is raised off the ground. Although I share it with Tante Tilde, I don't mind. It's wonderful. It has bed linens and a hay-stuffed softness I have only dreamed of. I can't even remember if I had a bed, a true bed, when I used to live here. I think momentarily of that house, cozy and comfortable, but it comes to me in fragments rather than whole memories: Mamma is telling us a story, and Mormor is chanting some incantation in the background. Mormor is in almost every memory I have, not just the ones starting when we ran, carrying as much as we could hold, the village and the sea disappearing behind us. She was there long before that, even when things were easy and witch burnings were happening in other villages instead of ours.

I bring my focus back to the bed and carefully slip off Mamma's shoes, which have turned out to be far more uncomfortable than I would have thought. The Sami along the coast trade with Norwegians and the Pomors from Russia, so they had shoes that look like Mamma's, which I was thankful to see, and plain brown wool dresses like the one I wear now. I didn't want to spend my silver on colorful threads. That felt like too much. But at least I'm not wearing the tatters of a girl who lives in the woods any longer.

I step out of the dress, too, and slip under the blanket, feeling the wool scratch against my skin. The bed is even plusher than it looks. But I turn over, suddenly afraid of what tomorrow will look like. Soon, Tante Tilde sinks into the bed next to me, and I am relieved at how kind and staunchly loyal she is, just as Mormor said she would be, but I know I cannot rely on her for everything. I must do the adjusting on my own. I must cast out the wild girl and learn how to live here, in this village, and act as if it's something I've known how to do all my life.

ᛁ
Minna

It's there as soon as I step outside the hut. I can feel it. It's in the new kind of cold. It's in the thinness of my breath. Most of all, it's in the tiny white flakes that dare to flutter down onto my nose.

It's late, this season's first snow.

We are always ready for it, and even though I am alone, even though Mormor is in the sky and Kaija has been gone for more than a month already, I will be prepared. I try to think about what else needs to be done if the snows decide to fall heavily tomorrow.

Dried bilberries are stockpiled in a basket along with some herbs. I've lined the floor with as many pelts as I could manage, though I could use a few more. I have had lots of luck with the hares this season.

I pick up a twig dusted with white and snap it in half when I think of the snares Kaija left me—one last pity gift. I wish I didn't have to use them, but I can't deny they have been helpful and will be even more now that the snow is here.

Later in the winter, when it's thick and pillowy under my fur boots, the hares will turn an invisible white, making Kaija's snares essential to catching them. It's the annual game they play with us, and Jörð seems to play right along, hiding them in low thickets and beneath bridged branches.

The old magic, Mormor taught us, is as moody as any person when left alone. It can be playful and mischievous as easily as it can be treacherous. Mormor carved the rituals, the galdrs, and the magic into us like runes carved into rock. We were born with the ability for witching, yes, but her lessons gave us power. *Sól is the goddess of the sun. Nótt is the night goddess, Njörun, the goddess of our dreams. Jörð is the earth herself. These are the ancient goddesses, and their magic runs through you both. Do you understand?*

I understand. The witching blood in my veins can be benevolent. It can be dark. It can be powerful, shake mountains. It can be small, contained in a hex bag the size of my palm.

Mormor's stern words come back to me: *Don't let your witching run wild. Keep your magic in check.*

I push the thought of witching aside for a moment as snowflakes fall on my hair, on my shoulders.

It would be really something if I could get an elk this year. It would be the first time trying it on my own, but I can manage. Kaija helped with hunting, but I was the one who did most of the work anyway.

I have a sense for prey.

I can always see it meandering between the trees, innocent at first and then eyes alert and frozen when we get too close. We lost a few that way, though Kaija never seemed too disappointed. And even though I could tell she didn't like it—mostly because she'd squish up her face whenever she saw the blood—she still dug the knife in and dragged it up the spine. She still stood on one end and peeled the bloodied hide off. It was satisfying, I always thought, but I could see she disagreed. I'm sure she thought it was men's work. Or maybe she just wished it were so she wouldn't have to do it. But letting a man do the satisfying work was the last thing I would want.

I laugh into the cold morning. Kaija may not like the hunt, but she liked the elk well enough once it was cooked.

I stop, thinking of the taste of elk meat. If I don't get that kill, it will be a long, hungry winter. I'm strong and capable enough, even alone. But I'm not taking any chances. I'll not leave anything up to the moodiness of earth magic. Witching has its place.

As I step between the gnarled fingers of bare birch trunks, snow-flakes thickening, I wonder if Mormor would approve of the spell I'm about to do. She had her own way of calling nature's magic to us, getting us the food we needed to stay alive. But I realize now that I have somehow developed my own method over the years. It's a bit more direct than hers: my words just a little sharper, my rune blood a little thicker, but that's just how the magic shows up for me—like the sting of a scorched needle.

At the clearing, the ground is hard beneath my knees. I tie a single knot in the piece of wool—I still can't find the witch's cloth I lost the night of the storm—and I speak the rhyme with my eyes closed. "Animals, come, for I hunger. Come one, come two, come three, come four. Meet my arrow and live no more. Arrive in number at my door."

It's not very poetic, but I hope it does the trick. The scratch of witching is content in my veins, happy with our little spell—so happy, I decide to do another.

"I call you, sleep, to close my eyes. That I shall rest through the long night. I wake with sun and sleep with moon. And with this wish, take this, my rune."

This one may be simple, too, but it comes to me as I say it. I spit on the rune stone and lay it on the ground; then I walk around it backward three times before picking it up and closing it in my fist. I'll put it under my pelts when I get back to the hut.

The spells, Mormor said, *they're yours. No two witches have the same exact magic.*

Every witch must make her craft belong to her. If she abides by the foundations of the ritual—uses the exact materials, counts the right number of times to walk backward or spit or yawn, doesn't douse the witch's fire too soon—she can perform them in her own distinct way. This is how it is with all magic, dark and light. I have practiced this ritual with Mormor several times before, usually when the snows came early and she wanted to be extra cautious. I tried to give it all the intention I could, connect deeply with the earth.

It will take this time. It has to.

Since Kaija left, I've been doing more spells than usual. Some of them have been necessary to make sure I don't starve, but mostly I'm just so bored. I haven't been sure what to do with my days once I've done my winter preparations. The spells have kept me going. When I feel the itch, I linger for a bit before performing. It feels good, the tingle. It feels like someone is here with me.

I caught myself—just once—trying to strike up a conversation with the witch under my skin. She didn't respond, which shook me back to my senses, but I wouldn't have been surprised if she did. It's all been a little off, like my magic is leaning slightly to the left, looking for my sister's, instead of standing straight upright on its own.

As I walk back, I notice the snow has gathered beneath my feet. It's thin and pillowy soft, a good first snow. It has the kind of consistency that will allow it to accumulate overnight. I know I'll light a fire inside the hut for the first time this season, and the idea of it makes me pick up my pace.

It's a long distance from the clearing to the small camp, but I manage it quickly, rune squeezed tightly in my palm. I pull my cloak around me a bit tighter as I feel the wind build.

Winter is on its way, the breeze seems to say. *Are you ready?*

By the time I see the hut, I'm fully chilled. I should put another layer on. The sun is setting now, and it takes me by surprise that the day is so short already. Between the coming winter darkness and the heavy snow, this winter will be full of fires in my little hut, and my feet will be warmer than they need to be.

I grip the rune stone tighter in my hand, grateful that my dreams will be quiet and I can finally get some good rest.

I'm close now, but something stops me.

The witch inside me has her ears pricked and seems to be holding me back. She's sent her tingling up to my face, as if she's trying to get closer so she can hear someone breaking through her enchantments. I listen, and all I can make out is the gentle sound of nothingness fresh snow makes on top of fresh snow. All is quiet.

But then I see it.

Something moving between two trees. It's a figure. A woman. She's so close, I can make out two pink cheeks and long brown braids that fall to either side of a fur coat, which is lined with red and blue. Those colors come from the Sami settlement to the north.

The woman is alone, moving gracefully and without worry, like she knows exactly what she's looking for, like she's well-known here. She's not careless but curious and only a bit impatient. I stay hidden as well as I can, crouching lower and opening my mouth to silence my breaths.

I don't quite know what she's doing here and how she's doing it. A person must be explicitly invited in order to even see this little camp, let alone come to it.

The woman walks around the fire ring, which sits like a ghost now, cold and empty, its black ash blanketed in white. Maybe she'll think this place is abandoned and be on her way. But then she spots my day-old hares, gives them a sniff.

Damn.

I should have brought them inside before going to do the spells. She grabs a foot, examines it, and then lets it swing back so it collides with the others. I see she's carrying a bag over her shoulder. It looks as if something is fluffed up inside it, though I can't see what it is.

"Minna?"

I'm frozen when she says it, and the moment grows.

She can't see me. I know she can't. I'm too well hidden. The snow is thick now, obscuring my vision just a bit. But my hearing is clear. This woman knows my name. How is it that she knows my name?

No one is supposed to know I exist except my sister.

"Your sister sent me." She says this in the direction of the hut in stilted but clear enough Norwegian. I can see the puff of her bag clearly from here. She doesn't appear to have a weapon of any kind. I scan the woods behind her. No one else seems to be with her. "Hello?" She spins around, and I duck lower. I can see now that she's older than me by at least a generation. Her pink cheeks brighten two gray eyes, and small wrinkles gather at the corners where her skin has browned from years in the sun.

She huffs. I don't move.

"Kaija asked that I check on you. She gifted me a pelt one month past, and if you don't come out and at least let me see that you're all right, she will have given me payment for nothing." She pauses, waits patiently. I imagine she's a mother, maybe a grandmother, since she's doing the type of waiting Mormor used to do. Quiet and knowing.

Then she pulls the bag around to her front. "I brought you some clothes, like your sister's." She pauses, waiting, again, for any sign of me. "Well, I will just leave them here." She pulls something gray out of the bag along with a few more articles and drapes them over the rack next to the hare carcasses.

She takes one more sweep around the camp but seems resigned because it only takes her a few more moments before she walks back the way she came.

⸭⟊⟊

I wait at least an hour longer than I need to before I come out. By the time I do, the skirts are already covered in snow, and I shake them off to look at them in the dark.

The bottom is simple gray, not too different from the skirt I wear now, except it's neatly stitched and clean. The blouse is white and flowing, and there's a pale apron that covers the chest, looping around the shoulder and tying around the waist. I lay all the pieces out in the snow, admiring them from above. It's not completely impractical, I'll admit. There's a flicker of a moment in which I think I may just try them on, see how they fit. But then I remember where they came from.

My sister wants me to come to the village. This is an invitation.

Kaija didn't want to stay here with me, so she invited a woman here to find me, to dress me as if I were a child, and to lure me to the village where she and I can play dress-up with the other young women. We can pretend we're just like them, that we don't bear the scars of their parents' decision to make coal out of our mother, that we don't carry their chains or know of their wretchedness.

And then the next realization comes to me, unwanted, like a cruel winter storm.

Not only has my sister insulted me with a piteous gift she couldn't even deliver herself, but in doing so, she has also revealed to someone that I am here. She has told someone, Sami or no, where I live. I am a witch, and I do magic here, and that is the reason no one is supposed to know.

I laugh. Kaija doesn't care. Kaija only thinks about herself, not about how I'm meant to survive. If they found out about me, the people of the village could come looking for me: the daughter of a witch, ripe with magic herself.

⊒⊁◇⟨⟨⟨

I don't burn the dress, though I want to. Instead, I sit in the hut, watching the flames spit and twist from layers of hacked birch logs and brush.

Beyond the fire, once in a while, I can see a little flash of white. The crown she meant for me to wear hasn't faded or crumbled. Its white petals shine fiercely, encircling the note underneath. They have been there since the night she left. I touched them only once, to move them to her side of the hut.

How could Kaija betray me like this? Just because she's gone doesn't mean I am. This is my home; this is where Mormor died. This is where I will stay until I am old and dying myself, if that's what it takes to stay safe. If that's what it takes to stay a witch. They've taken everything from me, but they can't take that. I'd rather die first.

I haven't read the note. Reading it would be condoning what she's done. But now I realize maybe she said something in it about the Sami woman coming to check on me. Maybe there is other information in there that I need to know before the whole of Norway discovers me and I'm forced to leave this little fell for Russia.

I stand up. Take a step. Sit back down.

The pelts are warm underneath me. This place is home, and I'm doing just fine on my own. I'm surviving just as we always survived, only there's a little less joy to it. Sometimes I find myself staring out into dark woods, after the butchering is done, before the cooking, and I can't help but miss her. I think of all the times we finished our tasks, elbow to elbow, without needing to say a word, and I long for it.

I hate that I do, but it's sometimes hard to see the point of all this without her.

The Sami woman. There was something that happened to me when I saw her. Of course, I would never risk being seen. Nothing is worth risking the fires of a witch burning, but she had such a gentle way about her that reminded me, even just a little bit, of Kaija. I had a moment when I wanted to go to her, to tell her how hard it's been. To ask her to help me prepare the meat tonight.

The fire groans as a log crumbles under its heat.

But no. That woman was just a tool my sister used to try to get me to leave this place, to join her in the village. I will never give those villagers what they want. They want witches to come to them, to stand in front of them, alive and itchy with it. It is much easier that way than to root them out, dig them from neighborhoods and friendships.

I am sure it's a very satisfying thing to see a witch burn when you're the one who discovered her.

I stare into the fire, wondering. If my curse against the village took, wouldn't Kaija have seen the destruction and come home right away?

I shake myself out of it. Of course it took. But maybe it's not quite so obvious, not yet—still too soon for Kaija to recognize the signs. Or maybe my sister has chosen a village of ashes over me.

Without meaning to, I've torn the hem of my skirt; I notice and release it.

I spot the note again and get to my feet. In a few steps, I'm there. I squat, and it's in my fingers, thin and fragile. The crown Kaija left on it, to ward off the evil spirits from this hut, falls to the ground beneath me as I lift the note toward my face. Instead of reading it, I fling it from my grip and watch it flutter into the fire. It burns until its ashes blacken the top of the hut.

Sleep comes easily to me tonight. My spell must have worked. They always do.

Kaija

I'm Kirsti Morgensdatter now.

I look at the window of a brygge as I pass, not seeing the fishing supplies kept inside the little storage house by the sea, but hoping only to catch a glimpse of myself. I want to see how my hair lies neatly in its braids, to see the hem of my skirts swing delicately with every step. It's not as if I'm a lady or anything, but I'm certainly not a girl of the woods anymore. It's late November now, and I have been here for several weeks already, though it feels like longer. The seasons used to feel like they shifted quickly in the woods, and there were too many immediate changes—changes I could touch with my hand and feel under my feet, year after year. Out there, my youth seemed eternal. There's something about the lack of trees here that makes me finally feel older, like the woman I am. It's only gray houses and rocks and the sea. The changes are small here. Even the snow, I remember, is minimal. And I can tell already, the expectations are nuanced.

The walk down to the beach isn't too far, but I start to hurry because I can already see the shadows of other women gathering around the hjell, a tall, pointed wooden rack where we will hang the freshly caught cod to dry. The sounds of the women's chatter are like pins in the ocean's calm breath.

"Over here," shouts one woman, who is taller and thicker than any tree I've ever seen.

"Use this now," says another, indicating a hook to a girl who takes a fish from her with silent obedience. It's midday, but the sun stays tethered just below the horizon as it's already mørketiden, the season of perpetual darkness that begins every year around this time. All the women are bathed in the lavenders of sunset.

As I approach, a few women quiet and stop their preparations to look at me. I search all of them for my old friends, and I think I spot Ingebor and Maren, but they don't pay me much mind, other than to assess my presence with all the welcome of a pack of wolves. I have only met a few of the others, but it feels as if I haven't met any as I stand here under their sudden gazes. They're watching to see what I'll do, and since I don't know what to do, I just watch back. The woman I felt proud to be as I walked down here has just vanished, and she's back to being a little girl, embarrassed not to know what's to come, shy in front of these grown women who seem to have a language, a way of moving, that's all theirs.

"Kirsti." Someone says my new name, and relief moves through my blood. Someone familiar moves toward me. Lisebet. She's familiar in more ways than one. I met her outside kirke recently. Tante Tilde tried to introduce me to young women around my age in the first few weeks so I would have some companionship besides an old woman. That was when I saw Ingebor for the first time, and Maren and a couple of the others whose names didn't come to me. They didn't remember me, of course. They couldn't know who I was—thanks to my new hair and eyes and name, I'm not much of me anymore—but all I could think of were those nights we used to spend running along the beach, trying to catch seabirds before they flew away, and then running back even faster, fearing we would be scolded by our parents for missing supper. However much I longed to dip into the nostalgia that painted my youth in the plain shades of white and gray, my conversations with these women were brief and stilted. As we spoke, children crawled up their bodies and peeked around their legs, distracted by the newcomer. Soon, I had the sense that the girls who once knew me as Kaija didn't much care to get to know me as Kirsti, and I eventually permitted them to drift off to walk home with their husbands. It felt off, trying to force new friendships with women whose lives were so unlike mine. When I met Lisebet and Anne, however, they both seemed pleased to meet another young woman. I think they may be Minna's age, though I can't be sure. All I know is neither of them has children, and neither is married, which makes them my only possible companions, I suppose, though they are both very sweet, especially Anne, with her fresh pink cheeks and playful spirit. I don't mind spending time with them. In fact, I love passing evenings at Tante Tilde's fireside, listening to stories about Mormor, but at this moment, I am grateful to have potential companions here. I can still feel all the other women's eyes on me. Anne pokes her head around the side of her friend and smiles at me, too, with the warm timidity of a sandy-haired child.

"Let's all stand near one another," says Lisebet, and Anne agrees with a fervent nod, giving me an encouraging look that calms my heartbeat a fraction more. Their faces are flushed from the cold breeze.

Soon, the other women are too preoccupied with the fish to pay me any mind. The hjell stretches along the beach, parallel to the sea, though not too close. It's made from imported wood that's been lashed together, and it's worn and gray from years in the sea air. Most of the men came back from a long trip early this morning, and the women have gathered to help with drying. We all work side by side— even Tante Tilde is here, though she's at the opposite end of the row from me—tying tails together and hanging the fish over the stocks.

It's tedious work, and it reminds me more of life with Minna than I thought it would.

I'm hot and tired within an hour, despite the damp winter wind. Lisebet shows me the difference between a pollock and a haddock, and she mentions Anne's upcoming betrothal. "Nothing officially ordained by the kirke yet," she says, nodding at her friend, who says nothing while she hides her shy smile, "but they've spoken about it."

I act interested, and I am, but I'm thinking of the hours spent on this beach as a child. Time was endless then, I realize as a splash of fish water wets the front of my apron. How happy I am to have had those nights, and how strange it is to see these women here now. I look down the line to watch them work. Their hands move deftly. Their mouths are mostly quiet, except for a few murmurs here and there. These women have beds that are raised off the ground and warm hearths and trinkets and skirts and washbasins and bonnets. But there is work in the curve of their shoulders, in the thick knuckles that swiftly tie and hang, tie and hang. These women may have comforts, but they're bound to the whims of the sea, and they're used to bending their heads against the strong northern winds. It's strange, but I suddenly understand Mormor a little more.

When we finish, it is even darker, though it's only midafternoon. The women are chattier now: some sharing stories about their husbands' journeys, and some shooing children home. I say good night to Anne and Lisebet and find Tante Tilde's stout figure in the crowd.

"Ah, Kirsti," she greets me in a tired voice, and I'm forced to slow my gait significantly to match hers. She's walking with two companions, I notice now: one, a stern-looking brown-haired woman, and the other, an older woman with a pointed nose and a distinguishable limp.

"Frøken Morgensdatter. Your tante has told me so much about you." The limping woman's words are like ice that has melted only at the top. It's mild enough, but bitter cold lingers just under the surface. I stiffen and hear Tante Tilde give a small cough, perhaps a warning.

"Yes, thank you. I am very happy to be here after such a long journey."

"I am Astrid Olsdatter. My home is not too far from yours. Perhaps we can walk to kirke together this Sunday." It doesn't seem like a very welcoming invitation but rather more of a command. I keep from glancing at Tante Tilde and choose my feet instead. She's told me all about Astrid Olsdatter.

"And this, Kirsti, is Mari Gundersdatter, Erich Pedersen's wife."

I can't see well, but I look up at the stern woman, who gives me the shadow of a nod through the darkness. "Nice to meet you, Frøken Morgensdatter. We are surprised and very happy to have another young woman here."

I don't respond because there's no question in there. I can't tell if Mari is truly happy or if there's a layer to her comment I can't quite reach.

"How old are you?" Astrid Olsdatter asks me.

I take a moment to adjust to the abruptness of the question. "Twenty-three." I am trying to find that proud woman who walked by the glass window just hours ago, grown and womanly, but all I can find is a girl too timid to speak a full sentence.

"About the same age as Jon then," says Astrid.

I get the sense from Mari's grunt that she's not too pleased with this information, but I keep quiet. It didn't feel too far to walk down to the beach just hours ago, but it feels like an eternity now, on the way back. The women move on to discussing the weather and the bounty of fish from today, but there's a solemnity that weighs down their voices.

"Such a shame about Johanne Henningsen," says Astrid.

Tante Tilde and Mari both tsk and shake their heads.

"You know, he was quite old," says Tante Tilde. "It's no wonder a simple cough took the last of his strength."

"He was frail, true," says Mari, "but it came on so suddenly." She leans in closer, lowers her voice. "He was coughing up blood in the end. That's what Pastor Thorkild told me."

"Too gruesome," says Tante Tilde. "I'd like to go in my sleep, thank you very much."

I frown, thinking of Mormor, but when I look up, I can see Astrid eyeing me sideways, her face shifting eerily in the lamplight.

I'm weary by the time we part from the other women, and I can barely make out where we're going. An unlit lantern hangs from Tante Tilde's belt. I suppose she must know this landscape as well as I knew the birchwood.

"You did well," she says to me when we're alone. "You were demure. They'll like that well enough."

I know there's fish stew and beer just inside Tante Tilde's door, and it can't come soon enough. I must find a place in this village, or I may drown in everyone else's judgments of me. But right now, all I want is to rest my arms and warm my toes.

"You'll do fine," Tante Tilde offers, and I can't help but wonder if there's a catch in her voice. Before I can think too long about it, she shoves open the door, and we file into the house to outlast the dark afternoon.

Minna

I squat to light the first candle.

My hands are ungloved, cold and exposed but prickly with witching. I hover them over the wick and close my eyes.

This is all of it. It's everything I need. Why would I need anything from anyone else when it's all here, the magic, right at my fingertips? I'm not counting or anything, but Kaija's been gone for more than two months.

I've been fine on my own. I can light fire without striking a match. I can ward off storms by bleeding on a simple rune stone and chanting a galdr. The power that lies just below the surface of my body is coming out through my hands, and it feels like it's all the power in the whole world.

The candle wakes, a yellow flame tickling the air around it, feeling its way in the dark. Light falls on the snow around me, illuminating the fur of my boots.

One candle done. Twenty-six to go.

I glance at the circle of unlit candles surrounding me. They're waiting for me to bring them to life. I'm impatient as I go—I can only light one at a time—but there's something rhythmic about the process. It makes me think about the night I cast my first spell. I was six. I caused it to rain in the clearing for just a few moments, though it took all my strength. I realized then that, for me, there is a rhythm to the magic that begins long before the ritual.

It begins right now.

The witch inside me swims with delight. She knows there are more candles to set aflame and more hours to play. She's trying to take control, make the ritual happen faster, but I scratch to quell her and push on. I can be just as stubborn as she is. This ritual will not be rushed.

Each candle lights a little differently, which interests me. Some are quick and bright, like a spark, while others start out small and blue and don't look like they're going to make it, but somehow they, too, survive. A flame full of magic will burn no matter what. I light one after the other and begin to move faster. My legs ache now from the squat I repeat to get low enough, but it's a sensation that comes with warmth, and it's welcome. My hands burn with the flames of magic on one side and the bitter cold on the other. I take breaks, but I refuse to look around again until they're all lit.

The clearing is windless and calm, and it feels as if the whole world is asleep tonight. All except the witches, who must be congregating now, wherever they can. They'll be disappearing under magical cloaks and away from watchful eyes to create some light in all this darkness because tonight is vintersolverv, the darkest night of the year and the start of winter. Spells will be cast on villages far and wide to keep the curious and the vicious asleep in their dark beds so those with magic can honor the light.

I wonder, briefly, what Kaija is doing tonight—if she's found a quiet corner away from all of them to light even a solitary candle for the solstice. I know her skin must be dancing, just as mine is. Another deep scratch keeps the witch within in check.

Of course, I realize, Kaija won't be able to get away. She won't be able to hide her magic from them.

She won't want to anyway.

She didn't even want to do magic here where there was no one to point a bony finger in her direction and scream what she was to the world. I know she won't be doing anything like I'm doing.

Maybe she never will again.

The last candle lights slowly, knowing its place in this ritual and bringing more spectacle to the moment. I don't mind any of it. I have plenty of time, and I won't need sleep for another few hours. I have been sleeping during the days in preparation for tonight.

Finally, I tuck my hands back into my coat and turn around to examine the circle. It's a dazzling sight. Every candle has its own dance, and together they're throwing light across the entire clearing. My inner witch seems pleased with me.

The days have been long and dark, and this marks the turning point, the middle of the darkness, the deepest, blackest night of them all. On the other side is light and spring and sunshine. I grab the flask of bilberry wine and take a celebratory sip.

There are more candles than I ever lit with Mormor and Kaija. Usually, we just do the typical nine—one for each of the ancient gods' worlds—and put them in the center while we circle. But this time felt different. It's somehow more significant this vintersolverv, which called for compounding the power of the fortuitous nine candles by three. Not because I'm alone. More because this place, this power, deserves to be celebrated.

If my sister is going to deny the witch in her, I'm going to make mine as mighty as I can. There needs to be balance in the world.

I examine everything I've brought. I have the horn, and I have my stave, which I carved specifically for this night. Another long sip of wine, and I'm ready to begin.

I sit at the center of the brilliant circle, and I put the horn to my lips. It's cold, but it feels familiar. It took Mormor a couple of years to fully embrace her magic out here, but once she did, we all lived in a world where we blew the horns of the ancestors and worshipped the gods of old. Our spells lit up the day when we needed sun and darkened the skies when we needed rain.

I grew up with almost as much freedom as I can feel now, as I suck air into my lungs, position my fingers for the first long note. It comes out of me smooth and loud, and it rings in my ears as the witch dances with delight just below the surface of my skin.

Normally, Kaija and Mormor would be here to sing or chant along with the note, and alone it's haunting, like a spirit missing its body. But since I can't sing and play at once, I keep going, bringing in more frigid air and letting it out in another hearty bellow.

When I'm done, my face is still vibrating with it, and I should sing, but I can't think of the right song—Kaija used to lead that part, and it feels strange to do it without her—so I stand and take another drink, and the sourness stings my tongue. Another drink, and then a bigger one.

Soon, I'm up and dancing. I twirl around, feeling the bright warmth that seems like it's from the candles' fire but is really from the magic moving through me. At least it feels that way. My limbs move me around and around, wildly and without me willing them to. I have the sudden desire to stop, to rest for a moment, but the witch inside has control now. She's not letting go.

I hear myself thank the goddess Nótt for this night, with a voice that's nice and loud. I imagine it sounds just as Mormor used to sound, but I know it comes out harsh, shrill even. I take another lengthy pull from the flask of wine. The witch is skipping me in circles now, her power like tiny burns all over my body, itches I can't possibly reach, and I'm imagining the sun shining brightly on me, and then my eyes are open, and of course it's dark, and I'm dizzy, but I take another swig of wine, this time not moving it from my lips until it's light and empty. I slump down into the snow.

My dancing has stirred up enough sweat for a thick chill to pass through me. *That's the magic releasing.* I want to laugh. Even though Mormor is gone, she seems to sit here next to me.

But I honestly can't tell if it's Mormor's voice I hear in my head or the witch who seems to have replaced me entirely.

I can almost feel myself becoming her.

I shake my head, an uncontrollable open-mouthed smile coming over me. When my loud witchy laugh dies, I can still feel her. I guess I can't get rid of something that's so deep in my veins.

And then I look up.

The spellfire glows, now a brilliant spring green against a deep-blue backdrop. It spins and streaks across the sky in one direction and then the other. I fall back, and some snow sneaks into my cloak, making me shiver. I look up, just like we used to, to see if I can see the entire wisp of color from end to end.

I wonder where it does end. Somewhere to the west, I think. But then it's spinning again, and I can't tell east from west anymore anyway.

Once the spellfire fades to a putrid gray against the black sky, the witch reminds me she's still here and forces me to sit up.

It's time for the sacrifice.

In one swift, blurry motion, I pull the knife from my belt and tear off my boot. My foot is numb to the cold for the half second it takes for me to slice the bottom of my toe, quick and shallow, and I barely feel it at all. My blood leaves dark spots on the snow as I grab my stave and smear it on.

"A dance for Sól, who will soon bring us sun—her strength breaking the cold nights into day." I slur slightly. "A sacrifice of blood to Nótt, the goddess of *un*light, in praise of her dark powers." The clearing spins, even though I'm sitting completely still, and I can't focus on a single candle. Whereas before they illuminated this ring with brilliant magical power, all I can see are streaks of yellow now, moving through my vision with a speed that doesn't seem to fit.

I know I'm not moving, but it feels like I'm flying, and then there's another sensation I can't control.

It's coming up through my gut, and then it's burning my throat, and I lean over to make sure it doesn't land on the fur of my coat.

‑‑ӜѺ҉Ӻ‑‑

When I wake, some of the candles are lit, but most have died out, leaving my circle looking like the inside of an old woman's mouth.

My stomach is rolling, and I swallow a sudden urge to be sick. I remember that I was already sick, and I wonder how long I've been sleeping. There isn't even a hint of spellfire above me anymore. I sit still until the last candle burns to darkness, and I'm so hungry and so thirsty, I could drink a whole river and eat a whole bear, but still I stay. There's a headache coming over me now, but there's more behind it.

I can almost feel Mormor's aggravated voice from the other side of the circle. *Control your magic—control yourself.* I nod at the woman who taught me how to be myself and tried to teach me how to rein it in but who died before she could finish her lessons.

I nod at the woman who isn't here.

And then I imagine Kaija's voice, soft and gentle, but her words sting nonetheless. *You're too wild. It's too hard to be around you when you're like this.*

It's vintersolverv, I think, licking my lips and feeling the cold biting at them. It should be a time of celebration, a time to be like the candle that bursts through the night. It's a ritual that's always been special. It's always been our favorite.

And the way the spellfire glowed, I remember now—it calmed me.

I should feel alight right now, but I'm not feeling particularly magical as much as dry in the mouth.

I look around at the ring of nothing where the candles burned. How much time I spent preparing those candles, and now it's all over.

I'm alone, and it's still dark.

I know the hope of spring is dawning, and I know Sól will be here soon, but she's not here now. No one is here now, not even the witch beneath my skin, who seems to be sleeping off the long wild night.

There's only the sound of my own breath and a steady throb that stretches from my head to the underside of my toe.

Kaija

I'm walking to kirke, and it's dark and cold. The sun hasn't shone for at least a month and won't shine for many weeks to come. But I'm glad to be out anyway. Kirke is an odd place to be, to listen to the pastor speak of God and his work and the evils of Djevelen, who is always tempting us. *Women, who are weaker of mind, are thus especially susceptible to his devious cunning. We must be wary. Let us pray now.* He seems to be speaking right to me sometimes, but I'm not sure if I'm being overly cautious. He cannot know what I am. He can't have any idea where I come from. I look so different now.

I have a good reason to watch my back, though. In the two months since my arrival here in the village, a story has made its way around the village, featuring me. Apparently, I am a long-lost daughter of Tante Tilde's husband, who picked up a mistress on one of his many trips to Bergen. "That woman has a mouth the size of a cod's," Tante Tilde told me just this morning as we dressed. "It's why I keep her close, even though I can't stand the sight of her big wobbly ass." She was speaking about Astrid Olsdatter and her propensity for gossip. It was the reason Tante Tilde sent me to walk the long way to kirke, rather than with her.

"Just because I must keep her close doesn't mean you have to. Go, meet some more people your age."

That change suited me perfectly well, though I said nothing. The truth was the way we usually walked took me right past Mamma's old house—our old house—which seems to be abandoned for now; it was the place where they put the stake and where I left Mamma all those years ago. I don't know what's worse, the memory of it ablaze back then or the sight of it now, plain and empty, a death not even worth commemorating. I'm happy not to have to see any of it. I want to be here and start fresh, but I'm not sure the memories will go away if I'm walking by all the time.

I watch Tante Tilde go in the other direction, and I start off on my own. I'm not alone for long, though, because from a house nearby, a group of people emerges and steps into my path. I see six dark figures turn in my direction, and I think I catch the shape of Mari, whom I recognize from our walk home from the stocks. All six of the figures remain still, and I sense they're waiting for me. Maybe they can see me better than I can see them. As I get closer, I start to make out their faces in the lantern light. It is Mari after all, and she's staring at me in a way I can't interpret but makes me look away. The other five stare as well, though their eyes hold more curiosity than anything else, and I can see now that they are mostly tall men—one man who looks to be Mari's husband and three younger men. One is slender, with arms he doesn't quite know what to do with, and another has the cherubic face of a boy. There's a little girl holding the hand of a third young man who seems to be the eldest brother. He appears to be just a couple of years older than me, and his eyes dance blue in the light from the candle his mother holds. And suddenly, I see it in the eyes. I know who he is. I had forgotten that face, but I study him for a moment. He still reflects the playfulness I remember from our youth, only his jaw is a little more defined. Jonny Erichsen was the teasing kind of boy, the kind who joined Ingebor and the other girls and me in games of chase along the seashore and pulled our hair while we obediently recited the Pater Noster for the pastor on Sundays. But Jonny was as gangly as the others then. He certainly wasn't the tall, broad man he is now.

"Frøken Morgensdatter," says the older man. "My wife, Mari, has told us how pleasant you are as a walking companion." It's subtle, but I see Mari shoot him an unappreciative look. He doesn't flinch. Instead, a warm smile broadens his cheeks. "I am Erich Pedersen, and these are my sons: Jon, Nils, and Peder. And this is Ellen."

"Pleasure to meet you," they all say, almost in unison. Jonny's voice is the deepest and softens at the last word. His gaze is so direct, I feel my face warm. But his smile broadens gently, just like his father's, before he turns to look back at his parents. He goes by Jon now, not Jonny.

The kirke is somewhere in the distance, waiting for us to come and pray in silence, but for now, all I can see are the swinging shadows of my companions and their sturdy shoes crunching snow beneath us. I'm warmed by the masculine presences that surround me. It's not something I'm used to, but there's safety in the low roll of the men's voices, and there's a nervous energy that keeps my own words lodged in my throat. Mari is saying something about Nils's coat and how it could use a stitch, and the men all reply to her kindly but without engaging her fully on any one subject. I get the sense they're used to this verbal dance. They simply let their mother ramble on, and together they fill the silences with kind words while exchanging looks over her head so she's never overtly offended. I suppose this is how it is with families. I try to remember conversations back from when Pappa was alive, but I can't think of anything. The only conversations that come to mind are the ones I had with Minna, sleeping head to head in the birch hut: reviewing spells and listing the next day's needs.

I don't want to think about my sister, so I try to think of a polite way to enter the conversation. When there's a long enough silence, I say, "How have you been finding the fish these past weeks?" I should have addressed Erich directly, I know, but I can't help indulging myself in the small thrill that the others will think I may be speaking to them.

"Ah, well, there's still much of the season left, I suppose," says Erich without hesitation. "Although these waters should be black with cod by now. They're usually plentiful in the winter, but I suppose there is still time."

"There are stories," says Nils, "of when the codfish disappeared for more than sixty winters."

"Nonsense," says Mari. "There will be fish enough to see us through the season."

"But the fish from the stocks are barely enough to eat, and the dark days have already started," says Nils. "That was our last catch."

"God will grant us winter cod soon, I have no doubt," says Erich with a nod of finality. "He will have to. The merchants in Bergen will be wondering where we have been these long months. I suppose it is like all blessings in life, however. We will simply have to wait for it."

"You must have more hope, little brother." Jon's voice cuts through the chorus of the conversation with playful command, and when he reaches out to shove his brother's arm in the way only older siblings can do without consequence, I force myself not to smile.

After the service, Lisebet and Anne find me and ask if I want to walk home with them. Anne and her mother have been making a new dress for her, even though she is still not formally engaged. Although she's shy about it, she wants to show us the progress. We have walked together from kirke for the past few weeks. It has been such a comfort to find friends after all these years. What Minna and I had wasn't so much a friendship as it was a necessity, and it feels nice to giggle and gossip without having to worry about fetching more wood for the fire or tempering my sister's bouts of rage. I thought, over the weeks, that Lisebet and Anne might start to remember me somehow. I thought, ridiculously, that the sound of my voice or my laugh might bring back visions of us running along these shores, though I can't pinpoint these two in any of my memories since they're closer to my sister's age. Regardless, if either of them does remember anything, they have said nothing. At first, I was a little disappointed, but I suppose it's as Tante Tilde says. The good women here don't look too closely at anything except their own kin. It's the ones who look too closely you need to watch out for.

"Of course," I tell Anne, and I squeeze in between her and Lisebet. Anne's face lights up with pleasure, and she hangs on my arm all the way to her home.

The dress is blue with flowers stitched onto the shoulders. The three of us catch only a glimpse of it pinned to the rafter before Anne's mother shoos us out, pointing at the door. "Take that setting dish in there and start churning the cream," she says without looking up from her handiwork. Her words are a command, but I can see her lips pressed together in a small smile she doesn't want us to see.

The three of us crowd the small room next door, where the butter churn sits waiting for us. Anne lights the lantern before she and Lisebet waste no time hoisting the dish off the table. Lisebet gives a small grunt, and I rush over to help scrape the cream on top into the tall wooden churn.

And then the work begins. Anne takes the first turn, grasping the plunger and pushing down forcefully.

"Are you excited?" asks Lisebet as she and I take a seat along the wall.

Anne laughs and looks up at us. Her face is small and delicate, but her grip on the churn is steady and sure, and she rotates the handle a quarter turn every time she pulls up, a trick of the hand no doubt honed over years already of doing women's work.

"Well, I'm excited for you," Lisebet continues. "And now that I've been polite, I just want to know when it will be my turn to become engaged."

"Same," I say wistfully, and I see genuine interest on my friends' faces. The churning stops for a moment, and there's a pause. I have the feeling they wonder about me, though not in a suspicious way like the older women. More in a way someone might wonder about a bird they've never seen before.

"Has anyone caught your eye?" says Anne shyly, resuming her vigorous plunging.

At this, Lisebet giggles, and I know they spot my instant flush.

"To be perfectly honest, it doesn't quite matter, does it?" Anne says before I can respond. "It's the boy who decides. And his family."

"You have the right of refusal, though, of course," Lisebet says, and I can tell she's attempting to infuse Anne's spirits with more positivity.

"Yes, but it all comes down to the mangletre," Anne replies.

"Which you can refuse to bring inside. You're perfectly allowed to say no, Anne."

I interject. "What is a mangletre?"

Anne seems delighted I asked and leaves her post, reaching over to grab something on a shelf behind her. "It's for rolling the flax into linen."

I'm looking at a plank of wood the length of a small arm with a carved-out handle on top. For a moment, I think it looks like a runestave, but then I remember where I am and shake the thought away. Lisebet takes the board from her friend and hands it to me. It's smooth to the touch, heavy. I'm sure it serves some purpose, but I'm not sure what.

"Don't you have these in Tromsø?" she asks me.

My heart quickens. "I—oh yes, of course. I just didn't recognize the name. We call it something different."

"So do you have the same betrothal tradition, then?" Anne asks.

"I don't think so, no." I try to sound confident, but I'm not sure I accomplish it. I'm certain neither of these young women has been to Tromsø, but that doesn't mean they can't know the customs, shared as stories passed along by their fathers and other men who have traveled the sea. I hold my breath, waiting for Lisebet to catch me out, ask me whether I'm really from Tromsø, but they don't seem to even notice my hesitation. They're looking at each other with mischievous grins.

"Well," says Lisebet, leaning in conspiratorially. "When a boy wants to ask for a girl's hand, he carves her a beautiful mangletre with shapes and animals and angels and sometimes different colors."

"They really can be quite lovely," Anne says reflectively.

Lisebet continues. "He leaves the mangletre outside your door as a sign. If you bring it in, it's a sign that you accept his proposal." She smiles, as if she cannot wait for the day this happens to her.

Thrilled by this romantic tradition and feeling comfortably part of the conversation, I turn to Anne, holding out the mangletre toward her. "Is this from him, then? From the young man courting you?"

I must have said the wrong thing because Anne stops churning and looks down at her feet. She shakes her head, embarrassment creeping into her voice when she replies, "No. This one is my mother's. I haven't gotten mine yet."

Lisebet speaks up next, a little too loudly for the small room. "But Anne is betrothed, to be certain. Their families have discussed the matter, and it's settled."

Unsure how to follow this, I simply nod. Anne looks so despondent not to have been offered such a gesture, I want to take her by the hands and tell her it will all be all right. That perhaps he is carving the most beautiful mangletre at this very moment, and he can't wait to give it to her. I don't know who the young man in question is, I realize, but she is so lovely that any young man would be fortunate to call her his bride.

I stand. Then I gently pry her fingers from the plunger handle and usher her over to the chair by the wall before taking over and letting her rest. She looks so grateful for this that I feel a stab of pity. I inhale it away, not wanting the mood to dampen further. "Now, then," I say brightly. "Do you think your mother would be willing to trade one of your sweet young cows for Tante Tilde's old goat?" When no one laughs or responds, I simply say, "I'm sure your mother will be pleased. This is starting to smell delicious."

Less than a week later, and it's Christmas. I linger a bit after kirke service, wondering if my new friends will want to walk together again. After our friendly afternoon in Anne's house, it's been a relatively lonely week for me, though the other villagers have been bustling around, busily preparing their Christmas suppers. Tante Tilde has kept me from venturing too far from her home, saying she needs the help, but there hasn't been all that much to do. We've passed most of the time discussing my backstory again as our faces glowed in the firelight. I get the sense that she doesn't want me mingling too much with the other villagers, but when I asked her about this, she shrugged and said, "People will always talk because you're a newcomer, but being seen too much around the village will only make it worse."

Today, however, we are out again. We cannot miss kirke on Christmas without raising suspicion, Tante Tilde says, so here we are. She has even given me permission to walk home with whomever I like again, though she admitted she will stay close behind. Her permission seems all for nothing, however, since Lisebet is tasked with wrangling her overexcited cousins and brothers, and Anne must rush home with her mother to help with the baking. She looks begrudgingly over her shoulder at me, pausing to stifle a cough with her apron, before dashing away down the lane.

I stoop to make sure my laces are tied tightly. I know they are. I've

checked already, but I want to look busy. I don't want the disappointment to show.

I notice the sky churning again. I recognize the faint outlines of
black and midnight-blue swirls that mean there's more snow coming,
even if it's just a dusting. I thought here, people might huddle around
their fires for days and weeks at a time, like Minna and I used to do
when the snow billowed, but the winter is milder here than it ever was
in the birchwood. Though by no means warm, it certainly beats winters
that could freeze your blood if you are out for too long. The people of
this village are not to be put off their duties by a little cold weather
anyway, especially not on Christmas when God requires their presence at kirke. They are devoted to their religion, or at least they seem
to be. There's a complacency here that I can't quite name, but it seems
to live in the colorless skirts of the women and the hard, pale faces of
the men. It doesn't feel exactly right, but it must be because I've got
so much excitement—I've been storing it up for months, maybe even
years—and these people are simply living their lives. I remind myself
that I wanted to escape to a mundane life after too much time in the
wild. It's this quiet, expected way of being that I craved. I'll adjust soon
enough, I am sure of it.

The thought of the birchwood reminds me of something else I've
been feeling lately—feeling but not naming. It's been happening for a
few weeks now, just a mild sensation right beneath the skin, like water
sliding over water right before it boils. I watch the faces of the women
as they walk by me: some offering stares that border on rudeness, and
others, curt nods. I try not to search too deeply in their eyes for the bubbling up of magic, which is why, of course, I see none. They either look
away too fast, heads hidden under winter bonnets, or their searching
eyes are a dull gray, too dull to have magic in them. It's too dark to see
well anyway, and I'm grateful I don't see anything I don't want to. Even
though I know I should stop thinking about it, I find myself wondering

what happened to all the other daughters of the witches who were burned here. Are their faces hidden among these women? But that is one thing I can never ask, and so I will never know.

When I first noticed the tingle of magic at my wrist, I ignored it. Then, about two weeks ago, Tante Tilde walked in on me charming my hair to blond. I had to get it done before the black roots began to show. I hadn't meant for her to see, of course. She glanced at my candle and my plucked strand and turned away as if it were nothing. I know I shouldn't be doing it, but now, when I feel the magic stirring inside, it's a little reminder that I can make everyday chores go just a little bit quicker. I can't afford to slip, but it's just easier to use a spell than it is to wash all the bed linens by hand or to milk Tante Tilde's solitary old goat. These little expressions of magic have started to creep into my life without my coaxing. I have been remembering little moments from the past, too: Mamma lighting a single fire in the hearth that would last the entire winter, using a spell to mend the hem of a skirt torn on the rocks or muttering a rhyme over a bonnet dropped in the mud. There aren't too many memories, but the ones that come back to me are of Mamma taking care of life's little conveniences with her magic, and so I suppose there's some part of me that does it simply because it feels familiar. Besides, it's not as if I'm causing anyone harm. I'm not doing the sort of witching that Minna probably is: trying to call up the wind or cause a hailstorm. I'm just making private tasks easier throughout my day so I can focus on more important things, like making the cheese just right for Tante Tilde and going to kirke and keeping my braids tidy.

I'm about to turn and join her when another crowd, men this time, comes out through the doors, lit by the kirke's lanterns. The first thing I see—the only thing I see—is Jon's tall frame and his smile. It starts to melt something in me, and I let it. Unashamed, he strides toward me as his father and brothers continue past me to greet Tante Tilde and Mari, who grips a squirming Ellen at her side. I don't know if I'm seeing things, but Jon seems to be hurrying, and I can't help but blush because the eye contact he makes is so intense.

"God Jul, Kirsti," he says. I flinch a little as he uses my new name, but it's intimate. He doesn't use my surname or put *frøken* in front of it like his father did. It's just Kirsti.

"God Jul," I say. *Merry Christmas.* Trying hard to look like I'm not trying hard—I think I manage it—I walk alongside him without showing my nerves. I can hear Tante Tilde's murmurs behind us between the beats of my own heart. She and her companions are not following too closely but following all the same. I suppose Jon and I will have a quarter of a blissful hour before he leaves me at my door, and I plan to make the most of it.

"So you're from Tromsø," he says to me. Our feet crunch snow. "I was there once, stopped on one of our voyages to Bergen. It is beautiful."

I try hard to avoid talking about my previous life in the village of Tromsø, mostly because I have no idea what the village is truly like. But I know it exists, this village, because Mormor spoke of it to me more than once, though Tante Tilde made me promise to keep my stories vague, as most of the men may know Tromsø.

"Not more beautiful than here," I say.

Jon's voice seems to drift off into wistful imagination. "Oh, you say that, but I think you're wrong. There are many places more beautiful than here. It must have been hard for you to leave it."

I want to tell him it was only hard dealing with the guilt. The actual leaving was one of the easiest things I've ever done. Instead, I laugh. "Yes, but there was nothing there for me anymore. I am glad I did."

I don't look at him, but I think I can detect a shy breath of laughter. "How is your Tante Tilde treating you?"

"Just fine, thank you."

"And how is her goat?"

"Pleasant enough." I stare down at my feet, which are illuminated only when Jon's lantern swings forward. We walk in silence because I'm suddenly feeling tongue-tied. I'm not sure if it's my fear of saying something wrong and being discovered for who I really am that keeps me quiet or if it's something else entirely. Tongue-tied or not, it feels right, walking next to him, even with the tension doubling over in my stomach. I wonder if he's feeling the same. It occurs to me that I am a newcomer to this village, and of course he is only being polite. Any nice young man would be.

I chance a look over at him, hoping not to catch his eye, yet hoping to in some small way. He's looking ahead, but I can tell he senses my glance, and it makes me blush again; I'm suddenly fresh with irritation at myself. These are the anxieties of a girl. This is the way I should have felt years ago had I stayed here and grown up in this village. I should have blushed as a girl in front of a boy, not as a woman in front of a man. I can't blame Mormor for this awkward introduction to adulthood, the missing era of my adolescent life that could have been spent strolling alongside boys and sneaking kisses, though I have the unfamiliar urge to blame someone. I spent my adolescence trudging along behind my sister, quiver slung at my back, furs wrapped around my shoulders, despising every minute of it. I spent my evenings listening to Mormor speak of Odin and the ancestors, roasting meat over the fire, and hearing the whistle of winter just outside our walls. I'm suddenly warm with a sensation I don't recognize. All the other women in this village had what I did not. They could do this little thing, walk home from kirke with a boy, anytime they wished. What a joy it is, listening to his steady footsteps beside mine, catching sight of his breath, white and wet with cold. Why couldn't things have been different? Why could I not have had this moment when I was sixteen? I don't want them to, but tears sting at my eyes.

Behind us, Tante Tilde's raspy laugh reminds me of her presence, and I realize I've been walking so closely to Jon that we're almost touching. I step away casually, though something inside me doesn't like that and tries to pull me closer to him.

Jon walks me all the way to my door, even though it's beyond his house. He steals a look behind him. We both see our chaperones are busy looking out over the churning ocean waters, pointing at the dark midday sky. Jon's brothers are still loping along, eyes only for their warm hearth that awaits them and a full Christmas supper. In this small moment that Jon and I have all to ourselves, he slides my mitten down gently so the top of my hand is exposed. Then he lowers his lips to my skin, giving it the lightest kiss.

"I hope I will see you again soon, Kirsti."

My bare flesh is cold, but the place where he put his lips tingles long after I close the door behind me. I can't tell if this feeling is from my inner magic or from his touch, but I find that I don't mind either way.

Minna

W olverines are nasty little things.

They spray something awful when they're caught in a trap. That's why I prefer to hunt them with an arrow. They're smart but not too fast, and that is just what I need today. If I can get one—even though I hate hunting them—it will give me a warm hide, and I could use another one.

My breath is ice in my chest, and I pull my coat even tighter around my neck. It's deep winter now, the days still as black as the nights. I've been lying here in the dark for hours, and my knees have melted holes in the snow. The deep-purple sky peeks through the pale tree trunks around me. I know the darkness will make it tough to see the wolverine when he comes, but I will be able to aim just fine.

As I lie here, I think again about how it used to be.

Before, Kaija would have been by my side or at least near enough to help with the return journey after I made the kill. She and I would take the animal and, together, make him into a pelt and several meals.

I rub my hands together and tuck them into my fur.

I never imagined what life would be like without Kaija. I didn't let myself think about the possibility that my sister would leave me here on my own, abandon me for a village that doesn't even want her. My hands are still cold, and I ball them into fists. I wonder what she's doing now. I can't even imagine anything beyond this snowy fell, these dormant birch trees, this unrelenting cold.

I know I don't need anyone else—I'm perfectly capable of handling myself on my own.

Despite that, the witch under my skin has become even more forceful lately. She seems to be enjoying this freedom of solitude a little too much. She bites at the inside of my wrist, and at the scarring on my hand, whenever she wants to do magic. It seems like that's every day now. And I let her win, even when I feel too tired to cast a spell to call up the wind or shift the clouds, thick with snow, away from this fell.

She is pushy, and I have nothing better to do.

I do sometimes wonder, after the hollowness that follows a spell done for no reason, if I could say no to the witch's demands if I chose to.

It's not like she's completely in control. She still needs me to carry out the ritual, to connect her with the old magic. But her scratches feel hostile lately, careless, untamable. I can't help but think what Mormor would say if she knew I can't control myself.

The thought enrages me, and I kick snow in protest of my own lack of control. I can't deny one truth: Kaija was always the one who helped temper my wild magic.

Kaija never did come back like I thought she might. In the months that have passed since she abandoned me, I have listened hard for her a few times when the wind snapped a branch or an animal scurried away from my footsteps.

I thought the rune stones were telling me my future. I thought they were telling me that Kaija would journey back here, that we'd take up life the way it used to be. But she never came, and now the snow is deep. I shouldn't be out in it for too long.

It's not that I miss Kaija's companionship. I don't.

It's just sinking in how much more than a companion she was. She was an extra body with hands and fingers that could mend and feet that could run, not to mention a calming presence to help control my witching, as much as I hated it at the time. While Mormor kept our home full of useful magic and I made sure we had enough to eat, Kaija seemed to be the one who kept us safe.

I still haven't remembered any of her protective spells, though I smeared blood on my stave and chanted a galdr that I made up. It didn't feel right. It didn't have any of her gentleness. It was all haste and hot blood, but it was all I could think to do. And the witch inside wasn't interested in gentle spells, so she stubbornly stayed away.

I didn't realize how much Kaija did when she was here, and Mormor, too, when she was well enough to be of help. Three people surviving the winter was much easier than one doing it alone.

I wish it wasn't true, but it is.

Though I would have loved the darkness to stay away, the winter has tossed a blanket over everything that won't lift for weeks yet. No matter how many spells I do, or how many times I go out hunting, or how many felled trees I chop, it's not enough to keep the quiet from settling into my bones. Plus, all the wild, pointless witching has made me stray from my necessary tasks. The witch doesn't understand what I need to survive.

This is the time for rest, Mormor always said, but it's not for me. I can only sit inside that hut and stew in my own resentment for so long, fighting as the inner witch claws her impatient nails into my skin. Thankfully, purpose has me chopping wood and sharpening tools in between meaningless spells. I have managed to keep up with at least some of the duties I can.

Never let your mind get the better of your body. Mormor used to say that, too. I roll my shoulders and snap my head from side to side, letting

Mormor's advice put the witch in her place. She quiets at that, maybe out of boredom, but it feels like bliss.

⸻ Ǝ⟩◊⟨Ǝ ⸻

Soon, I see a small dark shadow scurrying a few trees away, and a familiar thrill rushes through me. He's back. I situate myself near a small hole in the snow where I know this one's been hoarding his food for the winter. I lift my bow and squint out into the dark day. His face is pointed, a little pink nose at the tip. He sniffs around, feet plodding lightly on the thick snow. Then he spots his hiding place and digs his head down, leaning over with his catch, as innocent as a child hiding a toy.

I slide my hands free and pull back the arrow slowly, without making a sound.

This is a critical time, when I can watch the creature and pinpoint my shot. The moment right before a kill is the quietest of all, and the noiselessness that comes from stalking sometimes feels as powerful as magic.

I can see without being seen. I am invisible.

I am without the witch for now, which feels like pure freedom, and I loose the arrow with full control of my body. It thunks into the wolverine's backside, and the animal screeches and pulls his head out of the hole. He's frantic, but he's weak, stumbling with dark blotchy footsteps in the snow. I loose a second arrow, this time landing it as close to the heart as I can get. It's not ideal to have two punctures, but it's too dark to expect perfection.

I wait it out, but eventually, I see the confused little figure collapse into stillness. A few paces and I'm there, watching the life drain from his eyes, from his muscles, from his veins. I wonder what he thinks about as he sees me approach, wonder if he's angry that I've stolen the one thing he's always tried so hard to keep.

He only has a few moments of life left in him, so I don't have to wonder for very long.

━━━✦◇✦━━━

With the wolverine and his blood slung over my back, I make my way toward the hut. I'll clean and butcher him, make the meat tonight, but the hide will have to wait until the freshness of death isn't so strong.

A snake of red spellfire whips through the sky, and I see the hut in the distance. As I trudge closer, stepping high and trying to land in the holes of my old footsteps, I see a figure moving darkly around the hut.

I tuck myself down, hiding under the little wolverine's cooling body. The figure moves around, picks things up, and puts them down. The witch inside me wakes with a slow warning tap at my scar. I growl, a soft animal sound that only I can hear. The figure is probably the woman with the pink cheeks in her fur coat. She's come to check up on me again.

Kaija can keep an eye on her little sister from so far away, can't she? I don't need her, I tell myself again like I have a thousand times already. I'm capable, and I wish she would tell her friends to leave me in peace.

I notice that the woman's movements are strange, like she's walking bent over. At first, I think maybe she's hurt, and then the witch begins to gnash wildly beneath my skin. "Hey," I call out, unable to control myself. I stand, the wolverine heavy across my neck. I want to look her in the eye and tell her to go away. It feels like such an intrusion, someone I don't know looking around at everything I have, touching the sticks and stones I've collected and made part of my home. Does she think this is a place for visitors? I start to make my way over, pushing the witch down with all my might.

But then the figure stands, too.

And that's when I realize how tall she is. She looks to be about twice my height now, and the blood drains from my face, shooting straight to my limbs. It's not the pink-cheeked Sami woman.

Not at all.

It's a brown bear. What he's doing here in the middle of the winter is beyond me, but I don't have time to think because he's spotted me, and he's heard me calling to him, spitting anger where I shouldn't.

I set the wolverine down slowly and back away.

I know the bear has seen me, and I watch as he takes one step in my direction, still standing up straight. I take another careful step backward, keeping him in my sight. No sudden movements, or he may mistake me for a threat. I take another step, but the damn bear matches every footfall, and I'm no farther from him now than I was before. His face is wide. I wish I could get a good look at him. If only the sun were bright and the light could soften his features, I'm sure I would see curiosity on his face, but he looks nothing but menacing now, a dark shadow that should be hibernating but decided to come find me instead.

I suppose I did recently do a spell to call animals to my fell, but I meant for me to hunt, not for me to be hunted. My witching truly has spun out of control.

Another step, and he lowers himself to all fours. I don't know whether to be relieved or terrified now. It could mean that he's given up—or that he's preparing to run. I take another step. But this time, I back into a birch, hitting it hard. It's solid on my back, and I think maybe he hasn't noticed, but then I'm covered in snow that falls heavily from its branches.

The suddenness wakes up the bear from his curiosity. I try for another step, but a twig snaps as I do, and I know it's too late. I can see his gait quicken. I watch as his enormous claws trample the snow like it's only air beneath him, and piles of it escape behind him as he runs. Thankfully, it's deep enough that I can gain a little distance, and I know I shouldn't, but there's nothing else to do but get the hell out of here, to try to run.

Let him think you're dead already! I can almost hear Mormor shouting at me as I run away, birches whipping past my ears. But she isn't here; she doesn't know what this feels like. Fear is pushing my legs, not me. I'm not doing any of it, and yet I'm moving fast through the snow, which is trying its hardest to hold me back. I sneak a look over my shoulder, and he's much closer than I thought. He's made up the distance between us.

Still running, but knowing I won't outrun him, I reach behind me and grab an arrow. But in order to shoot it, I need to turn and face him.

I need to stop and be still.

It takes everything I have in me to do it, but I manage, stopping and raising the bow all in one motion. He doesn't care. He's bounding toward me. I can almost see the expression in his round black eyes. He doesn't see me as a threat. He sees me as his prey. But I am not his prey. I'm not anyone's prey. I'm not prepared to go down like this: mauled to death, alone in the woods.

I release.

Or at least, I think I do, but he catches the side of the arrow before it can shoot. His claw swipes and tears into the flesh on my arm. I still have a grip on the arrow, but the pain is deep, running through the valleys of my soul. A moment passes, and everything slows. I wish I could use magic now, send this bear to his death, make a meal of him. But there's no time for a ritual. There's not even any time for me to think of a banishing spell.

As if in response to my hesitation, he raises himself again onto his hind feet and bellows. It's a throaty sort of roar, one I have never wanted to hear this close. He's taunting me, and I know it.

I am swaying now, the pain taking over my arm, but I raise the arrow anyway, screaming. Then I send the arrow into his heart. I don't watch it sink in; I just pull out another one and send that, too.

He sways and his roar falters. He tries to take a step, but he's weakened. I stumble back, afraid he will find the strength to retaliate, but he just lowers himself to his front paws and examines me carefully, as if weighing whether I was a worthy opponent. He moans, and there's a relinquishing of power in it. He's surrendering, and then I move closer, confident that he's down and won't be getting back up. He continues to hold my gaze through the dark. It's as if he's seen the error of his ways and wants to undo it—if only he were given another chance.

But we don't get second chances. None of us do.

The witch suddenly takes control of my limbs from within and looses a final arrow. It's unnecessary. He is already dead.

And then he's buried in snow, which has started to fall on us again, freezing this moment in its delicate flakes of white. I scream, releasing everything inside me into the darkness. And just like that, there's no more bear. Even the witch has gone quiet again, satisfied with her ruthlessness. Now it's just me, alone with my own blood spilling red onto white.

Kaija

Jon's fingers are intertwined with my own. Our hands look like a bird's nest, safe and sturdy. I look up at him with real tears clouding my vision. This is it. This is the feeling I've always been waiting for. The blue waves glide up the sand toward us, and I can barely feel the snowy stones beneath me. This is the best place we could find to be alone for now, away from suspicious eyes, save for a boat in the near distance, dotted with the lamp of a single fisherman.

"That's Olen Bred," Jon says in a deep, soft voice. "Even if he could see us from all the way out there, it wouldn't matter to him."

The villagers won't approve of the two of us spending so much time together without someone watching us, making sure we're staying chaste. There's a part of me that wants to believe they're simply being protective, like the parents I never really had, fussing over my propriety but wanting me to marry a nice young man, all at the same time. Because I'm twenty-three, and it's time I got a move on, or else I'll be left behind. I'm not entirely convinced they have my best interest in their hearts.

These are the kinds of things I missed because I don't have a mother. But nothing can take away the bliss that runs through my blood now, not even the tingle of magic that's biting at my arms, trying to get out.

"Does he always fish alone?" I ask absently, feeling Jon's rough palm in mine. His hands are so big, I feel almost delicate in comparison, a feeling I never had in the years of living in the birchwood.

He inhales, picks up a stone with his mittened hand, studies it. "Olen is the only Sami in the village. People tend to stay clear of him."

I think of Riiga and the Sami settlement by the fjord. Her busy, bustling helpfulness and her practical, choppy Norwegian, honed over years trading with the non-Sami that surround her on all sides. I look down at the dress she made for me, the one that looks just like Mamma's.

"I would think it's hard to stay clear of anyone in this village."

Jon turns to me with a shy smile. He doesn't say anything, but he doesn't have to. We're alone now. Just us.

He and I have seen each other nearly every week now since Christmas, sneaking in a momentary hello as we pass, walking together to his father's boat. We have been growing closer between his fishing trips with his father—all of which have brought them back with empty nets. Through it, though, Jon and I have become more intimate with our conversations, our secret touches. Every moment with him has made me weak with excitement, though I can tell it makes Tante Tilde uncomfortable.

One afternoon, Jon prodded me to ask Tante Tilde if she would invite him and his family to her house for a meal. "What does Mari have to say about it?" she asked me nervously, closing the door behind me and ushering me inside. "Kirsti, some of the women—" She stopped as she faced me. I tried to hide my reaction. I was certain she'd be overjoyed that I might be courting a handsome young man who came from a respected family. Yes, his mother was particularly cold toward me, but I suspected Mari was like that with everyone. However much I attempted to mask it, I could tell Tante Tilde could see disappointment on my face. She exhaled and placed a tender hand on my shoulder, changing tack. "I will speak to Erich and see."

Shortly after that, I learned to make lefse on the bakestone by spreading the dough thin and flipping it over when it bubbles up. This was something Tante Tilde told me I should already know how to do, but of course, I hadn't had a mother or barley flour to help me learn such a thing. There was so much I didn't know. Every day I felt that I was a thousand steps behind the woman I knew I should be, and yet I still wanted to be her, with all my heart. I occasionally witnessed myself becoming withdrawn and quiet as well, fearing that I would be found out simply by my breathing. I did pray, however, that Erich and Tante Tilde would come to an agreement about supper, and so, days later, as I watched Jon's family finally shed their winter layers and sit with their backs absorbing the warmth from our fire, I knew my life was finally journeying in the right direction. That night, the lefse turned out slightly too soft and pale, but it was edible. Mari complimented it stiffly, thinking Tante Tilde had made it, and Jon raised his eyebrows and smiled down at his plate. We spent the remainder of the meal listening to Mari command that Jon's siblings sit up straight at the table and remind us again about the lack of fish out at sea, even though her husband was sitting right next to her, and he chose not to tell the tales himself.

"We all agree, there's something not right about it, Tilde," Mari had said, taking another bite of buttered lefse. The light was dim, but I could have sworn she narrowed her eyes at me just then, like she was trying to see me more clearly. Erich and Tante Tilde both tried more than once to change the topic of conversation while Jon and I remained quiet. Jon must have sensed my unease because he slid his hand underneath the table then and laced his fingers with mine. Later, when his parents were distracted by Tante Tilde pouring fresh cups of beer, he delicately traced my finger with one of his, and I surrendered to his touch, feeling suddenly as pliable as lefse dough.

That was a week ago now. Supper had gone well, despite Mari's coldness, and now Jon and I are here, closer than we've ever been. And more alone, too. There's a sliver of light now on the horizon, I can see. He looks over his back again, checking to make sure no one is watching us. I lean my head on his shoulder, and even through his thick coat, I feel his warmth.

"How many, then?" He asks this with a hint of mischief in his voice.

I look up at him, catch the glint in his sea-blue eyes. "How many what?" But I know what.

"Children," he says, bumping my shoulder with his and picking up a new stone with his free hand.

"Ten," I say. And then I laugh, as if it's a joke, but it's not a joke. I want little boys and little girls who will call me *Mamma* and cling to my skirt and run and play like children should.

As if sensing my bliss, the magic under my skin scratches at me sharply. I try not to flinch. I don't want to pull away from this moment. This—all this—isn't happening by magic, I suddenly realize. No love spell or potion could bind me to Jon and him to me, not like this. It's just proof that taking part in the world you can see is the only way to truly be happy. Happiness doesn't come from incantations or runestaves or vintersolverv rituals. Not for me, not anymore. Happiness is here, in the strength of this man's shoulder.

"Kirsti," he says, and his voice is a little hoarse. I look up at him, and I can see a hint of his teeth, a hesitation in his eyes. But as I'm expecting him to say something else, he just keeps looking at me, staring at my mouth. He reaches out a hand and touches my chin with such delicateness, I shiver. Then he runs a thumb over my lips, and I think I may melt into the rocks beneath us. I play with the hem of my coat while he moves in slowly, and then we both close our eyes at exactly the same time, and his breath is warm, and his mouth is soft but sure. Pleasure moves through me. Even the magic inside me is quiet, as surprised as me perhaps, and I breathe through my nose and let out something like a moan or a sigh and press against him, hard, as if his love is my life force, and if I don't get it all right now, I will die.

When we finally part, we don't say much else, but my lips feel full and throb slightly. We lean into each other and watch Olen Bred bob up and down in the twilight for a while before heading back to the village.

When we arrive at the first house, our steps in sync, I can see someone running down the lane toward us, holding tight to her bonnet. My throat clenches at the sight, and I take a step away from Jon, hoping I'm not going to be told off by whoever this is, hoping they aren't coming to chastise me for baldly overstepping the boundaries of propriety for an unmarried young woman. As the runner gets closer, though, I'm relieved and then delighted to see that it's Lisebet. The ties of her bonnet flap loosely in her wake, and I realize she must be moving quickly.

My smile fades as she approaches, when I can clearly see the features of her face. Where there should be scarlet painting her cheeks from the exertion, she has gone as pale as the full moon.

"Jon. Kirsti," she says breathlessly. Her eyes are large and round, and she looks like she may faint or scream; I can't tell which. She tries to steady herself, hands on her knees, panting and swallowing to get her breath back.

Jon puts an encouraging hand on her back. "Lisebet," he says. "What is it? What's wrong?"

The magic inside me senses something because a snap comes sharply at my wrist. I gasp. All the possibilities shoot like arrows through my thoughts. Is it Tante Tilde? Is she hurt? Could there be something the matter with one of Jon's siblings? And then, as Lisebet tries and fails again to get the words out, my mind careens into a void of dread. They've found out. They've discovered who I am, and they're coming for me. The sting of magic is suddenly overpowered by numbing fear, and soon, I'm grabbing onto Lisebet, and we're both giving in to the buckling of our knees, a heap of skirts on the packed snow. "Tell me, please," I manage to say in a voice that sounds like an echo. "Please, what's happened?"

"I can't—" she starts. "I don't—" And then, finally, sobbing into her hands, she says, "It's Anne."

Anne.

"It's her cough," Lisebet manages to say before sobbing into the snow.

Jon heaves us up, and we make our way back through the village. His strides are longer, and he paces ahead slightly, while I follow carefully behind Lisebet, whose steps are labored but steadfast. The magic is there, at my wrist, keeping her warning steady, though I am trying to remember the winter coughs Minna and I had as children. They were scary for a little but easily cured in the end. *Easily cured by a witch*, I remind myself, and I clench my fists lower on my skirt.

The wind moves past us as we run, and we don't stop until we're panting at Anne's door. There are candles lit inside and a very large fire in the hearth; that's easy enough to see from the window. A few shadows move around inside, but no one I recognize right away. I can see the worn old butter churn in a corner, and my eyes burn.

"Wait here," Lisebet tells us, and Jon and I look at each other for the first time since the beach. He's stuffed his mittens somewhere in his coat and clasped his hands in front of him. I can see his knuckles growing paler.

"Are you all right?" I ask him because I'm even more jarred by the deep depression of his growing frown, which is out of place, almost grotesque, on his normally bright face.

I'm expecting him to grab my hand and ask me if I'm all right, to run a hand over my head and tell me all will be well, that my friend will be fine. But, strangely, he just blinks at the closed door in front of us, biting his lip. His whole body seems to be quivering.

Dear Anne. Ever since my arrival, her sweet face has been like sunshine to me. She and Lisebet have given me hope that I will eventually have the life I want. With them, I have been able to be some semblance of myself—or at least of who I dream of being. They have been kinder to me than sisters.

"Jon, she wants to see you." Lisebet is back outside now, and she's staring down at her hands as she speaks. I presume, for a moment, that Lisebet has misspoken, that Anne wants to see me, that she wants her friends around her. But I can see Jon nodding beside me, understanding something I do not. She wants to see Jon? I hadn't realized they were very close. I had never seen them say two words to each other, and yet it's there, written on his face. I feel myself drifting into an aloneness I haven't felt in some weeks, as if I'm floating away from him, away from Anne and Lisebet, on a sea wave. Being with Jon has brought something to life inside me these past weeks, but standing here now, I am reminded, with clarity, how much of an outsider I truly am. I did not stay here. Anne and Jon and Lisebet and all the others whose mothers did not burn, who lived here, thriving on this sea air—I suppose they had years together after I disappeared into the woods.

"May I—" I start.

But Lisebet cuts me off with a no. Then, likely realizing she might have offended me, she puts a hand on my shoulder and searches my face. "I'm so sorry, but she doesn't want to see you."

"Doesn't want to see me?" I'm sure I've done something to make her want to avoid me, but I can't think of what it could possibly be. If only I could see her, find out what the misunderstanding is, we could mend it. Perhaps I could even help her.

But Lisebet has forgotten about me already. She turns to Jon. "Please go. I don't think she—" And then she buries her face in her hands and shudders. Jon disappears obediently through the door, careful not to catch my eye as the candlelight envelops him.

I put my hand on my friend's back and offer her a rub. At my touch, she flinches, dabs at her face with her apron, shakes her head. "I'm sure she will be all right," I say because I think it's what's appropriate. At least, it's what I would want someone to say to me. But then I hear Lisebet squeak before turning away from me quickly.

"The cough," she says with her back still to me. "It's taken a turn."

This cough doesn't have to harm her, I want to say. If only I could unleash the magic tickling at my forearms right now, I could turn Anne's cough into a laugh, and no one would worry at all. But she doesn't want to see me, I remind myself. I think back to the small smiles and stories we shared, trying to rethink hidden moments I may have misunderstood. Had I mattered to her at all? But yes, of course I mattered to her. She was genuine and kind, with a soft heart wide open, even for newcomers. She didn't have a pinch of hostility within her. That was what made her so different from my own sister. It was what made her friendship feel like home.

I hear a cry from inside the house.

"Oh," Lisebet sobs, and she's dabbing at her face again.

"Lisebet." I try to address her as gently as possible, trying again to rub my hand on her shoulder. "Should we not go in and see her? Maybe there's something we can do." This gets my friend to turn toward me. She looks me directly in the eye and keeps her gaze there, as if she's looking for something. An odd look moves across her face, and she lets out a sound that's more moan than sigh. She bites her lip, looking like she is fighting back a fresh wave of tears, and looks away again.

The door opens at that moment, and Jon walks out. His face is white, and his hands are in his hair. I see panic in Lisebet's wide eyes as she turns to him, a tremble on her lip. She's staring hard at him, trying to catch his gaze, but without looking at her, he exhales, his fingers still digging into his skull. He gives a tiny shake of the head then that sends Lisebet into a fit of sobs. She is clutching at her heart as if she wants to stop something from leaving there, as if she wants to keep whatever it is inside her. Then the pain seeps into my own heart. It hurts, this freshly broken thread of a friend's life. Lisebet and Anne are my only friends, I suppose, but I never realized the depth of the friendship I imagined for us until now. Anne and I will never watch our children chase gulls along the surf together or grow old enough to drink and gossip in front of the hearth. I will not toast to her on her wedding day. Not now. Lisebet's face is a wet mess, and she keeps sniffling and moving her apron up to wipe it. The genuine crumple of her face, the way she cries—it's unbearable.

Unbidden, a memory of myself crying so freely comes to me. Mamma is screaming as if the sky will hear her and open to swallow the men who hold her arms before one of them hits her, and she goes quiet. They grip her so tightly, they would have left bruises if she had stayed alive another day. I am standing with my back to the house as I watch them drag her down the grass-lined lane, right in front of her own house, and bind her to the stake. I haven't seen her for nearly a month, and she looks terrible. It took me years to understand fully what the look in her eyes was. I saw it in a wolverine Minna once took down with three painful shots, none of which hit the heart. But in my memory, I can't yet name this look. All I know is that it's the most ter-rifying thing I have ever seen—until, of course, they light the fire. And then, with my back to the wall, I do nothing but sob. Mormor grips my arms with a ferocity I can't feel, whispers instructions in my ear that I can't hear, and tears convulse through me.

The door opens, and I realize I'm clutching Jon's arm. He's holding me steadily, as if I may fall if he lets go. Lisebet drops her apron, but her face has all the red blotches of sudden, uncontrolled mourning. It is Pastor Thorkild who walks out. He is as pale as ice, and he wipes his hands on his cassock, which swings beneath him, black as night. He's missed a small streak of red on his finger, and I watch it dry slowly, becoming a part of him now. When I look up, I see he has caught sight of my arm linked with Jon's. Jon doesn't seem to notice, but the pastor gives us both a strange look. It's fleeting, but a sharp sting bites at my wrist as he does it. His eyes narrow just slightly, but it's enough to make the witch inside me squirm.

"This is the work of Djevelen," he says, looking now at the kirke down the lane, before he strides away, a shadow against the twilight.

M
Minna

The days are nearly as long as the nights now.

That's handy when you're trying to survive.

I spent the days following the bear drying as much meat as I could and preserving the hide. I now have a warm wolverine coat that I sling over my shoulders as night falls and a huge brown pelt that takes up most of the hut floor but keeps me warmer than I need to be.

My wound is healing, though it still bothers me when I wait too long between healing spells. It takes some coordination to perform the healing ritual on myself, but I do it faithfully day after day. I just need the blood of another—easy enough to come by since I had two dead animals to source it from—drawn over the gash in a straight line, to draw the ice rune. And a single cool breath to complete the ritual. Repeat at least once a day. I remember Mormor had a healing poultice she mixed for me all those years ago when I burned my hand on Mamma's fire. That would have healed me much faster, but Kaija, not me, was the keeper of that kind of magic.

My sister is flowers and herbs. I'm fire and blood.

It's nighttime now, and I'm in the clearing, hands igniting the witching candle. A waxing moon. It's very powerful out here. I can feel it pulling me, trying to tell me something, which is one of the reasons I have set aside so much time for the ritual tonight.

Witching is rushing through me, reaching my toes and my fingers both. I flex my hands, feeling it inside me, itchy and anxious to get out as usual. Tonight, I have decided, I will celebrate. It's not quite time for the equinox, but I sense that it's a good time to honor the ancient gods. I am alive—alone but alive.

Who needs a sister or a grandmother when they have two strong hands and a will that could snap a birch tree?

My rhyme is brief tonight, and the stones are lined up just right. It's a simple ritual, more release than witching, but magical all the same.

That's when I dance in the moonlight, shaking my hands and my head, freeing the winter from my bones. It's collected there, stiffened me. I've been walking around with my shoulders tucked up tightly ever since the bear. After that day, I've been looking behind me at every snap, every crunch, every wind gust. It wasn't normal, I came to realize eventually. It shouldn't have happened.

I haven't made any wine for the occasion, and I'm glad of it as I wipe my hands and kneel to tuck the stones and candle back in my pouch, which is tied tightly around my thigh. I may be dancing, celebrating, but tonight isn't like vintersolverv. The witch is within me, but she's not in control. Not anymore. Facing that bear together made me see that she and I are not enemies. I think she sees it now, too.

I am the witch, and the witch is me. Together we are stronger.

Kaija

A month after Anne's death, the village has become a ghostly version of itself.

Pastor Thorkild fills his sermons with warnings against Djevelen and the threats that surround us all the time. "Evil is not in temptation itself, for Djevelen does not cease. Evil shows itself in man's ability to be seduced. He who does not wish to encounter evil must seek to extricate it from those most susceptible, weak of intellect, and prone to base deception." His pale face and black eyes focus narrowly on the rear pews of women as he holds his palms up to ward off evil. Most of the women bow their heads in response, while a few clench their jaws and nod fervently. I reach out for Tante Tilde's hand to steady my own because I know he is stoking the coals of their fears. Graciously, she gives me a reassuring squeeze and offers a tight-lipped tilt of the head to the other women around us. *She is grieving for Anne*, her look seems to convey. And I am. But there has been something flickering in the eyes of the villagers, in their hearts, recently, that has the magic quivering in me. I see it in the way they avoid looking directly at their neighbors as they pass in the lane. I see it in the way their open, friendly faces have hardened and faded, like seaworn brygge. I see it in the way they no longer stand around after kirke to gossip but go straight home. Even Lisebet ignores me, turns away when I try to meet her eye.

This isn't mourning. Something has begun to decompose.

The shiver from kirke still in me, and with magic bubbling help-lessly at my skin, I catch sight of something leaning against Tante Tilde's door as we near home. I can't quite make it out yet because our approach is slow, our limbs heavy. It's been only lefse with scant gjetost and dried fish for weeks now. Thankfully, the salted fish stores are still feeding us, but they, too, are running low. Many of the men have not had a fresh catch the entire winter season. It's as if the sea has been emptied.

"The villagers' talk has become more sinister," Tante Tilde says in a low voice, as if reading my thoughts. "Many suspect Djevelen may be lurking about. I heard Astrid spouting rubbish about evil spells and asking the other women if they've noticed anything unusual." She lowers her head and leans in, even quieter now. "I kept my mouth shut, but I also heard Astrid ask Mari about you. She was wondering why you did not arrive by boat from Tromsø last autumn and how strange it was to wake up and see you wandering about the village with no chaperone or ship."

I glance at her. We had perfected my backstory over hours and hours, and yet never once did this detail occur to us. But it has been months. I thought I had at least relinquished my title as the newcomer. "It's like they're looking for deception," I say, raising one trembling hand to my hair, which I must remember to charm tonight.

Tante Tilde scoffs, trying for bitterness but exposing a slight hesitation.

I glance at the village around me and see neighbors trudging up to their doors, women leaning on men who look wistfully out to sea, children scolded too harshly by their mothers. And there she is: Astrid Olsdatter, who walks alone, pausing to perch her hands upon her knees.

She turns abruptly around toward the water just then. In the distance, bobbing up and down on thick black waves is Olen Bren, solitary in his boat, far from the kirke along the shore. Astrid watches Olen for a moment that stretches on for too long. Then she simply turns back to resume her journey home, though I catch her crossing herself three times and shaking her head.

I turn toward Jon's house. And there he is, one hand resting on his mother's shoulder and the other holding tightly to Ellen. The tightness in my chest unspools immediately. He looks toward me, and though I cannot see his expression from here, I know he is smiling at me until he follows his mother inside and shuts the door. I can think of almost nothing else until Tante Tilde and I reach our own house. The object I saw from the lane still leans there. I squat to observe it more closely. It is solid and wooden, about the length of my arm, with a woman roughly carved into the front of it, grasping a fish in one hand and holding a dove high above her head in the other. I swing my head toward Tante Tilde, whose small smirk tells me she knows what this is and what it means. I can tell she is almost as pleased for me as she is worried.

For me, there is no worry. The sight of this small token has suddenly lifted my heart off the ground, as if I am the dove in the carving. I feel as light as an angel, as loved as I've ever wanted to be. The pastor's words long forgotten, I cradle the beautiful mangletre in my arms and bring it inside.

Minna

I'm tending to the fire inside the hut.

I was able to dry out the bear meat in small strips—there must have been hundreds of them—but it's been enough to keep me full. They could use a little more salt, but I'm running low, and I will not be going to that Sami settlement to trade if I can help it. The bilberries are running low, too, but there are already wild onions growing, and soon there will be fresh berries and herbs to eat, so I'm not worried.

I think as I take another bite. This is what it's all about, isn't it? You don't have to look far for simple pleasures.

I lick my fingers and recall the last of the spellfire that stained the sky above me just before the bear saw me approach. It really was beautiful, its tail swirling back and forth across the black sky, never still. Never ceasing.

I must doze off for a second because I wake up to my arm stinging. If I remember to do my spell for the pain every few hours, it will be all right, though the itch hasn't completely disappeared. It's hard to do the ritual exactly right on yourself.

That damn bear.

I see a strip of its meat in my lap and bite down hard on it. I'm not actually hungry. I toss another log on the fire, and it hisses gratefully in response. I tuck the meat away and watch the smoke rise through the small hole in the roof, closing my eyes.

Then I'm with Kaija. Or rather, she's here. With me.

She's saying something to me, but I'm holding my hands over my ears so I can't hear her. I'm so angry with her. I can feel the steam of it forcing its way through me. Her face looks helpless and contorted, her lips circled around a word, or maybe it's a scream; her black hair is long and loose around her shoulders, and she is trying to tear it out.

There's a crack in the wood, and I am jolted awake. The flames sizzle comfortably in front of me. When I am sure nothing is amiss, I slam my eyes shut again, trying to bring back the vision, though all I can see now is an outline of the fire in front of me, dark behind my eyelids. I want to see more. I want to know what she is trying to tell me. Is something wrong? Is it my curse of fire and pain on the village? But she's not truly a villager, so it can't be that.

I hate to doubt myself, but I wonder if I should go under the cloak to see more. I've never done this kind of vision ritual, but Mormor told me how it could work. Under the darkness of a cloak, a witch should yawn to begin the ritual, say the galdr quietly, and wait for the vision to take shape in front of her eyes. I almost ask out loud whether I need a true cloak or if a pelt will do, as if the witch within me might give me the answer, but I already know it.

I crawl over to my runestave, which leans against the wall. I shaped this one from a birch that snapped in half under the unbearable weight of snow. It's only about the length of my forearm. In it, I carved runes for protection, for healing, and for survival. Now I grab my knife from my belt and carve another: two lines down, parallel to each other, connected by two crossing lines between them. It looks like a series of fresh scars, and a faint birch smell fills the hut. I clutch the stave to my chest.

If I remember correctly, there is no sacrifice necessary for this one—only my words and absolute concentration.

I tuck myself underneath the bearskin, trusting the power of this instinct. It's impossibly warm under here, and I'm instantly comforted. I yawn, and though it feels like an odd way to begin the ritual, I know it's right. It's a signal to awaken the magic within and connect with the air around us. When my yawn is finished, I lie as still as I can, and I start the galdr. It's slow and steady, quieter than a whisper. "Bring me news from afar. Show me how things are. Show my sister to me. Show me how things might be."

Only my lips and tongue move. The rest of me is as still as a corpse. I repeat the words over and over, until they take on their own rhythm and I'm finally lost in the vision.

I see Kaija again. The sea is slapping at her ankles, and she's crying. She's grabbing at her apron, bringing it up to her face. Her cries are terrible. They're not the soft tears of loneliness or nostalgia. They're fierce, like she's trying to call up a great storm or release a deep pain. But she's not doing magic. She's suffering, and it's nothing but human.

I'm in the vision, too, standing near her with my hands pressed hard over my ears, and even though I'm trying as hard as I can to keep her voice from my ears, I hear her say something.

Her words come as clear and stubborn as the midnight sun. "Minna, please. It hurts."

I shake my head, not wanting to let her words in for some reason, squeezing my ears harder and harder, but it's no use.

I can see now that she's standing with her back to a tall pyre of wood, and there's a single flame growing ominously at her feet.

"Minna, please." The flame grabs her skirt and climbs it. She is screaming, and she thrashes, but she's somehow tethered there, unable to escape the fire.

I fling my hand toward her, realizing she needs me, trying to take hers in mine.

I want to pull her down, away from here, but I can't find anything to hold. Kaija is still crying, and her face changes as the fire finds the ends of her hair and begins to consume her.

"No," she screams, and her eyes go blank, fear melting into blind terror. I can feel the fierce heat of the flame scalding my hand, but I move in closer. I can't grab her. "Please, make it stop," she screams. I grasp at the flames, digging in as deeply as I can, trying to find her, but she's not there. My arm is suddenly black and solid and then turns to ash as it crumbles from my shoulder into the fire.

A sound claps me awake.

I sit up, gasping for breath, and fling off the bearskin. A log pops again, sending a spark onto my arm. I climb to my feet, and I feel the sweat that has matted my hair to my face. It makes my shirt feel heavy on my shoulders. The flames in front of me have grown tall, too tall, and I examine my arm in the light of the low fire in the hut.

It is intact. It was only a vision.

I'm alone here without my sister, but I could hear her pleas as if she were standing right next to me. It takes time, but my heartbeat slows, and I'm able to think again. Finally, it's just me and the fire, and the sweat steaming off me.

I want what I saw to be some exaggerated hallucination, not a vision. I want it not to matter, I want to blame it on the damn moon, but I realize I'm shaking as I slide a log away from the others, spreading the flames a bit, dulling the heat coursing through me. My hands won't stay still until I tuck them underneath me.

There's a new feeling surging through my body. It's like the vision woke something that has been dormant for too long. I close my eyes carefully, allowing myself to feel it fully.

It's not rage or joy. It's something much rawer, something I thought peeled away long ago but, for the past few months, has clawed at me even more than the witch inside. I know what it is, too. I felt it with the bear, but even then, it was familiar already. It was familiar because I knew it as a child, when I heard my mother scream, when she couldn't escape their rigid fingers or their iron chains, no matter how she tried. I felt it when the hungry hands of fire melted the threads that held me together. When the scar from that day lingered long after the smell of smoke left my skin.

So, this feeling, I know it well.

I don't wait for the morning. The moon is light enough. I gather the rest of the dried meat, all the berries, all the herbs, my knife, and a few choice pelts, leaving the bear. I stamp out the fire, bury it in snow. The act is so final, but I'm not even paying attention to what it all means. I'm racing. I'm fighting this feeling inside me, and I know what I must do. The witch within gives me a brief simmering signal to let me know she's here with me, too.

Bag slung over my shoulder, runestave and walking stick in hand, I head north until I see a slender path, and I know my instincts have brought me the right way. I walk for more than a full day, until the watchful sun hovers over the horizon. That's when I start to see some huts with smoke trickling out the tops.

The sea lies beyond, Sól dancing on the waves with white-hot flames.

I don't know which hut is hers, so I sit on the small hill and watch them all, scanning each one for motion, until the sun disappears behind a low cloud and a sturdy woman with pink cheeks emerges.

Kaija

The time between the mangletre Jon left at my doorstep and our wedding is less than two months.

I'm standing on the rocks now, just next to the sandy beach, surrounded by Jon's father, Erich, and his brother Nils on either side. Tante Tilde is behind me, patting down my braids after every gust of wind. The sun is back out during the daytime hours now. Spring will arrive soon, though it's still cold, and there is still snow in the shadows where the sun cannot reach. I can see the small gathering of villagers approaching the beach, and soon I can make out Jon at the center. I stand a little taller when I see him looking so handsome in his coat.

My heart pounds, just as it's been doing all morning. I feel nervous, of course, but it's more than that. I simply can't believe this is happening. I always dreamed of a wedding, but did I really think it was possible? Every night before I went to sleep in that dim little birch hut, I tried to see myself in the village, celebrating something like my wedding, watching their smiling faces turn to me, watching me twirl in the arms of a man. But it didn't occur to me—not really—that it would be real one day.

The waves suck at the shore behind us. I wobble a little as I make my way onto the patchy snow and grass, but Erich gracefully catches my arm. He's my new father, I think, and I return a look that I hope conveys all my happiness. I want to say something, but I'm afraid I may not be able to get the words out without my chin shaking. He doesn't seem to mind, and his arm is sturdy beneath mine as he and Tante Tilde walk me up to meet my groom on the beach.

Together, we journey along the lane to the kirke. I didn't dare stick the small white flower into my braid, even though I yearned to, even though I brought it all the way from the birchwood for a day just like this one. It would be too obvious, I realized as Tante Tilde helped dress me. Still, I snuck my flower into Mamma's shoes, and I'm glad I did. I feel a happy little crunch with every step, and the feeling under my skin bubbles softly with contentment.

We're all bundled up in spring coats, and even the kirke is cold. Pastor Thorkild unites us in a flat voice that seems to drive all remaining warmth from the building, but none of that matters to me. The sun is out right now, and Jon dazzles me with a bewildered smile every now and again. There's a childish excitement between us, even though we're as adult as others our age who already have children of their own running around. I wonder if he's ever dreamed of this day like I have, though if he hasn't, he'd be forgiven. I'm not sure anyone has ever dreamed of this day the way I have—at night, lying atop pelts I skinned myself. For no good reason, I remember now that small hut with its fire radiating from the center, warming my toes and lighting my sister's face. A wave of loneliness moves through me, taking me by surprise.

I glance back at the parishioners, hoping to see angelic bliss reflected at me, but most of them are as solemn as God worship requires, despite the sun glinting through the window. Jon's mother, Mari, is looking at the cross that hangs over our heads with a sternness beyond anyone else's. She flicks her gaze to me, as if she feels my eyes on her, and the expression on her face changes into something unreadable, but it sends a shiver through me, and the tingle under my skin crackles in response. Unable to bear it a second longer, I look around, trying to spot other familiar faces. That's when I catch sight of Lisebet, who is sitting alone toward the back, behind rows of other women. I watch her for a moment, along with the empty seat by her side. There seems to be a hole right through the middle of her, and I know that's where Anne should be. I turn back to the front, sensing that the loneliness has crept through my insides and made a little nest somewhere near my heart, apparently there to stay. I smile up at Jon, and all I see there is everything I've ever wanted, but even still, I can't seem to shake this feeling.

The way the pastor speaks, I can sense his reluctance with every word, every emotionless movement of his arm to consecrate our union. But he does not stop; he does not refuse to marry us. He only strips this moment of color and light, taking care to cast a shadow over us, and the congregation follows suit.

After the service, there is a modest line of chattering villagers preceding us as we make our way to Erich's house. Little Ellen and her friends wave to me as Jon and I walk by hand in hand, and then they run ahead so they can greet us again. Ellen giggles as I pass through the door, and then she calls after me, "You're much more beautiful."

I stop to thank her, thinking she has said something sweet but not sure exactly what she means. She must sense my confusion because she puts a hand on my sleeve. "I only mean that I am glad Jon married you. I'm sad Anne died, of course, but you are so pretty. And you're my new sister." She seems delighted with her own good fortune. Before I can say anything, she scurries inside to join her friend.

The wedding feast is not grand at all, nor is the mood joyous, and

I wonder again if having a wedding a few short months after the death of my friend is too much. Maybe that's what Ellen meant by her words, which seem callous after a few moments of reflection. But she's only a child. She doesn't understand how cruel she sounded. And yet she does seem to understand something I do not. The magic in me stirs, brushing against my skin where it's the thinnest. I scratch gently as I glimpse Jon beaming at me from the other side of the room. I beam back. This is my wedding day. All will be well.

The fire is lit, and we squeeze in at Erich's table. It's tight, but it keeps the room nice and warm. The table and the drink help everyone settle in. Soon, we eat a small meal of dried fish and cheese that I made fresh this week. Men come up to Jon with full tankards to toast the new marriage. My tankard—a gift from Erich—has been filled many times, too, of course, though I have received almost no congratulations. Even still, Tante Tilde's beer is delicious, and I allow the cheer and Jon's easy contentment to soften my disappointment.

Later, when the respectful crowd has thinned and only the drunk and spirited remain, someone begins to play the fiddle. Little Ellen grabs my hand. I watch her more carefully than I let on, following her steps in case there's some kind of dance I should know but don't because I grew up in a birchwood far away. My steps are slower than hers, and I try to speed them up, but my head is light from the drink, and I can't concentrate hard enough. I laugh as we spin around, in part to hide my growing concern. What if they see that I don't know the dances? On the next turn, I bump into someone. It's just Jon, thank goodness. I lean into his arms, feeling him support me. Ellen laughs and twirls away into the crowd. With Jon holding me like this, I manage to steady myself, to reorient my face to be as bright as a bride's should be.

"Hallo, min brud," he says, only to me. *My bride.* He leans down for a kiss on the cheek, and my face goes pinker than it already was. We ignore the sparse whoops from other dancers who circle around us, and he stares into my eyes with a hunger so intense, I feel my knees shake. And then he is playful again, guiding me around the room in a dance I don't know. But it doesn't matter this time. I don't feel afraid. I catch glimpses of villagers as we spin and laugh, and then I see Tante Tilde, who is looking at me over her beer with the kind of look Mormor would have had, both wistful and approving. With the next turn, I imagine Mormor at Tante Tilde's side, nodding and sipping and tapping her toe along with the music. And then I imagine Mamma, tall and proud, holding Mormor's hand and watching me with so much love, I feel a tightness in my chest. On the next turn, I look and I imagine Minna. I don't mean to, but suddenly she's there, with her arms crossed tightly, all stern and pinched and angry.

I watch her lips, and they start to move. *Kaija.* She says my name, that reproachful look still painted on her face.

Jon and I clatter into a chair. Someone laughs good-heartedly, and Jon gets a haughty pat on the back. But I let go of him. My dress has caught on something, and I can see a tear that started at the hem and traveled upward. I grab the dress and turn back to where Minna was just moments before. But she's not there, of course, because it wasn't really her. It was nothing at all. I was just being stupid.

"I—I'll be right back," I say to Jon, giving him an adoring smile and a quick peck on the cheek. He doesn't seem to notice anything amiss, thankfully, so I turn and head outside.

The moon must be new because the sky is charcoal black by now, and I find a place behind the house where the light from the windows cannot reach. I can feel that the tear of the dress goes all the way up my leg, exposing the black stockings underneath. I curse, sensing the familiar itch intensifying, then pour the poppy petals out of my shoe, careful not to let any drop. I pluck a hair from my own head.

I blindly tie the hair into a knot with skill mastered over years of practice and roll it up with the petal remains before stuffing it all into the thick hem of my dress. I pinch tightly and close my eyes.

I whisper the galdr as quietly as I can, knowing it's the ritual and the intention behind it that will make the spell work, even more than the rhyme that goes with it. "Thread and needle, end to end. Trust this dress is yours to mend."

As I say "mend," a bang rings out around the corner. Footsteps approach slowly. My free hand flies to cover my mouth, and I'm frozen. My eyes are still closed. I can only hope I'm as well hidden in the evening darkness as I think I am.

I feel my heart vibrating in my throat. The footsteps stop for a moment somewhere nearby, and I do not twitch, I do not flinch or even open my eyes. I do not breathe.

There is no sound. The silence continues for so long that I begin to think I imagined it all. Too much beer and merriment, though my eyelids squeeze tighter, and I dare not even swallow.

Then there's another creak on other side of the house, someone opening the door. A laugh, voices, the trill of the fiddle all waft out into the night. It breaks the thick silence, and I am suddenly glad I didn't breathe.

Though now I hear shoes on snow again.

The sound is so close, I know that whoever stood there was holding their breath, just as I held mine. Then, after too long of a pause, the steps fade, heading back toward the house, and whoever they belong to is greeted by someone at the door. I hear a new song start up from within, and then the door closes.

When I open my eyes, I look down. I'm still gripping the hem of my dress. I finally permit myself an exhale and release my fist. The tear is completely gone. The hair and the poppy crumbles slide out into my palm, and my hands eventually steady themselves. The itch, too, has been quelled, though out of fear or satisfaction, I cannot tell. I breathe in deeply and tuck the pieces of the flower into my shoe, crushing one remaining petal between my fingers before I do. Whoever that was could not have seen me, could they? We were both veiled by complete darkness. I'm almost sure of it. Still, I can't help feeling it was so careless to do magic at my own wedding.

"Fru Morgensdatter?"

I jump, slamming a knee against the side of the house. The voice is one I've never heard before, and it comes from somewhere behind me. I look around, my heart thundering and my knee throbbing.

"Are you all right?"

I can see now that it's a young man, about Minna's age. His expression is one of concern. He stands all alone, holding a small lantern. I search him.

"Congratulations to you and your husband." He pauses, and when I say nothing, he fills the void. "I'm Olen. Olen Bred." I feel a strange relief at hearing his name. He's the man who spends his Sundays fishing alone on the seas when everyone else is at kirke. There have been hushed whispers that he is the only fisherman who has caught a single thing for weeks, Tante Tilde has warned me. Despite that, his eyes flicker with kindness in the lantern light. "Shall I walk you back inside? It's very cold out." He motions to my dress, and for an instant, needles of fear prickle me all over. But then I realize he's referring to my lack of a coat. I nod and grab his arm as we walk around the house.

I exhale everything and try to conjure the joy from earlier. It's there somewhere. I can feel it, deep down. It's just a matter of getting it back. "I have seen you out on your boat, Herr Bren," I say.

"I am out there most days." His tone is not overly friendly but somehow comforting all the same.

"You seem to have found those elusive cod." I feel him flinch under my hand, and I instantly know I have said something wrong. I try to correct course. "I mean only that you seem quite skilled at the art of fishing. Or at least dedicated, not even sparing a Sunday for kirke."

"Kirke," he says simply.

When he doesn't go on, I try for politeness again. "Well, you are welcome at our home anytime. Once we have our own."

I am curious about him, about what drives others away from him, but I know as much as anyone the fortress that barricades the hearts of these villagers and how cold it can feel on the outside. Now that Jon and I are married, I sense this may change for me, but for some reason, I'm not sure it will change for Olen.

As we peel open the door, we're greeted with a rush of warmth from the fire. The fiddler continues to play, though I sense a shift in the sound, maybe a faint sharpness to it, and the handful of men who are circled around Jon turn to look at us. Jon smiles, but the other men do not. I intend to offer Olen a drink, to thank him for walking with me, but before I can, he releases me and backs away through the door and into the night.

The sun has risen again by the time Jon and I are finally all alone and the last of the drunk men have gone home. My new husband and I slide quietly into his room. Once the door is shut, he lights a candle and then turns, picks me up abruptly. I'm startled at first, but it only takes me a moment to settle into his strong arms. "Min brud," he whispers gently. That's when I see the mischief that has crept back into his eyes, and I finally relax. I feel the fear and tension leaving my body as he carries me over to the bed. "Shall we get started on those ten children?" he says, then closes the door with one steady stockinged foot.

Minna

My sister.

Taking off in the middle of the night. Not saying goodbye, not caring about any of it.

All those years together, our bond as sisters, stronger than anything she's found in that forsaken village. I know that must be true. But of course she left. She's afraid of who we are. She's afraid of being a witch.

I don't feel bad for her, even if my vision of her did awaken a deep, sharp fear that pierced as close to the bone as an arrow. I couldn't help but think of the curse I cast to the village and how she hasn't yet come back. Something isn't right. But there's no possible way Kaija would fall victim to my curse—if it even worked. She is not one of them. I aimed it specifically. Or I thought I did. There was a storm to contend with that night. That could mean some inaccuracy or wildness, as Mormor would have called it. Either way, if Kaija had never left, she would not need my help now.

I realize I'm stomping my way through the heath, trampling stubborn snow that won't melt until the sun forces it to. It occurs to me—and I wish it didn't—that my sister has this hold on me that I can't shake, no matter what. This is the reason I'm traveling north toward her. It's the reason I left home, something I swore I'd never do, just to find her and bring her back. Because she walked straight into the fire. It's not my fault she left and went to find a new life that didn't include me. But I guess it's my responsibility to save her from it.

There have been miles between us for months now, one entire winter, and I'll never forgive her for that. Yet I can't ignore the vision. I must go if she needs me.

I lighten my footfalls as much as I can and take in the white fells dotted with green around me. I'm reaching a place I've never been to. Though I guess that's not true, is it? I came through here with Kaija and Mormor, but that desperate race for our lives thirteen years ago wasn't really my choice.

The closer I get to the village where Kaija is, the more I feel the repulsion sliding around inside me like a bilious snake. More than once I had to stop and heave into the stones. I've been taking it as a sign that I'm getting closer.

I'm not sure if I'll be able to handle it, being there. And when I do get there, I don't know if I'll be able to keep my witching contained. I'll try for Kaija's sake, but the tingling I feel in my fingers, the feeling that grows sharper with every step, tells me it won't be easy.

I know the way because the Sami woman told me how to go. Her name is Riiga. She was kind enough in the end, and I tried to trade a wolverine pelt for her troubles, but she took nothing. She only looked me up and down and pointed me west, undoubtedly noticing that I hadn't bothered to wear the clothes she had brought me. I couldn't tell her they would make great kindling, so I just nodded my thanks and left. I had her send me the long way so I wouldn't be seen traveling along the coast.

Now that I'm going this way, I realize how much longer I'm making the trip. But part of me wants to see what I may recognize along the way.

Did Mormor trample this patch of heather with me in her arms as she ran from her daughter's charred body? Did Kaija kick over an ancestor of this thick-stemmed buttercup? Did yellow petals scatter at her feet? The thoughts that run through my head as I walk are ridiculous. This is what's become of me. I'm a girl who lives alone in the woods, with no one to talk to, and I'm going mad trying to conjure memories that just won't come.

It's Kaija's fault, of course—all of it. But I can't dwell on that. I just have to find her and get the hell out of there.

Mormor used to tell us the stories the villagers made up about witches, how they thought them to be true. She told us women even used to confess to things like drinking beer with Djevelen or becoming a bird just to fly to a sabbath gathering with witches from other villages.

I wish those things were true. I'd love to drink with a devil-man, see if I could match him. I think I probably could.

I would also love it if witches could fly. That would be convenient.

I look out across the expanse and wonder why women confessed to stupid things like that—women who weren't even witches. But I know why. I can almost see a holy man whispering his deepest fantasy in a chained woman's ear and then scalding her breasts until she admits she'd done it. I assume these are the kinds of things men in villages do to women just because they can. This may be why I've never had much interest in men.

I stop to take a drink of water. It's spring now, which means the midday sun is high, and the weather is mild, despite the remaining snow on the ground.

I look up to see two foxes run into my line of vision.

They're far away at first, but they race closer at a startling pace. Their fur is bright red, but they're both streaked with a stark white underside. I can see their backs and their bellies clearly because one grabs the other by the neck with his teeth and throws him against the ground.

I drop my water and stand. The bottom fox thrashes, and he tries to shove the fox on top off, but the top fox just tosses him more from side to side, the grip on his neck relentless.

I move closer to get a better view, until I can see their faces, their pointed snouts, the ferocity in the top fox's eyes and the desperation of the one he has pinned. He's still got the other one in a tight hold, and it looks like he's going to end him, right here and now.

I wonder what started all this. Was it territory? Was it a female? Neither of them notices me in the slightest. It's not over yet; the bottom fox is still fighting for his life, and the top fox keeps whipping him about.

Then something changes, and I don't know if it's that the wind picked up and distracted them for a moment, or maybe it was just sheer exhaustion—I imagine it takes a lot of strength to keep up that level of intense violence for so long. Either way, something shifts right before my eyes, and the bottom fox is now edging his way off the ground. I can't explain the change, but now they're spinning together in a flash of red and white, and it's not clear how it happens, but the bottom fox is free. They're facing off now, baring their teeth. And then the bottom fox lunges and catches the top fox by the neck. It's just how he was pinned before, only in reverse, and it feels like sweet justice from where I'm standing. The bottom fox seems to have kept his energy in reserves because he's light on his feet and heavy with his jaws. He's tired the top fox out so much that he's pinned to the ground.

It's enough to get his message across. It would be enough for me. But the avenging fox doesn't let up. He doesn't just call it a fight and let his opponent slink away, ashamed of the brutal loss and afraid to cross him ever again.

No, he doesn't loosen his grip at all.

Instead, he keeps his opponent pinned, and it doesn't look too hard, since the fox that's now on the ground is too tired to fight back with any real strength. He stays like that, at the mercy of his opponent, until his legs stop churning in the air altogether.

He's pinned there until his head slumps to the side, until his body is heavy and lifeless, and the top fox is victorious.

After a few long moments, the animal lets go. He eyes the still body for a moment, and I think I can detect a little surprise in his behavior—the way he nudges the dead fox with his nose, tries to coax him awake so he doesn't have to be burdened with such a thing as murder.

It's almost like he didn't mean to do it. He didn't mean to kill him. He meant it as a game that just got out of hand. But there's no denying the corpse that lies red and white and dead, alone on the bloodied esker. The fox backs up a few paces, and it looks like he's not sure what he's going to do now.

That's when he spots me.

I'm close enough to see his eyes, which I'm sure are blacker and more afraid than he wants them to be. He bares his bloody teeth at me once, then runs away down the fell and out of sight.

I approach the dead animal he's left behind and examine his neck. It's caked in his own blood, thick and tangled in his white fur. Despite it all, I grab him and sling him over the bag on my back.

I won't have bear meat forever. Maybe I can enjoy some fresh fox tonight.

I continue my walk, a trail of blood behind me. Even though I'm happy to have supper killed for me, I'm unsettled. It's rare to see two foxes fighting, and I know it's not a good sign.

Foxes tell the future.

It takes days, but I'm not prone to sitting and waiting when there's progress to be made.

It's getting late when I reach the village. The sun has dipped below the sea. I can see the houses made of stiff gray wood, their green moss-coated roofs in the near distance. I can smell the smoldering of hours-old cooking fires.

The kirke is at one end, and the houses and barns and brygge all seem to be built facing it. They want everything to be regular and everyone to be as uniform as they can be. There's comfort in routine for some people. It helps them feel protected, close, safe from the long cold night. But it's not the night they should be afraid of.

I turn away, head toward the rocks the earth stacked behind the village. I need to be far enough to make a fire without anyone seeing me. I scramble up, making sure I'm well out of sight. On the other side, there's a small beach that's completely hidden from the village by the land. I can make a fire there. I can keep warm and cook my fox meat. I can set myself up until it's time for us to go.

I will give it two days. She'll find me.

Kaija

Tante Tilde loves her beer.

She pours me one as soon as I sit. I accept, grateful for this time with her. I feel like I haven't spoken to her much in the past few months. It's all been such a whirlwind since our betrothal. Then the preparation for the marriage, then moving into our new house. It stands at the end of the lane, just next to Jon's parents, and it's more than I could have imagined. Sometimes I just walk around it and run my fingers along the walls. I sit at the table, then stand, then lie on the bed. It's all so surreal, having a house this big that's all ours. When Jon's out with his father and brothers, they sometimes spend days searching the seas for fish. I do feel a bit isolated, especially now that Lisebet doesn't want to spend time with me. She says her parents need more help with their small plot of crops now that spring is here, but I can tell there's something else, too. She and I used to lean on each other, link arms, braid each other's hair, and walk in sync. But that was before Anne died. Since then, Lisebet doesn't touch my arm. She doesn't even meet my eye.

It has been difficult to lose a friend to death and then another one for no explicable reason at all, and I feel it most when Jon is gone. Even still, I am usually able to find some solace in little Ellen, who has taken to me like a sweet younger sister, but the loneliness is starting to peel away at me, exposing something raw underneath, like wind does to a weathered tree.

Today, it's Tante Tilde who keeps me company. We sit at her hearthside, just as we did when I first arrived. She is already telling me a story about how Astrid Olsdatter wants to walk with her to kirke on Sundays, to rekindle their friendship, and how Tante Tilde is going to do it even though she still can't stand the woman.

"It doesn't do well to have neighbors as enemies," she says meaningfully before taking a swig of beer.

The conversation turns to the cough, which has hit the village harder this year than it has in generations. It seems to be outlasting the cold weather. "Two dead," Tante Tilde says with a shake of the head. "Of course I feel for their families. Of course I do. But you know, I'm always worried when things like this happen. We must watch our step. Be extra diligent." She asks me about Jon, who is out fishing with his brother Nils. I notice her face go stern, and she peers at me over her cup as she does when she's about to say something serious. "You know, you cannot be who you are when you are there."

I don't know how to react. She motions to her hair, pinches a few strands between her fingers, then raises her eyebrows, holding my gaze.

"My hair?"

She just stares at me. Then she puts her cup down. "If you want to change the color of your hair, for instance, you should do it here, at my house. Not at your house. You never know who may see you."

I stiffen.

"I cannot impress this upon you enough. You should practice as infrequently as possible, if you can help it. But when you must—and I realize you must, sometimes—you should only do it when you're in the company of others you are sure are like you. My door is always open for that, but again, only when necessary. Oh, and you must never speak of the ancient gods. That goes without saying. I know you have been to kirke, but Kirsti, you are a Christian now, do you understand me? One word about Odin and his ravens or the blessings of Jörð, even in passing, will have them questioning your fealty to God. No one has practiced the old ways around here for centuries. At least not openly." And then she clears her throat, as if to end the conversation there. She moves on to discussing what the men have told her—how few codfish there were over the winter and how desolate the spring catch has been, too.

I nod along, playing my part, but my mind wanders back to the idea of magic. I must admit, I'm scaring myself a little lately. The itch feels closer to the surface than it did when I was with Minna and Mormor in the birchwood. Maybe the strength of their magic was enough to keep mine satisfied. Minna certainly had enough of it in her for us all. But now, I can't seem to go more than a couple of days without a ritual. If I wait, the itch becomes too strong, too uncomfortable, and I worry that I could lose control of it. So I do the washing up, the mending, the cooking—I've become particularly good at magical salt-cod stew from what little is left from the winter—with just a little help. It's not like I ever do it with Jon nearby. He doesn't know. I know no one can know. That's my number one rule, of course. But I will take Tante Tilde's advice—she's rambling now about the benefits of salt water for aging skin—and try to only do magic when I'm with her.

I especially want to take care because there's something else on my mind. My monthly bleed is late by more than a week. I keep watching for my belly to stretch as I know it eventually will, but it hasn't happened just yet. I've kept this information to myself. I haven't even told Jon because it's another thing I can't believe just yet. I need to confirm it's true first. I want to see my body changing before I let myself believe it. This will be the first of ten, and the thought makes me smile to myself, pretending it's a reaction to Tante Tilde's story.

Then I notice she has gone silent. Daylight peeks in through her windows. Spring is on the other side.

"Are you all right?" she asks me.

Of course I'm all right, I want to tell her. I'm teetering on the edge of absolute bliss.

"I know what it's like," she says. "That feeling."

I pause, try to read her face. Does she know?

"The itch, I mean."

My heart sinks. We're back to talking about magic. I'm not the only one who can't seem to stay away, apparently. We have never truly talked about it, but here we are, in her house, caught in its slack net.

She sighs, and I can tell the beer has gone to her head. Her words are slower and less careful. She sways in her chair a little. "I nearly broke in half when you all left. Your mormor was my dearest friend. You know, they said your mamma and all those other women they killed, that they had a pact with Djevelen. Well, no witches have a pact with any devil. No real witches, anyway. Witches don't need a devil. We know there are demons and angels, right inside all of us. We embrace it. Magic isn't like their god. It's not like their devil. It's more real than all that. But those witch hunters are right about one thing: you cannot be a witch and a Christian both. We pretend, though, don't we? We must survive somehow."

I blink in her direction. I have never heard her talk this way, and I can't help but sneak a look at the door to make sure it's shut tightly. The beer has lifted her voice a little, too, and I wish she would stop.

"The real devil is that they didn't accuse us," she goes on. "They didn't get me and Inge—your mormor. We knew it could end badly for us, but we were getting older, and the itch is strong in this village, as you may have felt, so we practiced magic here and there. Not that we ever did any harmful spells. Never. Only small spells to shift the wind in our favor or heal a sick animal." She stops, misreading my silence. "How do you think my goat has lived to be this old?"

I respond with a small smile because I know that's what she wants.

"But your mamma never did. Beautiful Sigri. Sigri was always careful. She was never careless. She barely did any witching with us at all. I don't know how she controlled it, but she was too protective of you girls to slip like that. But, in the end, they named her a witch anyway. Even though they had no clue about what a witch was and made her admit to disgusting lies—how she danced with Djevelen, turned into a raven, poisoned innocent children. It was so terrible. I'm sorry every day that it was her and not me who burned. She had you girls. I had no one. And I know in my heart, Inge never forgave herself."

My skin scratches unpleasantly, and my heart beats wildly. "My mamma," I say, and it hurts to talk about her. "She didn't do magic in front of you?"

"Hardly ever."

"But she—so they didn't know she was a witch?"

Tante Tilde finishes her drink and sets it on the table. "Sigri—all those women—burned because of every tiny drop of magic that ever wafted under the nose of a fearful man or a jealous woman. Not all of them were witches. Most weren't, you know. Your mamma was one of the only ones. It was just luck, really, that they actually got one. But the way they tortured them… There's no doubt in my mind that those poor women were forced to turn on their friends and neighbors. No one knew your mamma was a witch, and yet someone said her name, didn't they? These saintly men. They did it all in the name of this god they fear so much. It's like they invented Djevelen just so they could watch women burn."

Instinctively, and I don't know why, I lay one hand across my belly.

"That's why—" Tante Tilde hiccups. "Oh, I think I've had too much of the beer. That's why you must be careful. Do you understand? And not just with your magic. You must be careful not to get on the wrong side of anyone. Blend in, don't stand out too much. Stick to being Kirsti, plain and demure, and you may just survive."

My skin still itches, and I really don't want to talk about this anymore. I feel momentarily like I'm back in the woods and Minna is telling me about how I should stay low and walk in a crouch if I don't want to be seen, if I don't want to go hungry. How I must make the first cut as she holds the animal taut. How I can grab one end of the fur to better strip the animal of its skin. This village isn't supposed to be about survival. It's supposed to be about Jon and babies and knitted mittens and steaming salt-cod stew.

"Thank you so much for the beer," I say, standing suddenly. The room feels too small, too hot. "Please come by for a meal once Jon is back." I'm speaking quickly, trying to keep the itch to a minimum. My control is slipping. It's becoming almost painful. I have to get out of here before it gets worse.

I close the door quickly behind me and hurry up the lane, leaving Tante Tilde's house behind. I'm sure she was shocked at my abrupt departure. The look on her face said as much, but I don't have the patience to care right now, and I'm sure she'll be happy to finish my cup of beer. The tingle is still there, and I'm scratching hard through my coat. I can't help but think about the crushed flower petals I wear in my shoe. I put them in there every day now. And I won't stop until after the baby comes, to make sure it's all safe and everyone's healthy. I slide up my sleeve to scratch at my arm, not knowing how I'm going to make this feeling stop.

When I look up, I see Olen Bren watching me from across the street. He gives me an odd look, and then our eyes connect for a small second. It's the strangest thing: the itching seems to calm.

But I turn away, afraid of what he might see in me, and hurry off toward home.

ᚾ
Minna

Just because I'm waiting for my sister doesn't mean I have to sit still. I've already carved a point onto the end of my walking stick, and I swear I saw a fish just past the froth of the last wave. I know fishing can't be so different from hunting, and I have a sense for prey.

The water is calm as I approach it. A little wave tests my ability to withstand the cold, and it wraps delicately around my ankle.

I strip off my dress and toss it onto the rocks, away from the water. The waves are so gentle, it's like they're calling me in, and the cold is invigorating, turning my skin hard and white. It's been so long since I've felt cool relief like this, and it draws me in farther. There is no itch, no fiery sting inside my skin.

I walk in up to my knees, and I feel the water working its way up my legs. Every step takes me by surprise, but the surprise is a blissful reprieve from the heat I've been scratching at for so long. Even the scar on my hand feels soothed. I know I must keep going deeper, past the bubbles and mist. I can feel the cold sink deep into me as I do, filling my bones.

I glance behind me, making sure I'm still alone, but I know I am. There's nothing on the shore but my runestave, a pile of fur, a ring of stones where my fire was, and a crumple of a tent that was propped up with the birch stick I now hold in my arms—my weapon. I would have put up some protective charms, but I still can't remember them, and I know the one I did manage to do wasn't effective at all. If it had been, a bear wouldn't have found its way through it.

I think about the bear's regretful eyes, about my knees that shook uncontrollably. I can't believe no one was around to see that. I can't believe no one was there to watch me take on an animal more than twice my size.

Once I got over the shock of it, which took much longer than I'd like to admit, I could have shouted about it from the hillside, if there were anyone there to hear it.

And I am still alone, even here. All I've seen all day are dots of fishing boats far in the distance. Not a soul has passed by this beach or come nearby, which is why I don't let my glance behind linger for long. I turn back to the sea, reminded by a small clap of cold on my thighs that I'm taking on a new challenge now. But, again, there will be no one here to witness this either. I search the water for signs of fish, but it's too cloudy here. I go out farther.

The frigid water surrounding my legs slows me, and I find that the small waves that meet my naked torso are even colder. It feels something like bliss as I push on until I lose my breath a little bit because the water is up to my chest now, and it numbs me in a way witching never does. Once my shoulders are under, I can barely feel my body beneath the surface, and the joy of it rises inside me. I never could have imagined the sea would be like this. It's always been so far away, so distant. And even when I did see it, when I glimpsed it over the tops of Sami huts on my recent visit there, it seemed just like an extension of the land. I didn't think about it much beyond its practicality. Men rowed out on it in search of fish just as I trod on the snow to find the perfect position to catch a stag.

But now.

Now I can feel that the sea is more than an extension of the land. It's not an extension of anything but is its own thrumming soul. Walking through it feels impossible on the one hand, and yet it's somehow also the easiest thing I have ever done. It feels necessary to be here now, to relinquish some of the heat that's always lived within me. Suddenly, I want to somehow take this feeling back with me when we go. Or maybe I'll just have to take more trips to the coast and let Kaija tend to things at home while I'm gone.

In the distance, I see a dark wave rising, like a small mound pushing its way toward me. The way it just levitates out of the rest of the sea is astounding.

How does the water decide which bits of it will become a wave and which bits will have to wait their turn?

The mound grows, in part because it's moving closer but also because it seems to be gathering more water into itself, sucking in unknowing smaller waves. I think about turning back and swivel my head around, but the shore is farther away than I thought.

The wave is coming closer, and I decide to try for land anyway. It's far, but I don't have any other choice. If this wave meets me and my shoulders are still underneath the surface, my head will go under. So far, the heavy blanket of water around me has felt safe, but I'm not sure I can handle plunging underneath a wave. My knees move forward first, lifting my feet off the sandy bottom. I try to force my first leg ahead, but it won't move as fast as I want it to. It feels like the harder I push, the more the sea resists me. A quick backward glance tells me the wave is almost on me, and it's grown into an ominous dark roll, reaching higher than I anticipated, and I haven't made any progress back to the shore. I try to stab my stick into the sand beneath me, but it doesn't catch.

The sea is fighting me, and I can't push my way through. There's a sort of pull that's grabbing my feet as I try to plant them in the sand

and rocks below, trying to get some grip, but they slip free of where I place them, offering me nothing and surrendering my body to the water completely.

It suddenly feels like I'm even farther out from the shore than I was before because I have to stand on my toes in order to keep my mouth above the spits and slaps where the sea meets the air. I try for one last push, knowing it won't get me anywhere, knowing I can't fight whatever power the sea is using against me, and when it doesn't work, I sneak another look back toward the wave.

It's here now, big and dark and ready to crush me. I can sense its ruthlessness, its power. I wish I had time to think of a spell that could harness the wave, soften it, shrink its menace, and turn it around. I know there's something from Mormor's lessons.

But all I can do is hold my stick tighter. The rest of my body is reacting now without my help. The water is paralyzing, gripping me so fiercely, I have lost all control. This wave stretches in front of me so it's the only thing I see.

The chill of the wave's roll over my head sends a crackle down my spine, but it's over so quickly, and it's behind me, crashing into the rocks and sand in a spray of white. I'm able to gasp in a breath just above the surface, and I try to make my way back to the beach.

But I feel the wave starting to come back now. It's pulling me out the other way, to where I can no longer touch the earth underneath. Soon, not even my toes reach anything, and I try to climb with my hands, but I can't get a grip on anything. There is nothing to grab. I don't even have hold of my walking stick anymore. The sea is elusive underneath me, and yet it holds me so tightly. Then I'm under the water again, holding my breath and trying to push myself to the surface, but I have nothing to push against, and the surface is out of my reach. I open my eyes, and I can see green-hued sunlight shining down through the bubbles, but I can't seem to get to it. I claw upward, but my hands find only more water, and then I have to breathe in, or I may explode, and so I do, and it's nothing but heaviness invading my insides, filling me in a way that feels like death, and I'm getting farther from the surface, and there's nothing I can do but surrender.

It's tough to say who will die first, me or the witch inside. She's powerful, but I'm a fighter, and I won't let things get the best of me if I can help it.

That's why we can harness unbelievable magic and do impossible things.

But right now, the witch is quiet. We are both in shock, not understanding why we can't fight this power that can only be the gods' power, and so there's no spell that comes to mind, no rune that will save us now.

Instead, we wait for it all to end, together.

As it's ending, I feel something struggling to pull me ashore. I can feel now that there is air around me, not just water, but I am so cold, I'm shaking, and I'm sputtering, and there are splashes and sand everywhere. Somehow, I am on the beach again, breathing, and I can open my eyes, but they're too swollen to stay open. They catch a shadow hovering over me, blocking out the sun. They catch the sea getting farther from me as I'm moved away from it. They catch something being pulled over my head and down my body. And then they catch newly born flames, creaking and spitting. Warmth pours over me, and I can feel that I'm underneath a thick pelt, and the fire is melting the frigid sea from my bones. My throat and chest are sore, and the shake is still there, but I think I can make out a man sitting on a rock near me. I want to say something to him, ask him what happened, but I'm not sure he's even real. All I know is I need to close my eyes now and sleep.

I wake up there all alone but wrapped in a pelt and back in my dress, drying out by a fire. My lungs burn, and my throat is raw, but overall, I can't deny that I'm safe and warm on the sand, head resting on a rock just next to my tent, which has been newly propped up with half a wooden oar, worn and splintered.

No one is here with me, but I can see footsteps leading up the bluff. I don't remember a face at all, just the shadow of him and the certainty of his strength.

I sit for a long time, watching the waves come and go in front of me—back and forth, steady as ever, as if nothing happened. They don't seem to care that they almost killed me. They don't seem to even know.

As I sit, the discomfort grows into irritation. That damn walking stick is lost forever now. I'll never get it back. I crawl to peer into the tent, and I see my runestave. At least I had the good sense not to take that into the sea with me. And then I'm suddenly on my feet, grabbing stones from the beach and hurling them into the waves as hard as I can. I'm not sure what I'm aiming for—the sea wave that took me under or my own strength that sank somehow to the bottom of it. I look again at his footsteps, and I should feel grateful, I know, but all I can feel is rage.

I couldn't save myself. What kind of a witch am I? I kick the sand so it goes flying in the direction of the bluff, and it's picked up and tossed even farther by the wind.

My anger is white-hot, the cool reprieve of the water long gone. I am not powerless. I will not let the elements control me. I will get back control.

I inhale deeply, letting the witch within spark to life. She digs at my salt-stung insides—parts of my body that should never have felt the flood of liquid.

Her presence reminds me that a spell can make this feeling go away. I'll feel like myself if I can make magic flow though me.

But I sit and think about Kaija instead, closing my eyes and wondering if she has felt my presence here yet.

Whoever the stranger was who dragged me up here, I am alone on the beach now, and I already know it wasn't my sister.

Kaija

Tante Tilde and I stand with our eyes facing the sea.

The men are coming in from their fishing trip, and I can see the waves, white like reindeer moss, splashing against their hull as they trudge up to shore. Jon looks exhausted, I can tell from here. His face is sunken, and he won't meet my eyes, though I'm watching him with as bright a smile as I can muster. Nils looks tired, too, as does their father. None of them makes a wisecrack like they sometimes do when they return from a trip, carrying their heavy net up the beach.

I have a sinking feeling as they haul up the boat and let it rest on the sand. They're wet, and I can see Jon's blond waves teased up by the wind. He and Erich pull a small bag along the sand, but it doesn't look heavy enough to need two men. I look at him as they come near, trying to find light somewhere in his eyes. He gives me a small smile, and there's his usual flicker of mischief in them, though it's buried beneath clouds of frustration. I exhale, grateful the sea hasn't taken everything from him, at least. He and Nils and Erich pass us without a word and make their way back toward the village.

Tante Tilde and I follow, careful not to get too close. The sand sinks beneath my feet, and I feel it gathering in my shoes. We know, somehow, that it's the right thing to do—to give them their space. Their shoulders are slumped, and their heads are low. They're lost in something together—worry, disappointment, shame—I don't know what. I watch Jon, though I don't speak to him. As he turns to look at his father, I see he wears the gray smears of weariness beneath his eyes, which makes him look more like Erich than I've ever seen him.

The thought of the news I have for him bounces around inside my head again as I watch the back of him. I haven't said anything to him about how I am late, not yet, and I certainly don't want to burden him with that now. I will wait for it to be perfect before I say it out loud. I want us to be happy, to be in each other's arms.

"An empty sea is bad for the women of this village. It's even worse than the cough that took Johanne Henningsen and your friend Anne." Tante Tilde is plodding alongside me, even though I couldn't feel any farther away from her at this moment. "More yields like this one," she says in a whisper, "and not only will we be hungry, but they'll be looking for someone to blame."

I glance at her, awakened from my thoughts. I can sense that the word *trolldom* is at the tip of her tongue. Witchcraft. I know it from that grandmotherly look in her eyes. She won't say it, I know she won't, but I still brace myself for it, just in case. And, of course, she's right. Even I know enough about the history of this village to admit that. When things are going well, the neighbors are all smiles, women like Lisebet are as pleasant as they were when I first arrived, enjoying the company of the other women near them. It's when things go wrong, like friends dying and fish disappearing—that's when you must watch out. I shake my head silently because it's Minna's voice I hear in my ear right now. She's the one telling me to be careful, that the village is to blame for every morsel of my fear, and yet they want to blame someone like me for every morsel of theirs. But I know I have brought on my own doubt.

I try to brush Minna away, but now it's like she's walking alongside me. I can almost feel the heat of her, she's so close. She's telling me to be watchful when I'm in the village, to see the fire behind their eyes. It's not the village, I want to shout at her. I just want her to go away. It's not the village. It can't be. It's me. I'm the one with the secrets and the lies and the fear. I'm the one who's afraid.

Suddenly, Mamma's face, flanked by two long dark braids, appears in my mind so clearly, it's as if she's right here walking up the beach next to me, too. Mamma and Minna and me. I look toward them, fending the sunlight off with a hand. Mamma doesn't look sad. She doesn't look afraid. She was never any of those things. She was brave all the way to the end.

"It's strange, you know. It's like they can sense what I sense. I think there's some dark witching going on. I can feel it in the air, Kirsti. Can you?"

Tante Tilde's words, the name she uses, blots out the images of my family. They're just thoughts, I tell myself, rubbing my own arms. I want to tell Tante Tilde that I've felt it, too, but I don't know what I've felt. I need to remember there's nothing to fear. Mamma was brave. That's how I need to be. I look again to my right, but all that's there is the sun.

At home, I heat the water so Jon can wash the chill of the sea from his bones. He stands behind me, puts his arms around my shoulders, rests his head on top of mine. "I don't understand it. We were out there for days. They just never came. We'll try again early next week, see if the currents have shifted at all."

"I hope so," I say as he moves his hands to my waist. The evening sun glares at me through the window.

"Is everything all right, min brud?" He gives my body a gentle turn, dips his head low to look into my eyes. I look away, smiling shyly. I don't want him to look too closely, in case he can see the worry starting to collect there. I want to keep the playfulness between us.

I consider telling him about the baby I suspect is growing within me, and I almost do, but something stops me. Fear is starting to bloom, and I decide to wait until I am absolutely sure.

The water is warm now. I feel the steam at my back. It's a luxury to heat it for him, but I want to repay him however I can. He's given me this chance at happiness.

I doubt it's because he senses I need it—it's probably just all the days he's spent away from our bed—but he leans down and kisses me. It's so gentle, it feels like our first time. I'm momentarily whisked away to a place where none of this matters. Where it's just our bodies and this steaming water, his lips on mine, and my hips on his.

The pot is boiling, but now we're busy, fumbling with each other's clothes on the floor. His are wet and cold, but the sun still peers in at us through the window, warming the house as much as it can. Soon, I'm on top of him, and he takes a blanket and throws it over me. It's exactly what I need, and we rock together, just like that, in unison. I allow myself to look into his eyes now, knowing he won't see the lies I'm hiding. He won't see who I really am. All he'll see is his own pleasure. He'll be blinded by it, and it occurs to me that this is just what I need—I need them all to be blind to me, to just let me be.

Soon, though, every thought disappears. All that's left is my own pleasure, and I'm deep in it, pressing my warm body as close to his as I can get. If we could crawl into each other's skins, we still wouldn't be close enough. His face is flushed, and his flirtatious smile is gone, but so is mine. We're so intertwined—our limbs, our hearts—it would take the world's strongest spell to pull us apart.

Minna

Her hair is different.

That's the first thing I notice. It's blond now, almost as blond as mine. Even though the braids that fall primly over her shoulders make her look younger than she really is, I know it's her.

She's walking arm in arm with a stout woman who seems to be going on about something serious, and Kaija is listening intently, like she actually cares. She's nodding along, even responding with words I can't hear, and I can't help but wonder if she is acting or if she's being genuine.

I know how I would be.

I can't see too closely, but I can see now that she's not moving with the same freedom she used to. She looks different somehow, and it's not just the tidy dress and the tidy hair and the tidy smile. It's something else.

I gave it a few days, but she never came to the beach. I sat there, practicing small spells. It gave me some comfort after the fear I had felt in the water. I never saw who saved me, but I will be keeping a sharp eye out, that much I know. Once my rage reduced to a simmer and the itch was contented enough for now, I put aside my witching because I remembered my vision under the bearskin back in the birchwood. I came here to save my sister, and if I am going to do that, I must find her first.

And here she is.

As I watch, the witch beneath my skin is either anxious or afraid, or maybe it's both. She started lighting up as I left my small beach and snuck through the village. Then the feeling grew as I saw house after house. At first I thought it was because my witch was sensing her own magic, but I did not see the effects of the curse anywhere. I heard no wails of sorrow or pain. I saw no fires. Strangely, the day appeared ordinary. And so, when I felt the itch again, it didn't take long for me to understand. It was sharp and put me on my guard. It felt like a warning.

I'm here now, and I can't really believe it since it's someplace I swore I'd never be again, and I'm watching my sister, who hasn't even realized I'm here. I thought she'd somehow sense I was close by. I thought she might be waiting for me.

But then I thought maybe the vision was more literal than metaphorical. Maybe something happened to her, I thought, and she can't come down to the beach.

I can see now, though, that she's doing just fine. Seeing her like this makes me remember why she probably didn't sense me. It's because she's not doing magic anymore. She can't feel the witch who lives inside her.

She's becoming one of them.

"Kirsti!" A little girl calls the name, and Kaija and her companion look behind them. I can't see their faces clearly, but I can tell by their postures that my sister is pleased to see this girl, who is now all but skipping toward them along the lane. She's small, no older than ten, and she links arms with Kaija on the far side. The three of them continue like that all the way down to kirke. They pass through the doors, swallowed up by the bodies that crowd in behind them. The whole village is there now, too, which works just fine for me.

I slide back behind the wooden house, out of sight.

That name. Kirsti.

There's something familiar about it, and I realize it's the name Kaija used to use when we were girls, whenever we played pretend in the birchwood. She would imagine she was a girl called Kirsti and had fine dresses and a maid and a husband, and I would pretend I was a polar bear, a big white animal Mormor told us about that lives on the islands even farther north of here. It would always end in an argument, since I would inevitably attack her—I was a bear; what did she expect?—and she would pout because I ruined the game.

But that name.

I know she could never have gone by her given name, but I don't like that she's erased it. I don't like that she's the pretend version of herself. It feels wrong.

I walk around the houses while the village does its praying. Each home looks exactly the same. Growing green rooftops; graying wood walls. I wonder which one is hers. Surely, it's one of the smaller ones.

I know she'll have come here pretending to be Tante Tilde's niece or something. She'll still be playing the part—of that, I'm sure. I just don't know what she's telling them her childhood was like. She wouldn't have mentioned the hunting or the full moon rituals. She probably told them she was a lady from a village far away who left her maid and fine dresses to seek out her aunt in the north because her dying parents wanted her to have some family, even if it meant living right up at the end of the world. She always loved tales of princesses and ladies and lords.

I spit into the grass.

Without its inhabitants, the village almost looks innocent. It's as quiet and still as the birchwood. A few seabirds land on the rooftops, forming neat rows while they look out across the expanse. The sea watches back. I am starting to recognize its power. This is some of what

I've been working on down at the beach. It hasn't been easy, but I'm finally seeing the water for what it is.

That's the first step to control.

I turn back and examine the homes again. Unwanted questions creep into my mind: Where was Mamma's house? Where was I born? Where did Pappa greet us when he came home from all his trips before that last storm that kept him from coming home? The questions come to me without my coaxing them, and there are no answers.

I'd rather these thoughts go the hell away, actually. But here they are.

None of my footsteps recall anything like a real memory, I know that, but it's still familiar somehow.

I can still hear the sea from here, even now that I'm not staring at it, though it's pierced with an echoing of prayers from kirke. I shake my head. What a joke. I guess that's what you must do when you can't rely on magic to change the world around you.

You must pray to some god to do it instead.

Behind one of the houses near the beach, I spot a man. What is this? Someone not at kirke? But he doesn't look bothered. Nor does he look guilty. He looks like he's simply going about his own day, just as he normally does. He's a young man, I can see from here. Around my age. He closes his door and heads down toward the beach. Before I think too much about it, I'm following, bending over as I run so I'm not seen.

He loads himself into a boat, and I lie in the sand to watch him, obscured by a helpful piece of driftwood. The sea looks choppy today. The waves are higher than I'd think a boat like that could handle, but I don't really know too much about boats, and he doesn't seem to be bothered at all. Instead, he heaves two oars, a fishing line, and a net inside. Then he leans over the side, getting ready to push it out. But he takes a quick glance around him first. I don't know what he's checking for, but I follow his face toward the kirke. No one is there.

I bring my gaze back to the young man. He's staring right at me, and I can't tell exactly, but I think he gives me a small nod. I slither behind the log, but I know he's seen me. I curse myself for being so careless. I shouldn't have followed him here. Idiot.

When I chance a look back, he's in his boat, rowing away from the shore. He's probably a witch hunter, that one, and he doesn't go to kirke so he can check for runestaves and herbs in the women's homes, see if any stragglers skipped their weekly prayer session to do spells instead. Strangely, the young man is rowing away from the land but still staring in my direction. He's getting smaller and smaller. There's no way he can see me from that distance. And yet he stares, like he's got me pegged. Like he knows exactly who I am and what I've come to do.

After kirke lets out, and the crowd is back on the village lane, I watch, well hidden, from behind a house at the opposite end. From here, I can't make out individual faces. People break off from the group as they disappear into houses along the way, but some continue toward me.

The men and women are mostly all dressed in a sky gray, and even though there is some chattering coming from the groups of walkers, there's a solemnity about them that I can see, even from here.

I see a young woman grab the arm of a tall striking man. She leans into him as they walk.

Can't a woman hold herself up on her own?

The way they're talking, it's intimate. She lets out a laugh that's rich and deep, and her mouth is wide with it. It's strange because that laugh has something familiar in it. It cannot be my sister. The man laughs too then, gives her side a squeeze.

They're much closer, and now I can see them clearly.

It *is* Kaija. But I don't understand it. Who is that man she's with? I can see now the roundness of her cheeks and her eyes, which used to stand out a deep blue against her black hair. She always looked like a witch, more than I ever did. That's what Mormor always said. Kaija had a look they'd be suspicious of in a place like this. But the fact she looks like me now is hard to bear. It's like a solid slap in the face.

And she has no problem laughing with this stranger, letting him touch her waist, her shoulders, the back of her neck like that. His touches become so intimate, I find myself gaping. When I realize my mouth is hanging open, I also realize how much closer the pair is to me now than before. In fact, they're about to go into the house. This house. The one I'm hiding behind. I slide my body back so just one eye can see.

Kaija lets out a teasing giggle, says something too quiet for me to hear, which has the man pulling her inside the house by both hands with an urgency that can only mean one thing.

I want to run away.

I want to tear through the sea spray and huddle next to my little tent, put my hands over a witch's candle, and brew up something powerful. I want to yell and scream and call up the magic inside me. I didn't expect to see my sister like this. It's deep and unexpected, like the knife she dug into me the night she left is now twisting.

I wonder now if she has even thought of me once.

My feet don't leave this place, even though my heart is telling them to. My body wants to stay. It wants to see more. It likes the pain of the twisting knife.

I step toward the window ledge and raise my head just enough so I can see inside. She unlaces her shoes; then she undoes his. She's preparing something busily, with her back to me, while the man tells her something. The boil of their laughter has turned to a low simmer, something akin to comfort. Kaija soon turns and puts some plates on the table. They aren't talking now. She's watching him eat. There's a look of fondness on her face, and hot jealousy races through me, even though it's the last thing I want to feel right now. What is she doing in this village, with this man, eating this food at this table? I want to climb through this window, take her by the hair, and charm it back to the witchy black it should be.

But then I see her lift her white sleeve just enough to scratch at her wrist.

She scratches and scratches, like there's an itch there that no fingernails can reach, and that's when I know.

I haven't lost her yet.

Kaija

It's nearly midnight, and I'm standing outside my house, looking over the sea toward the north, toward the glinting summer sun. It's shining right into my eyes, but I don't care. I'm always in awe of this time of the year, but standing here looking out over the dazzle of sun-speckled water, I realize I've never seen anything so magical. It's the way the sun plays with the waves on the surface of the water, like a dream, and I don't want it to end.

The sun itself is warm on my face, and I close my eyes, trying to bring all its light inside me, to soak it in through my skin and warm this chill I've been battling since I came here. I want it to heat my insides, to make a fertile home for a baby. I am struck with the idea that I don't know what to expect now that I am likely with child. When will I begin to show? What will it feel like, to carry another person inside me? I have no one to ask, not truly. Mari is certainly not one for questions about motherhood—not from me anyway—and I cannot see myself speaking to Tante Tilde about this. Besides, she has never had children. Would she even know what to say? I exhale and rub my wrists together, gently soothing my own magic. I wish Mamma were here.

The rhythmic tapping of magic on skin is part of what drew me outside tonight. I left Jon sleeping soundly with the curtains drawn as darkly as I could get them. But I didn't want to sleep. I wanted to see it with my own eyes. I wanted to feel Sól's light on my face. It's quiet, and I know no one else in the village is awake. It's too late, and people here have learned to sleep through this time of night—that's what Jon told me—even with the sun reflecting off the sea.

I didn't plan to leave the village, but I feel myself wanting to go closer to the sun now, as close as I can get without burning. I decide to walk down to the water. The rocks are steady under my feet as I do, and soon the sand sinks beneath me, giving way to this feeling that overwhelms my senses. I'm comforted by the gentleness of it, by the hushed lull of small waves running up the shore toward me and then back again.

I'm surprised to find that the water looks inviting. I slip off my shoes. As I do, the soft sand squeezes between my toes, and I push it away to get at the sheet of a wave that slides across the beach like a blanket. The cold water jolts me momentarily, but it's like an energy that wakes something in me. I realize this is the first time I've touched the sea since I've been here. This is what I've been missing all these years. Strangely, I think of Olen Bren and his solitary boat out in the middle of the water, waiting for the fish to come to him, all on his own. I think he must feel like this when he goes out fishing. There's magic in being alone. No noise, no worrying, no pretending. It's just you and the water. For now, it feels right.

Even though the water is soft and cool on the tops of my feet, I could do without going in any farther, and so I turn and walk along the sand. I'm rewarded with an inviting blue twilight that fills me with brightness, and I let it sink in, feeling whatever it is that has been dormant in me waking up. Beyond, there's nothing but a bluff, and then the sea stretches for miles. The bluff is far away, but I don't want to go back home. I want to stay out here, maybe all night. I want to stay in the sun's healing light. I want to walk.

I turn my head to the left, away from the sun. I see there the pale white ghost of the full moon, hovering between my house and the rocky hill. And that's when I see the antlers, bowed toward the sea. A solitary reindeer stands along the edge of the beach, and I can see him clearly, even at this distance. He's nibbling at something along the water's edge, paying no mind to anything else. His legs are knobby, though his hooves are wide and steady. I take another step in his direction, and I think then that he senses me. He raises his proud head and turns to me. Strangely, at this moment, I feel the tingle grow stronger. Of course, it's the magic, but it seems to blossom under the placid gaze of this animal.

He doesn't appear to mind that I'm here. His movements are not afraid or cautious, but fluid and knowing. To him, this village is a place he has simply come to graze many times before, and he knows what the sand and rocks feel like beneath him just as I know the crunch of flower petals in my shoe. To him, these lanes taste only of sweet green grass, the shoreline of salty seaweed and algae. And now I watch as he turns away from me completely and walks toward the full moon.

I feel a pull at once, toward the moon, toward this animal, that makes me think of my home in the birchwood. The magic vibrates inside me, reminding me of the life beyond the village, the life I used to live with my sister and Mormor. It's reminding me of where I have been. I walk on, feet falling softly on wet sand. It's like the reindeer is pulling me forward, away from the village, and the moon and the sun are propelling me ahead, energizing my footsteps. Each step I take feels lighter than the last, and I don't even realize how far I am from the village. I don't even realize how much of the night has passed since I left my bed. How much of it I have left behind. I only see solid antlers nodding their way up the bluff and then over some rocks. I follow along the hooved path, muddy and narrow. He is guiding me to something, and it feels right. Out here, I realize, the worry is fading—the worry about my loneliness, about my happiness. Everything I've ever wanted feels within reach.

When I reach the top of the bluff, I look down at a beach I have never seen before. It's rocky and harsh, and the reindeer doesn't venture down there. Instead, he stays high on the bluff and curves around until he dips out of sight on the other side, leaving me alone again.

And that's when I see her.

She's crouched over a small fire, tossing dried sea kelp onto it and raising the flames with her hands. Even though the sun shines on her, she has her back to it. She's facing the moon. I can't see that closely, but I know her eyes are closed, and I know what she's about to do. I expect a chill to rise inside me. I expect surprise and even anger, but it's mostly awe that I feel, and my feet keep up their steady pace. Maybe she was the pull I felt.

I'm close enough now to see that her feet are bare like mine and her hair is tangled, falling vine-like over her shoulders. She turns to me with fury in her eyes and a hand reaching toward the knife on her belt. There's a spark between us, like something long cold has been suddenly kindled, and then she stands. Flakes of brown kelp fall from her lap into the sand. She wipes her hands on her dress, leaving the knife sheathed. I can see it's not the wool dress I left for her. I don't know why I notice that, but I do. It's the torn and tattered dress she always wore in the birchwood. It's loose and practical and has a belt perfect for keeping her knife close by her side.

"What are you doing here?" I've stopped, and I'm too far away, so it comes out as a shout. Even as I try to stand still.

She doesn't respond. She's trying to read my face. I can see her trying. Then she lifts her head with a small smile and gazes up toward the moon.

"What if I were someone else?" I say, but I think it's just because

I want to get her attention again. I know we're too far from the village to be seen by anyone. And if I know my sister, she will take care to stay well hidden during the daytime hours when the men venture out on their boats. She doesn't give me her attention but continues looking at the moon. Frustration starts to build in me.

"Minna." I allow myself to take another few steps closer. From here, the shape of her eyes and the strength of her arms are clear.

This word, her name, seems to have the desired effect. She turns to me, and I don't see that smile anymore. I see something seething, something feral. "Kirsti."

That's all she says, but she might as well have cut me with that knife of hers. Still, I give in to the pull, expecting her to say more as I approach, but she doesn't. With ferocity still behind her icy eyes, she lifts a questioning eyebrow. I pause a moment and understand. I'm not done with this conversation, but the pull has turned into an itch now, and I know what she is going to do, and I know now why I have come.

We stand like this—together and yet not close—for too long. But it feels like we have all night. It feels as if we have all of eternity to determine what will happen next. The decision seems so much in my control that I feel strength building in my muscles, blood rushing to every part of my body, filling me because it knows what it takes to do this kind of magic. This is the kind of magic that is neither benevolent nor evil. It is neither aggressive nor defensive. It's an offering, a recognition that's subtle, but it is somehow the most necessary of all. Celebrating what is, and the power of what can be, is as simple as speaking the galdr to the moon once a month. And yet this reciprocity, as basic as it may be, is at the heart of all magic.

Minna starts the ritual unusually. She is standing, and her eyes are wide, fixed on me.

"Máni of the moon," she says loudly, in a sort of command.

She draws in a deep breath, as if she's allowing in the magic that will replenish her for the days and nights ahead. I do the same and let her continue.

"Brother to Sól. Chased by wolves through the skies on high."

We bend down together so the fire sits between us and the moon. The sand near the flames is warm on my toes and my knees. I pull my skirt up so I can feel it on my bare skin. "Journey and guide." I'm speaking now, still watching my sister. Though I wasn't expecting them to, the words come naturally. I don't have to think about them at all. It's like they've been preparing all night to finally escape from me. My blood runs smoothly underneath my skin. My words come out just as they always have, and not for the first time, I notice they're softer than my sister's. I continue. "Men and witches, our kind, along your path of light."

Then Minna does a sort of squat-to-stand motion, over and over, coaxing up the flames in front of us with her hands. I follow suit. This fire is low and hot, not tall and pointed like the birch fires we grew in the forest, but it releases a winding fog of smoke that curls up and out toward the land. I wonder if I'll see the spirits of Mormor or Mamma in the gray billows before me, and I can sense myself trying to look closely, and then, when I see nothing, I attempt to conjure their faces out of the shadows the fire throws onto the rocks at our feet. But they don't come. It's just my sister and me now, alone with this moon ritual we've done a hundred times. I know she has been doing all the rituals. I know my sister, and she will have kept up with every one, if only to make Mormor proud. I catch her eye again, and in it I see a contentedness I'm resisting. Peace wants to flow through me. My magic is happy it's being recharged, and so I decide to let go and be the witch my sister wants me to be—the one I need to be right now.

At some point, she reaches out to me. I'm ready to take her hand, so I do. Then I reach out for her other one, and she grabs it with a hunger for touch I've never felt from her. I rub my thumb softly over her scar, and she doesn't pull away. She doesn't flinch. And then, starting slowly, we spin each other around the flames. Eventually, one of us starts to laugh. It's not an evil laugh but a laugh filled with joy. Soon, the other one joins in, and it's all merriment as we dance around the fire, smoke and flame rising between us, warming the circle we create with our bodies. Here we are: a couple of witches, dancing like fools in the light of the midnight sun, under the watchful gaze of Sól and the illumination of Máni, our bare toes scratched and calloused by the earth.

Freedom washes over me. I replace the wonder about what we must look like with a knowledge that we've stirred the power in the heavens. At this moment, my heart is so full of witching, it feels like I might as well be flying—like I'm not human anymore but magic itself.

Minna

When it's over, we sit on the sand.

Our feet are covered in it, and my pulse is quick. It's been so long since I've seen a full moon during the midnight sun. That's what has made it feel like it was the first time all over again, I think. Or maybe it was seeing my sister show up. It's like she felt me getting the ritual ready and couldn't resist it. I knew she'd come one of these days.

She's still a witch, no matter how hard she tries to deny it.

Now that we're quiet again, still thrumming with the dance of magic, I want to ask her about the man she was with. I want to know who he is. It's strange that she can have such intimacy with someone I don't know. Strange, when we've only ever really known each other. I want to ask her about it. I want to tell her about my curse and ask her why it didn't work, and I want to find out if she likes this life here in this village more than she liked her life with me, but these feel like a child's questions, and so I just push sand away with my heels instead.

"I changed my name because I had to," Kaija says. Her breath is fast, interrupting her words, and I feel a little satisfaction from that. She's become even softer here. "I'm not a different person."

"But you have a new life," I say, unable to stop myself. I try to keep the whine out of my voice, and because I do, it comes out more like a snarl. But why shouldn't I snarl? It's the obvious response, especially after I saw her with that man whom she let squeeze her like that. I saw her carefree laughter, and it didn't seem to fit. I thought she'd be miserable. I thought she needed my help. It's enraging, her happiness here.

She stiffens. "I left the birchwood, yes, but I'm still me."

I can't tell if this is a statement of fact or if it's a plea. She wants me to forgive her. Truthfully, I don't care. If she wants to pretend she's not a witch and leave me for a village that forces her to hide her magic, that's fine. I don't care at all. She's entitled to do whatever she wants. It's just that I know the truth. I know she is a witch. I know what runs through her veins. I know her real hair color. Her real name.

She doesn't look at me. She's squinting at the sun on the horizon, which has slid a bit to the east. "I'm sorry," she says. "You must hate me."

I let out a laugh that's brief and sharp. Of course I don't hate her, but that's what I hate most of all. I can't bring myself to say the complicated truth, and so I instead say something childish, unable to keep it in. "So that's it? You just live here, and I live there, and we don't see each other unless you can sneak out of your husband's house in the middle of the night?"

She turns toward me, eyebrows raised but saying nothing.

"I saw you with him," I admit, and I realize for a moment that I don't like that I've said it. It's out loud now, hanging between us, and there's a fresh wave of something familiar—rage probably—welling inside me. "How could you get married and not even tell me?"

"I couldn't very well send a letter, could I?"

"You could have found a way."

Her face is pink with the sun on it now. "Minna, I asked you to come with me. You knew I wanted you here with me. You are just acting like I abandoned you so you can have something else to be mad about.

You know, I thought for an instant when I saw you out here tonight that you came because you wanted to stay, that you were ready to give up the loneliness of the birchwood and come here to be my sister. But that's not why you're here, is it? You're here to torture me. You're here to make me feel guilty for what I've done. I've said I'm sorry, and I wish you'd change your mind, but you're too angry all the time. There's so much rage emanating from you, it's like a poison."

I'm not sure she meant to say that last part because she looks away quickly. I feel the sting, but it's not deep. "I was attacked by a bear." I don't know why I say it, but it just comes out. My chest is rising and falling quickly now, like we're still doing the dance, only it feels a lot less like magic and a lot more like something else. Besides, I really was attacked by a bear, and I almost drowned. They both seem like facts she should already know. It's strange to have to tell her any of this because she should have been there.

Her head turns back like it's on a swivel. She searches my face, and I can see it there. She doesn't believe me. It's not fine, but I pretend it is. She can think what she wants.

"You sent that woman to check on me," I say. "Why did you do that?"

"Who, Riiga? I don't know why I have to say this, but I wanted her to make sure you were okay."

"Our home is supposed to be a secret, Kaija. The only people who can find it are those who are told about its location. That's how you enchanted it, remember? What if she tells someone else there's a witch living in the birchwood? What if they decide they haven't had a woman to burn in a while and they come after me?" My hands are clenched so tightly, the sand in my hand starts to slip through my fingers.

"Riiga doesn't care. She won't tell any Norwegians about you. Why would she? The witch hunters would be just as suspicious of her as they would of you."

She says this like I'm paranoid, like I think about being caught all the time, not because she sent some stranger to do what she should have done. But then I remember I saw her scratching furiously at her own skin, like there was something inside her that wasn't getting enough attention. I remember the vigor in the way her nails pulled off the top layer of skin, leaving streaks of white and still not satisfying the itch.

"You're not doing magic, are you?"

She fidgets with her dress without answering.

"Are you?"

"No." And suddenly her eyes are like fire. "I don't do that anymore. I'm Kirsti now, and I live in this village with my husband, and I'm just a woman. No magic, just a woman."

Her anger feels like spring rain. My laugh comes easily. "You're lying. But you're not doing it enough, apparently. I saw you scratching yourself like you were digging up the roots." She looks surprised but hasn't looked away yet, so I keep going. "You think it can be cured by your clean, delicate fingernails that haven't touched earth in months? You think it can be cured by anything other than witching?"

She looks like she wants to say something, but I can tell she's holding it back. Good. I don't want to hear her excuses. I don't want to hear how she's changed so much and has no time for the thing that makes us who we are.

"Tell me," I say. "How do you feel right now? I bet your skin is as calm as the sea after that ritual." Finally, she wrenches her gaze away from me. I'm satisfied with that, but it also scares me. I want to see the fire in her eyes again. I want her to see me, even if it is through waves of heat.

Instead, we sit there, side by side, and stare out across the sea. Soon, the fire beside us starts to smolder, glowing only with gusts of wind. Eventually, I let my mind wander, and I imagine I can see the snowy island with the polar bears out there on the sea. I imagine the bears standing on the ice, looking straight back at us.

Like she's reading my mind, Kaija says, "Were you really attacked by a bear?"

I think for a second, rub my forearm. Another faint scar, raised delicately off the surface of my skin, is the only reminder left. "It's fine."

Something has cooled between us, and I can't decide if I like it or not. It feels final, like a severing of something that's healing over on both sides.

Then she looks at me with those witch's eyes, a new kind of fire at play in them. I'm intrigued. She hesitates, prepares herself for what she's going to say. And then: "I'm going to be a mother soon."

Now it's my turn to study her. I know I'm not hiding my surprise very well because she starts to laugh. It's that same head-back, mouth-open laugh she gave to her husband, and my head swims, jealous and angry and thrilled all at the same time. I let a tight smile cross my lips and a breath of air escape through my nose.

"You'll be an aunt."

I'm smiling for real now, and it's part shock, part relief, and part confusion. I shove her on the arm, and she bends away from me and then bends back. "Are you going to name her Sigri?" I ask. I'm thinking of the imaginative games we played as girls. The times she pretended to have a baby—a small blanket or a bundled hare fur was all it was—she would call it Sigri.

When I glance back at her, I can see her smile has dimmed slightly, and I feel like I've said the wrong thing. The sun ducks behind a cloud for just a few seconds, and she pulls her knees close to her chest, wraps her arms around them. "Why did you come here?" she asks, and I know she's talking to me, but it looks like she's talking directly to the sun, which is bright and white again, busy warming the rocks around us.

I want to tell her the truth. I want to tell her I came because I had a vision that she was burning, screaming in agony, because I thought she needed my help, that she was begging me to save her. Instead, I say, "I don't know."

There's a long pause, and I feel the old irritation start to come back. It seems like the answers to my questions were right there, within reach, just a moment ago. But now, it's gone cold again, this connection between us.

"I'm happy here, Minna."

Now that she's said it, I know the conversation is closed. Even if I think she's lying to me, maybe even lying to herself, I can't bring myself to hate her for it. I can damn well try, but it feels weak, forced. My sister is going to have a child, so I can't wish her too much ill, can I?

I don't respond, but I stand, and she looks up at me for a small moment before getting to her feet. Then she nods, looks like she may reach out a hand toward me, but I move backward slightly, and she nods again.

I turn away so I don't know whether she's hurt or happy. Either way, I eventually watch her walk away, back lit by the sun and front facing the village ahead.

Kaija

When I get back, there is a group gathered outside Erich's house. Four or five villagers crowd around the door, peering in. I hear someone calling something from inside the house, and one of the crowd outside runs away. I look at my own house. It's dark and quiet. Jon is in there sleeping, I know, and I can't wait to crawl into bed next to him, to share our warmth and nestle my head underneath his arm. I imagine him grunting in playful annoyance and then grabbing me even closer, not letting me escape. I vow that I won't escape anymore. I'm his. In fact, I think I'll tell him in the morning about the baby. I know it's coming, even though there's no bump yet. We deserve to revel in the happy anticipation together anyway.

As I approach my own door, I hesitate. The commotion at Jon's parents' is quite lively, and it occurs to me that if I show my face for a few minutes, it will be easier to explain to Jon where I've been in case he asks, claim I couldn't sleep thanks to all the noise.

I walk past my own door and make my way to his parents', trying to see inside as I approach. The small cluster of gray-clad villagers doesn't part for me. They hardly notice I'm there. I'm surprised to see anyone here, it being so early in the morning. They're looking inside, concern painted on their faces, but they don't go any closer than the threshold, where they stand crossing themselves over and over. I don't want to be rude, so I stand back a foot or so, lifting myself on my toes to see if I can catch a glimpse of what's going on inside. I can see the top of a woman's head, wisps of brown and gray. It's Mari, Jon's mother, and she's leaning over something. That's when I notice a wail, low and rumbling. At first, I'm taken back to the birchwood, back to the time we speared an elk but it didn't die right away. It called out with a sound just like this one, desperate for help and yet recognizing its fate nonetheless. The wailing is so loud, it sounds like it's all around me, and it takes me a moment to understand that it's coming from inside the house.

"Kirsti, oh, goodness. Where have you been?" It's Tante Tilde, and I notice for the first time that she's one of the people gathered outside Erich Pedersen's doorway. The expression on her face is complicated, too complicated for me to put my finger on right now. I just want to know what's going on. If Jon's parents are hurt or something has happened, I should do something. I try to see past her, but Tante Tilde doesn't move.

"Should I go get Jon?" I ask. "Has something happened?"

Her look grows in complexity, and I realize it's fear pulling her eyes wide like that.

"Kirsti," she says, and her voice is stern like a grandmother's. "Where have you been?"

I feel a jolt. Did she see me leave the village? She couldn't have. Everyone was asleep. My house is the last on the lane. The chances of her having spotted me are slim, and yet her face seems to show she somehow knows I haven't been at home. Even though I don't have to lie to Tante Tilde, I choose my words carefully, well aware of the company we are in.

"At home," I say. "Asleep."

She shakes her head slowly. Bites her lip. "No, you weren't. You were out for a small walk, weren't you? You went out to see the midnight sun because you couldn't sleep. That's it, isn't it?"

I don't understand what's going on. She doesn't sound accusatory, even though something inside me senses that she knows something. I watch her head bob up and down slowly, holding my gaze steady. She wants me to nod, too. She wants this to be my story. I want to ask her why, but I can't right now, not with all these people around. Instead, I dip my head in sync with hers.

"I'll just go get Jon." I phrase it like a question, thinking it's the right thing to do. It's what a wife should do in a situation like this. "Something's happened, hasn't it?"

She looks around, still biting her lip. Then she grabs my arm. "You were out for a walk to see the midnight sun. You couldn't sleep. Do you understand?"

I nod again, and I'm starting to get annoyed. I'm not a child. But before I can insist she speak to me like an adult, she pulls me toward the door, pushing people aside without excuses.

As soon as we step inside, I see Mari. She's hunched over, just like I saw before. Her head is low, and I realize now that it's she who is making that moaning sound. It's louder and even stranger to hear it within these echoing walls. A moan like that is desperate and powerful, but it's intended to reach far distances, as if someone might hear and come and save the dying, even though he's been speared in the gut by a predator who has outwitted him. Indoors, the sound is terrifying.

And then I notice what she's hovering over. There are two bare feet sticking out from underneath a blanket. I recognize those feet. I take a step, wrenching myself free of Tante Tilde's iron grip. As I do, I start to see his familiar shapes emerge. It's Jon's body underneath that blanket, and it's his raspy breathing that's cutting through his mother's wailing. His blond hair is streaked across his forehead, and there's a pillow beneath him, but she still holds one arm underneath him, cradling his neck like a child. Erich is pacing nearby, not looking at Jon, not looking at anything, just running his hands over his beard again and again. Neither of them notices I've entered the house.

I fall to my knees next to Mari. I'm not bold enough to force her to move, though it's all I want to do. I want to shove her aside so I can hold him in my arms. His head is my head. His shoulders are my shoulders. His breath belongs to me, doesn't it? I'm his wife. Instead of doing that, I simply look at him and put one hand on his stomach, gently as I can. His eyes are only half-open, and he's trying to draw in air through his open mouth, but he can't seem to get enough. His arms are by his sides, still and lifeless. I grab one, notice it's still warm, and relief washes over me.

"Jon," I say, and it comes out like a squeak. I must do a healing spell. I have to say the galdr. I have to help him, but I cannot think of what to say. I can't remember.

Just realizing I'm there, Mari turns toward me, blinking me into focus. But there's an emptiness behind her eyes. It's an emptiness I haven't seen for many years, and it splits my heart in two.

"What happened?" I manage, but Mari can't hear me. She's resumed her low wailing. "Jon," I try again. "I'm here. Jon." Why can't I think straight? I need to do the breathing and then the galdr. What is it? My eyes are foggy, and I blink to clear them.

And then, for a flicker of a moment, he sees me. Our eyes meet.

"Min brud." *My bride.* It's him saying it, but it's not his voice. It's a scratch more than a word, and it touches the exposed wound that's my heart.

His mother stops crying, sniffles, grabs his hand, and looks into his eyes. "Jon?" she says with a small tremor of hope in her voice. "Jon?" But he's still looking at me, and I hold his gaze. I hold it tighter than I've ever held anything. I see the boy who chased me down the beach and splashed water in my direction as I screamed and ran for cover. I see a strong, dry chest hovering over me before his lips lowered to mine. And then a thorn touches the thin pink skin of my heart and starts to sink in, pushing deep inside my flesh right where it hurts the most. Jon is blinking slowly, but he still looks my way. What could have been moves between us like a cloud—Jon splashing in the waves with our first son, Jon sitting at our table toasting to his own daughter's wedding, Jon growing old and still placing his arms around my middle, his head resting on my hair. They're there, all these moments, but they pass by so quickly, like a gust of wind, and I can barely hold them. He keeps my gaze, and I know we're both living them for just a few more seconds. I know he's still here because I can see a hint of his playful smile. I believe he may be using the last of his energy to hold that smile there, to make sure I see it. I reach out and feel his chest with my hands, and I imagine I can feel his fingertips move from his sides to my belly. I imagine he holds me there with a look of such delight and love, and neither of us can believe how lucky we are, and neither of us can keep from laughing.

But then the cloud disappears, and so does the vision. His chest heaves, and he coughs once, then he starts an uncontrollable spasm of coughing. Waves of them come, flexing his muscles and forcing his body to expel whatever poisons his lungs. There's an itch somewhere within me, and the reminder to do a healing spell washes over me, but I still can't think straight. And then the thorn in my heart is joined by another one, and piercing pain radiates through my chest. His coughs are persistent now. There's no stopping them. His mother has her head flung back and cries, screams maybe, but I can't hear her. All I can hear is the air leaving Jon's body with such force, I think Djevelen himself must have his claws in my husband. Suddenly, on the next cough, I'm covered with a splash of blood. It's hot on my face and slides down my neck until it drips under my shirt and down between my breasts. It's coming out with every one of his exhalations, spraying me like the sea, but I don't move. I stay right where I am, even though I can feel a third thorn shove its way into the softest part of my heart, underneath my ribs. Pain rips through me because I know what is happening, and I know there is nothing I can do. There's no time. People are yelling. Someone is crying. Someone else is trying to pull me away, but I hold him. His blood slides down my lip and into my mouth, and it tastes like fire, and that's when I realize he's not coughing anymore. He's gone still, and his hands are pale and loose at his sides. His playful smile is now a slack, drooping frown. And his eyes—his beautiful eyes, like the sea. I see now that they're closed.

Minna

I manage a few hours of sleep, which is all I can ask for when the sun is shining over my shoulder all night.

I'm not sure if it's morning or midday when I hear a thud of something falling near my feet. I feel a slight tremor move from the earth to my body and the spray of sand on my ankles.

Instinctively, I reach for my knife, wield it before I even know which way to point it.

"Hallo."

It's a man's voice, and I point the knife in the direction of his figure. He stands above me, shadowed by the sun, while my eyes adjust. I knew I shouldn't have camped out in the open like this, but there's no tree cover in this forsaken place, only rocks and sea, and I had to sleep somewhere. I blink at him, keeping my hand steady.

He's got light-blue eyes, like mine, and soft brown hair twisted up over his head like a tangle of branches. Not too menacing. He looks—actually, he looks amused.

"Thought you might want something fresh to eat." He's dropped a pair of fish at the edge of the fire ring. "Mackerel."

I'm speechless, still getting my bearings. What is this person doing out here, and how has he found me? Do I know him?

Gripping the knife tighter and raising it toward his face, I see his amused expression hasn't changed. I glance briefly at my weapon, wondering if maybe I've picked up a shoe or a stick instead, but no, it's a knife, notched and jagged but sharp enough to slice through skin.

"I was hoping you'd avoid going swimming for a while. Happy to see you the other day, healthy and moving about while the villagers were all at kirke." He doesn't say it as an accusation but with a hint of curiosity. I feel the knife lowering a bit, so I grip it tighter. I shift my feet beneath me, preparing to lunge at him if I must. If he makes a single move, I swear.

"Okay," he says. "Fine. Well, you're welcome for saving your life. Enjoy the fish." He turns to leave. He's walking back up the rocks.

"Wait." I curse myself as soon as the word is out because I don't know why I want him to wait. This is the man who saved my life? He barely looks older than me, and his arms are too lean, his hands too small. A flare of heat rises in my chest. I was rescued from drowning by a scrawny man-boy. Pathetic.

I think about lunging at him, cutting him deep enough for me to run from here and stay the hell away. I have to stop him from telling people about me, if he hasn't already. But he's too far away from me now, so I lower my knife just slightly.

"What were you doing here? When I—when that wave—"

He looks down at his hands and the small net he's balled up in one of them. "Fishing."

I stare at him longer than I want to, but I realize now there's something familiar about his face that I can't pinpoint. It's a deep recognition, some kind of warm memory, maybe. And I'm not used to warm memories, so I shake it away, but now he's walking back toward me. He looks casual, pleased even.

It's like I'm not even holding a weapon in his direction.

Then he smiles a simple, friendly smile with absolutely no mystery behind it, and it catches me off guard. "I'm Olen Bren." He dips his head in a formal greeting. He raises an eyebrow at me, but I say nothing. I'm not well versed in pleasantries.

I sheath the knife in a swift movement, more to show him how quick my hands are than to take away the threat. But, again, he looks unfazed, and I'm annoyed now. Maybe I should show him some of my other skills. Maybe if he sees the consequence of a binding spell or a curse, he'll show a little bit of respect.

Instead of that, he shoves his hands in his pockets and stares at me. Then he speaks with a sigh like we're old friends. "No one knows you're here but me, I swear."

He sits, starts to build the fire. I study him from above and see he has brought nothing with him except his fish. He's not like I imagine men here to be, and I can't quite wrap my head around it, but I sit across the fire from him, watching his every movement closely because I'm starving and the fish he's brought are huge. They stare up at me with their terrified eyes, and suddenly, I can't wait to sink my teeth into their flesh.

I'm wondering what fish taste like—I'm sure I ate fish when I was a child, but again, I'm short of warm memories.

"And you? What are you doing all the way out here?" He tosses the fish right on the fire. They sizzle.

I can't think of anything to say, not a single clever lie or a masked truth comes to mind. I didn't think I'd be speaking to anyone except for Kaija. Otherwise I would have prepared. I decide not to answer for now, but I'm beginning to wonder if I'm giving off the wrong impression. Maybe he still thinks I'm lost or need help or I'm in danger. I'm none of those things.

If he only knew what I'm really capable of.

Soon, the fish are charred. The smell is rich and makes my mouth fill with want. He peels back the skin with quick fingers, revealing a steaming center that's as white as midwinter snow. Then he unceremoniously digs a couple of fingers into the pale flesh and picks out a piece, pops it into his mouth, and sucks in air.

"Hot," he says.

I could have told him that.

I pinch a piece between two of my fingers and slide it onto my tongue. I bite down far too hard the first time. The meat is so delicate, it's almost not even there. I only need to chew it a few times, letting the salty, watery juices settle in my mouth before swallowing. All I want to do is eat more of this, and I do. Without asking permission, I grab another piece and shove it in my mouth.

"Why are you here now, Olen Bren?" I say it between chews, not wanting to swallow too soon but needing to get the question out.

He licks his fingers, tilts his head to one side, then back upright. "You're alone, right?"

I'm not alone. I feel a scratch of resentment. My sister was just here, and we were raising magic right out of our own blood, casting it out into the summer twilight. I'd tell him about it, and maybe about the witch who lives within me, if I were feeling more reckless, but for now, I just nod.

But then I remember the finality of our ritual last night. My sister isn't coming back. She's not coming with me, and I must leave for the fell soon, so I guess in a way, he is right. I guess I am alone. I stab a finger into the second fish, dig out a chunk. Part of it falls in the sand, but I eat it anyway, feeling the roughness sharpen my teeth.

"What about—" I say, raising my chin in the direction of the bluff and the village beyond it.

"I'm not from there."

"No?"

"Well, I am and I'm not. I suppose it's both."

So he's mad. I wonder for a second if he's going to tell me he's a child of God or something else like that, but then I remember when I saw him the first time.

"You don't need to go to kirke like the rest of them?" I can't help the venom in my voice, and why should I? I don't know him.

He laughs, and something in me stirs. I know that laugh.

"No. I tried for a while because my father made me, but I couldn't do it anymore after he died."

I squint at him. Is he going to give me a sob story? Because I know all about parents dying. I can match him word for word if he wants to play that game. Only my story would involve so much fire and pain, he would probably run away crying.

"I should get back," he says and gets to his feet.

I'm startled and realize I don't know if I want him to go.

His hands are in his pockets again. "The rest of my catch is for the family."

When I don't respond, he goes on. "A man died last night. Some kind of cough. Sudden. Just got married, too. His wife—" And then he looks at me strangely. "His wife and his parents will want some fish to eat."

He looks away for a moment, then adds, "You'll stay here, right? Out of sight?"

I narrow my eyes back at him. "Why?"

"Well, I imagine, soon, they'll have a whole lot to say if they see a strange woman walking around. You may want to avoid walking straight into the hungry wolf's den."

He leaves me with the bones of the fish lying out, exposed on a sunny rock, and turns to go. I don't acknowledge him, and all I can think is how much I hope he won't be back.

Only, I'm not sure I put enough energy behind this hope because disappointment slithers up my spine as I watch him walk away.

Kaija

I t's hard to do anything. I don't want to. Tante Tilde brings me more beer, and I drink it because I can't think of anything else to do. The pastor took Jon's body away. Jon's mother went with him, but they wouldn't let me go. Instead, I was instructed to stay home and let them take care of things, so I did what I was told. I sat in my house and looked at all the things that were Jon's. His bed. His hearth. His clothes. His shoes. All of it was his, and none of it was mine. I stayed alone in that house for as long as I could stand it, and no one came. I realize now why they didn't come. They took my husband away from me like he was one of theirs, as if he were not mine at all, and then they left me there to carry on alone—an outsider—while they all grieved together.

It felt like I was on my own for an eternity, but Tante Tilde told me it was just a few hours. She grabbed me by the arm, tenderly this time, and pulled me to her house, sat me down by her fire, and fed me. I remember Olen coming to the door with fresh fish and a word of concern, but I couldn't get up to thank him. Tante Tilde put the fish on the table and tended to the fire. She knew I was cold even though it was summer, even without me having to tell her.

Time has passed, now—though, again, I'm not sure how much. Maybe weeks? I may have missed the kirke services, I'm not sure. Tante Tilde didn't try to convince me to go, and I couldn't be more grateful. To think of sitting on that hard bench, listening to the man who took Jon away talking to me about Kristus. If God is so powerful, why didn't he save the one good thing in my life? It doesn't make much sense. Tante Tilde hasn't made me do anything but eat and bathe, and I'm grateful for that, too. But she sits with me here now, and I can tell she wants me to pull it together. I can tell she wants me to pick up my head, walk out the door, and move on. It reminds me of Mormor. It's in the fidgeting of her hands, in the up and down of her knee under the table. It's in her silences that I don't want to fill.

We sit with beers now, and she continues to say nothing. The quiet moments allow the darkness to creep in. I imagine the way it might have been. I imagine this stone-gray day being how I would have wanted it to be. I imagine him here with me now. Tante Tilde would be telling some story—not staring into the flames, waiting for the house to cave in—and Jon would be nodding along, playing with the seam of my skirt underneath the table. He'd be running his hand along my thigh, gathering the wool in his hand, and I would be dangerously close to slapping it away.

"I could have saved him," I say.

She looks at me with curiosity, shaken from her thoughts. She's still twitching a bit while she takes a sip from her cup and eyes me. "You can't think like that."

"I should have cast a healing charm. I know the perfect one for illnesses of the lung. Mormor taught me. But it didn't—I couldn't—"

She stares at me again, taking in this information. Until now, I haven't spoken to her about my magic—I've only listened—and I can tell she's surprised. "I know I asked you this the night Jon died, but where were you?"

I fidget in my seat, debate keeping it a secret, but only for a moment. I don't have the strength for a secret beyond that. Not now. "I saw my sister. We did a ritual to celebrate the full moon." I feel the sting of tears at the back of my throat. "And while I was dancing and laughing, Jon was dying. He was coughing up blood and wondering where I was. He had to go over to his parents' house because his wife was out playing witch on the beach."

"Keep your voice down."

"Why? There's nothing to hide now. It's all over."

I try to reach for my beer again, but Tante Tilde grabs my arm. She tries to tell me something with her look, but I can't hold her gaze for that long. Now that the memory has arrived again, all I want is my beer and the silence we were enjoying before.

I grab the cup, and I'm staring into the fire when she speaks again. "Listen to me, Barnebarn." Her voice is low as she calls me *granddaughter*, just like Mormor used to, and it wakes something inside me. "There is everything to hide right now, do you understand? This is not over. It is just beginning."

I'm listening as she asked me to, but I don't understand. How can this be the beginning when he's gone? My future here is dark. It has all but disappeared. "But he's dead. What am I supposed to do now?"

"That's what I'm trying to tell you."

"You have the answers, do you?" I can't keep the bitterness from my words. Why can't I keep it together? I know she's only trying to help, but if she would just leave me here with my beer, then I could—the tears pour down my cheeks and fall into my cup. I could have saved him. If I had only been back in time, he wouldn't be gone. And why had I gone out in the first place? To see my sister? Because the pull of magic was so strong, I couldn't resist it? I take a swig, hoping to wash down all my choices. I wish to forget that night. If I hadn't gone out, everything would have been fine. Tomorrow morning, I could have sent him off on a day out at sea with some scraps of salt cod and kisses and lightly charred lefse, which he would have taken and said, *Will I have to dip them into the sea to soften them up?* with that smile like warm butter.

I'm back where I started. Here I sit in Tante Tilde's dark house, despite the bright early morning sunlight, despite the windswept love that's kept time soaring like a seabird, not stopping for anything but sailing over miles to reach its destination. I suppose all that bliss, all that hope, was for nothing.

I can't help but think of the look on Jon's face as the light drained from him. He still had that playful glint in his eye, bless him, even if it was for only a moment, even if I was the only person to see it. It was the same as the day I met him. And now, suddenly and without realizing it, I'm sobbing. The words come out wet and slurred. "I never told him. I didn't get a chance to tell him. I wanted to wait until I—"

Tante Tilde is hovering over me, taking the sloshing cup from my hand, rubbing a knobby hand on my back. "Now, now," she says. "Shh." She keeps rubbing my back, and my heart is still in pieces on her floor. Her touch is soft, but she's not a mother. She's not accustomed to being the source of comfort. I can tell by the way her hands move—all jerky and stilted.

"Listen to me, Barnebarn," she says finally, with a meaningful pause that hushes me.

I answer with a sniffle and a silent heave as I draw in air.

"This village isn't safe for you right now. I don't have to tell you that there have been rumors, and talk like this isn't harmless. Astrid and Mari are snooping around, asking questions, spreading stories. They've even been speaking to Pastor Thorkild about it. It's how it began last time."

Last time. Last time we didn't mourn. We couldn't. We just held Mormor's hands and ran.

"They start to cry witch every time something bad happens, you know, and it usually fades. But now, with three deaths from the same bloody cough, hungry bellies from the first-ever winter with no codfish, and the spring as hungry as the winter—even I am starting to suspect there's dark magic behind it."

I hate that she can list out Jon's death like that, brushing past the vibrancy of him when he was alive, the hole he's left in my heart now that he's gone.

"Are you listening?"

I nod, not thinking.

"Then you know what you must do?" Her hand is still moving back and forth across my back. It's comforting, even if it is unpracticed. I release a fresh wave of tears. I know I'm being ridiculous. I should have some composure. But I can't seem to stop it. I can't seem to get back control. Maybe it's the beer, and I understand why Tante Tilde drinks so much of it now. The sharp things feel duller, even when they make a deep cut.

Moving is hard, and I haven't managed much of it since I sat at this table—only to bring my cup to my lips and back down again, only to heave the sorrow of what could have been out through my eyes, letting my woolen skirt soak it up. But I must move now. My arm itches, awake with understanding. It's slight at first, and then it grows more urgent—a reaction to Tante Tilde's warning. The itch becomes a sting, and it's burning soon, and I'm thinking of Mamma, but I don't want to think of her. I don't want to think of the flames that came between us. I don't want to think of the look in her eyes, so unnatural, when I last saw them. It's like Minna said. I want to dig this feeling out at the roots.

Before I realize what I'm doing, I'm tearing at my sleeves, wrenching the fabric free at the seams wherever I can. I want it gone. I want this witch out of me. I don't want to feel it anymore. I don't want to feel anything, let alone this persistent, irritating itch. Without Jon, without this place, there can be no more magic.

"Barnebarn, I need you to calm down." Tante Tilde's voice is like a grandmother's again, and it finds me just as I'm about to lose complete control. It somehow snaps me back into my body. I'm breathing unevenly now, and even though the itching lingers, I'm able to sense the world beyond it. I look up into her face. "It's all right, Kaija. You'll be all right." She has me in her arms. It feels like Mormor, especially the way she calls me by my real name, like I'm hers. I close my eyes and pretend it's Mormor now, and then it really is her. She's got me in her arms. She's rocking me. Her arms are so warm and so tight. I don't even think to ask how she's handling this grief. I don't even think about how it must feel to lose your daughter to the flames like that. I'm only thinking about how it feels to lose a mother—

I stand. Tante Tilde is there, shocked and sorry, and Mormor is gone. The vision of my grandmother was a memory. And now the touch of her sears my arms, my neck. This pain is about Jon. It's about the man who would have been a father to the little baby growing inside me. It's not about Mamma. It's not about Mamma. It's about Jon. I reach down and put my hands on my belly.

"I'm going to be a mother."

Tante Tilde stretches a sturdy hand out to me. I know her intentions are good, but I still can't bring myself to touch her again. I don't tell her anything more. I just let these words absorb the space between us, wishing I wasn't saying them between sobs. But I know I am going to make Jon a pappa, even if he is dead. "We are a family, and this village is our home. You cannot take that from us."

"Barnebarn, please. I must warn you. Childbearing can be fickle for a witch, especially when she cannot use magic. I lost all four, and your mormor lost two. You would be better to go—"

I hold up a hand to stop her. I know what she's going to say. I know what she's going to ask me to do, but I did not come all the way here just to leave again and have my baby grow up in the birchwood, hidden away from the world. A small shake of the head, and I'm moving toward the door with a swiftness I haven't felt since the night of the full moon. I'm not waiting anymore, and I'm not hiding. I'm still heaving back the tears, but I manage to sweep myself up. I'm not sure whether I should look at her, but I decide I can't bear it, so I don't. Instead, I leave her house and close the door behind me.

I go home first to bathe again, to dress. I fill my shoes with crushed flowers, and I wipe the wildness from my face. Once I resemble Kirsti again, I'll be ready to face the villagers. I will head to Mari and Erich's first and hold their hands. I'll show them what they want to see: the plain, sweet girl who married their son and, maybe soon, the swell of this new barnebarn.

Minna

I walk down to the water and stand with the gentle waves rolling over my bare toes. The sun is low and heavy, and I have no idea what time of day it is, but my belly is full of fish, and I'm suddenly aimless. My mind wanders, and I think of Olen's words. The wolf's den.

My hands are balled up at my sides, and my knuckles are turning white. I have known almost my whole life that this is a village doused in fear and coated in evil, the kind that even witches can't conjure. I can feel it now that Olen has reminded me, even from all the way out here.

In the vision under the bearskin, my sister burned and cried for me to help her, to make it stop. But it's clear there are no fires here. Not yet anyway.

In this moment, I just want my sister to come back so we can leave before it all ignites.

Spread to eternity in front of me, the sea is so peaceful, the color of a spring moss, but it doesn't feel right. I wonder if a little magic might signal the warning I need. The witch within snaps happily in response. She's pleased at this development.

I run up to my tent and dive into it. A few torn pieces of wool and stones, one white, one red, one black. My hands. This is all I need. My feet carry me to the water's edge again, only now the waves don't feel like gentle caresses—they feel like slithering hands. But I let them slip over the tears in my dress, wrap themselves around my calves. I let them pool beneath my legs and slink away, cold as ever.

My eyes close, and I know I don't need a candle for this one. If I can't go to the village, I just have to get my sister's attention.

"Waters shall rise, waters shall fall." I tie the first knot, tight and sure. I can't go backward now, and something about the finality sutures together what might have split open. The second knot is tighter still, and in the pocket between them, I stuff the white stone.

"Churning madly and growing tall." The third knot is tied swiftly, like second nature. "Red winds shall grow, a violent tack." The red stone slips in snugly. Then I tie the final knot. My hands and the wool are both soaked by now, but I know that will only make the knot tighter.

"Turning gray clouds, like hearts, to black." I force in the black stone, and it's almost too big for the pocket of wet wool, but I don't give up. I make it fit.

Still, I feel like something is missing, though I have done the right ritual, said the words I've been reciting quietly to myself. I'll feel better once the ritual is complete, I'm sure, but I can't swat away the feeling that lingers.

I stay on my knees, clenching the wet wool in my hands. Suddenly, I recall Mormor telling us about the water ordeal. I remember her face glinting in the sunlight, on a summer evening made for laughing and flower picking—but we had finished with that for the day—and it was time for Mormor to tell us a dark story. She told us about how when they wanted to prove a witch was a witch, they would bind her hands and feet and toss her into the sea.

Just like that, as if she were a worthless pebble.

If she sank, she was not a witch. But if she floated, if she rose to the surface, well, then, that was just another excuse to burn a woman alive.

I remember Mormor's wrinkled face soaking in the patch of sun that shone on her through the birches. The evening was warm, but her words were ice-cold.

I asked the question because I knew Kaija wouldn't. I knew she wouldn't want to know. I asked if that's what they had done to Mamma. And Mormor closed her eyes then. She picked up a flower petal between her fingers and rubbed it gently, muttering something to herself. I remember looking at Kaija, who was sitting and staring at Mormor just as I was, but after I asked the question about Mamma, she had closed her eyes and started rubbing a flower petal, too.

I never understood the obsession with flowers. I never understood why Kaija loved them so much, why Mormor didn't discourage that soft magic. It's the big heavy witching that works the best—the kind of witching you can see.

I grip the wool and the stones in my right hand and hurl them into the tranquil water. Then I wait for the sea to rise.

Kaija

The waves have been rising ever since I drank beer with Tante Tilde and listened to the beat of my own heart. It's been over a week, I think, and they're even higher now. I watch one billow and curl, black as ink against the storming sky behind it. And then it crashes down hard, relentlessly, into a receding one, and they tumble together in a splinter of skeletal white.

I know my sister is still here. I can feel her. The strange seas and this rain make me think of her kind of magic—imposing, brutal, wild. She has always burned hot, and now more than ever, I have no room in my heart for that heat. I have no room for much of anything anyway.

Today, I decide I should walk with Mari and Erich and Nils and Peder and little Ellen. They're my family now, and I suppose a part of me wishes one of them will mention Jon so I can feel the ache of his absence and share it with someone. I feel as if I'm the only one who truly understood Jon and what he wanted as a man, and I can't shake it, though I know it's vain. At least I know Mari and her family are thinking of him, too. Today, that feels like enough.

I hurry to catch up with them as they gather and stride away from the kirke. I push past a few people to get there, and I brush shoulders with Astrid Olsdatter. She doesn't look too pleased at being pushed aside, and I reach out to steady her, in case she's lost her footing. I notice her flinch away from me as I do it, and she reaches for the arm of her companion instead. The acid in her eyes makes me do my own flinching, and I'm about to say something—anything—to placate her, when I hear Tante Tilde's voice.

"Astrid, dear. Let's walk." She takes the woman's arm in hers, but Astrid is still staring at me. "You know," Tante Tilde says, louder this time, "I've been wondering when we're going to be able to brew more beer. It's been ages, and my stores are running low."

"Oh, Tilde. You drink too much," says Astrid, finally releasing me from her sight, but the chill from it stays with me.

"I'm an old widow, so whatever I want to drink, I must brew it myself. Just like you."

Astrid laughs, and I think this must be a long-standing joke between them because even though Tante Tilde is stiffer than usual, the conversation has lightened, and they walk together like that, arm in arm.

As I approach, I notice Mari move to the other side of Nils, pretending to fuss with his shirt. She does not want to walk beside me. She has been avoiding me just as she always has, although now I know I can't be the only one who notices. I put my head down to hide the pink I'm sure has flushed my cheeks and to watch my hands, to see if they're shaking. Politely, Erich takes up the position at my shoulder without hesitation. He may have missed his wife's rebuff, but he doesn't seem to notice much these days. At least he hasn't lost his mind like I have. Like Mari seems to have. He's a man, and he has livelihoods to think of. I watch him glance out over the sea. His look carries a longing, though I'm not sure if it's for the fish that aren't swimming freely under the tumult of waves or for the son he won't be sailing with again. A sting blocks my air passage momentarily. I let the tears prick my eyes, but I open them wide to dry them out before they can fall.

"It was nice that the pastor spoke of Jon today, during the service." It's Nils who speaks. His voice is forced, like he's trying to be the eldest son in the absence of his brother. I see Mari flinch and fiddle with her bonnet.

"It was a good service," says Erich.

We walk in silence for a bit longer, listening to the thrash of the waves on the shore. They're not too far from us, the waves, and I catch myself glimpsing at them to make sure they're not rising above us, ready to take us all out to sea in their frothy white recession. Once or twice, it seems likely, and I think I can even feel a faint mist on my face after one particularly voluminous wave, though I'm sure I'm just imagining it.

"You're coming by for supper, Kirsti?" It's Nils again. He's leaned forward to peer at me beyond his father's broad chest. That face is just like Jon's, but where Jon had a flicker of mischief, Nils has an earnest innocence. For a moment, I think of Minna and how earnest innocence is the only thing she ever lacked. I nod back at him with a polite half smile. My hands go to my belly again, which makes me feel even more alone. Thunder rolls overhead, and we all look up.

"Those clouds are too black," says Erich. "There will be no fish until this storm has calmed." He's right. There seems to be an endless layer of thick clouds, each one in the shadow of another. And then, as if in response, rain falls on us, ruthless and sudden and cold.

"It's unnatural, this," says Mari in a sharp voice. "A storm like this to last for over a week? The seas to rise like this under the midnight sun?" Her voice is deep with mourning, and she tsks with disapproval.

Erich lets out a low groan. "Mari, enough. It is weather, not witches."

My shoulders go stiff. My neck straightens. I feel my eyes widen and force them to soften. I must act naturally, of course. Tante Tilde told me there was talk. I will have to find a way through it without betraying anything.

"Erich, you're blinded by politics. You just don't want the district court to have any more say in our village affairs than they do already. But that is how witch trials are dealt with, you know that. We must root out this evil magic, whatever it takes."

I was mistaken, I realize. It isn't mourning that has darkened her voice. There's more power behind it than that.

"Enough." Erich's voice is a warning, but it's drowned out by a clap of thunder that resonates from one end of the sky to the other. The rain falls harder. Soon, I can barely see Erich beside me. I can't even see my own hands. The drops are a cold thrumming on my head, and I'm soaked though within seconds. There are yelps and shouts from a group that has been walking near us. People are hurrying into their homes, taking cover from the sudden storm that seems to be building.

"Kirsti!" Erich shouts at me as I separate from them. "Come to our house, please."

"I couldn't," I manage to say. It's a wet response, dampened by the roar of rain and the crackle of thunder, and I know it's better than facing Mari around the supper table, listening to her dig a grave for a burned witch she hasn't named yet.

His shoulders slump as he watches me peel off from his family group. I steal a last look over my shoulder and catch Mari's face glowing in the next bright flash of lightning. She is wearing a satisfied expression, and it's pointed directly at me. And then the rain comes down in torrents, and I can't see her anymore, so I open the door to Tante Tilde's and walk inside the cool, dry house.

Minna

I'm not itchy anymore, but I feel my blood moving like icicles through my veins.

I am watching the water rise and fall in front of me. I've had to move up the beach until I'm sitting on the rocks, soaked from head to foot as cold rain splashes against my skin, my hair, my clothes. But my body still tingles from the spell, even a week later. And yet Kaija has not come back.

It's not in my nature to not be prepared, but somehow Olen catches me off guard. Again. He's standing behind me before I even notice I'm not alone anymore.

Incredibly, he holds up a line with two fish dangling from it. I don't know how he's done it, but he's gone out in the chaos I created and caught some fish. I'm impressed, but I make sure not to show it.

He says something, but I can't hear it over the rain. Then he's walking over to my tent, which is pulled taut with the fabric from the dress Kaija tried to make me wear. He sits inside, like it's his. Then he leans out and waves me over.

All I've been doing is watching these damn waves grow and sink and crash against one another. There's some satisfaction that comes from seeing a wave you created curl and collapse from its sheer height. I guess, when you get too tall, there's nothing left to do but come crashing down on yourself. I thought Kaija would see the waves and understand I was reaching out to her. I thought she would recognize this kind of magic, feel the warning, come back, and find out what it's all for. But I haven't seen her. I've seen no one but Olen.

I run over to him now, giving the witch a break, and as I do, I'm suddenly aware of the chill in the air. I duck underneath the tent, and it's dripping in spots, but I've pulled it as tightly as I could this time, lashed it in place with stones and stakes and twine. He looks at me with a smile, and it is so out of place, I return it with a laugh.

He keeps catching me off guard, and I don't like it, so I wipe the smile from my face before he can say anything and examine what he's brought.

"How is it over there?" I ask him. My voice is loud under this small stretch of wool, and I already feel warmer, and I realize it's not from the prickle of my witch's blood but from Olen.

"Well," he says without looking at me. "Well, the seas are rough. They suspect witches."

I nod. Of course they do.

"It's not the only thing that has them talking," he goes on. "There have been three deaths from the same cough—two since Christmas—and there have been no fish in the sea for months."

I glare at the dead-eyed fish at our feet. They're slick, and I wonder how we'll cook them with all this rain. "No fish?"

He smiles and shrugs, offering no explanation. "There's also a big storm that's been going on for a week. If you haven't noticed."

I eye him. "What's your story, Olen? Why do you come down here and bring fish to the strange girl on the beach?"

He laughs now that I've caught him off guard for once. "You're not a stranger."

I feel another smile rising, but then I see he's not joking. He's completely serious. In fact, he seems to be trying to send me some kind of message with his eyes. Either that, or he's trying to see me for who I really am. Good luck there.

"You're Minna."

My name sounds strange on his lips. I'm not sure how it got there exactly.

He hesitates. "You don't remember."

It's not a question but a statement. I'm meant to agree with him. I'm meant to remember, but remember what, I'm not sure. I'm the one searching his eyes now. Is there something I'm not seeing there? The way he's looking at me tells me there's something he wants me to see.

He sighs instead of pushing it, and I'm glad. My heartbeat slows again.

"Were you trying to spear fish out there, the day you almost drowned?" He nods in the direction of the sea, changing the subject, maybe sensing my reaction.

"Hm." I can't tell if he's making fun of me or just curious. Either way, I don't want to give him the answer he's looking for. I can already see a small smile starting to crawl over his face, raising his cheeks. I won't let him get at me that easily.

"Spearfishing is near to impossible here. It's not your fault," he says quickly. "There's a sharp drop-off not too far out, and the rip current is strong."

I don't look at him because I know what he's doing.

"I'm glad you're not dead, though."

To this, I turn and face him. I'm not sure I agree. I could have died out there in those waves, and it would have been a very cruel way to go—but it would have been very witchy if you ask me. I was fine with it. I don't have much to keep on living for anyway, do I?

"How do you know my name?" I make sure there's a sharpness to my words, so he doesn't get too comfortable.

He shrugs. "I've known it as long as I've known my own." There's something modest and shy in the way he says this without looking at me. If I didn't know any better, I'd think he was waiting to see me again for quite a long time.

"My sister changed her name. She's Kirsti now." I don't know why I say it, but it slips out.

Olen doesn't miss a beat. "Ah, I did suspect. She looks the same as you, you know."

"Well, that's not her real hair."

"What do you mean?"

Though there's no point—she won't be coming home with me, I am starting to realize—I still can't betray her this easily. It's on the tip of my tongue, telling him about what kind of women we really are. He thinks he knows so much about who I am. Admitting the rumors are true would be a real shock, wouldn't it?

"Nothing. She just wanted a new life."

He's wringing his hands in his lap, passing one set of fingers over the other. "Where have you been all this time? I thought I'd never see you again." The way he says it makes me think he's probably been wondering this for thirteen years.

I shrug and sigh, and I feel as noncommittal as Kaija as I do it, but there's no good response.

"Do you really not remember me?" he says.

Why did he have to ask me that? I would have said if I did. Now I have to admit that he was so insignificant to me that I didn't even take the memory of him with me to the birchwood.

Before I can think of how to respond, my gaze travels to his pocket because his hand is in there, and he's digging for something. He pulls it out and places it on the sand between us. It's a stone, smooth and black. For a moment, I wonder if he saw me doing magic earlier—if he knows I've bound up a black stone, just like this one, into a makeshift witch's cloth and tossed it into the sea as my witching pawn. But I can't tell what he's thinking because he's not looking at me. He's looking at the stone, and his hand is back in his pocket. He pulls out a second stone, then a third.

Delicately, and with obdurate concentration, he sets the second stone on top of the first, but the way he's placing it is at an impossible angle. That stone will never stay. He's gentle but persistent with it, and neither of us breathes. And then he lifts his hands away, and there it is, stacked impossibly on the bottom stone. It only balances on a tiny edge, but it stays, even after I stare at it, waiting for it to wobble and topple over.

Olen is getting the third stone ready to stack on the second one. I can tell by how carefully he picks it up, rotates it in his hands, examines all its edges. As he does that, a vision of another man's hands flashes through my mind. Instead of the sand, the base stone lies in the grass, and the man's hands place the edge of another stone right on top, and it stays there, as if it's suspended in midair. I must be small in the vision because I look up to see the man, but his face is shadowed by the sun behind him. I turn back to look at the stones, and I hear a laugh. There's a boy there with me, and we're laughing together.

This vision seems sweet in a way. It makes my pulse slow. It's short-lived, and soon I realize Olen has put the last stone on top, and he's looking at me again, patiently, with his hands in his lap.

"I can do it now," he says. "Almost as well as my father."

And suddenly, I understand. That man and those stones and the young boy's laugh—it wasn't a vision at all. It was a memory.

I scramble to my knees, knocking over the stones as I do. They tumble soundlessly into the wet sand. Olen looks shocked, but I don't care. I can't deal with this right now.

I squeeze my head to block out the memory, but it's there now, and it's not going away. I want to tell him to leave. I want to tell him to leave me alone. Once he's gone, I will enchant this small beach so no one can find me. I should have done that from the start, but I couldn't in case Kaija came looking for me, and she did come looking.

But even that is done now. The full moon came and went, and now I don't have a sister who will be going back with me, but I have this thing, this new memory.

"What are you doing here?" I ask him, furious. I look him straight in the eye so he knows I'm serious. He doesn't shy away but looks back with a determination that unsettles me momentarily. Kaija never had that look.

"I told you. I wanted to make sure you had enough to eat."

"Last time, you said you were and weren't from the village. Both. Why did you say that?"

He's on his knees now, and we're so close, I can feel his breath when he speaks. "I'm alone. I'm alone because of my father. They found a ceremonial drum in his house one day while he was out fishing. I'm alone because they burned him like they burned those women, only he was not a witch." He pauses, and his breaths are quick now. He picks up a stone and squeezes it. "He was a Sami man. Not even a shaman. Not even a healer. Not any of that. He married a Norwegian woman. That drum was for music, but they see what they want to, don't they?"

A beat passes, and we don't say anything to each other. "My mamma was burned," I say without thinking. It's as much a defense as it is sympathy, but it's as much as I can muster. Something in his face tells me his pain may match mine, and that's something I've never seen in anyone before.

"I know."

"So I guess I know how you feel."

He picks up the other two stones, stuffs them all back into his pockets, and shakes his head. Then he ducks out of the tent so suddenly, I sink back to the ground. All he says is, "No, Minna, you don't," and then he's gone.

Kaija

I'm praying. I'm not doing a spell, as I know Minna would have me do, but I'm talking to God the way the villagers do, the way Jon did before bed and around the supper table. I wonder if there's someone out there who hears me or if I'm talking to myself.

"Bring me peace," I say over the small wooden cross that marks Jon's grave. I'm crying lightly, but it's still raining, so the tears and raindrops muddle together as they fall to the ground. It feels strange to pray, and though I've heard others asking for peace in this way, I feel nothing. At least when I say the words of a spell or do a ritual, I feel the tingle rising inside me. In a way, it's validation that I'm doing it right. This—I have no idea if I'm doing this right. Pretending to do something and actually doing it are certainly not the same thing. I wonder if the other people in this village truly feel something when they do this. I decide they must. Otherwise, why would they continue to do it over and over?

The ground is wet, and I feel a little rebellious since, unlike most of the village women, I'm not afraid of the rain. There's still some of the birchwood life left inside me, I realize, and for once, it's serving me. Storms aren't to be feared. They're life-giving, aren't they? They clear the way for blue skies and new things to grow. These are the things you're more grateful for after a harsh storm anyway.

I am careful to avoid the fresh dirt that I know marks the place where they laid his body. He was tall, but the mound doesn't do him justice. It looks small below me. I try to imagine his face and the way he might look now, watching me pray. He was certainly devout but never made too much of a fuss over God and kirke and the like. Just as his father before him. Jon did his duty, but beyond that, he was more interested in the people alive right in front of him. He was the one making jokes to his brothers about the pastor's pinched face during the sermon. But he did what was required of him, and it's not like there were any other options for a man like him. We never discussed his beliefs in earnest. I'm not even sure there were any. He would never divulge something as indulgent as what he believed happened after someone died, for instance, just as I could never tell him about my magic. There are some secrets we only think we keep and others we truly do.

Thunder overhead reminds me of where I am. Erich and Mari will be waiting for me, and I should go back. I am sure, more than anything, that it was Erich's idea to invite me to supper tonight. Mari has always looked at me with disapproval. Only now, she wears the look of someone who has had something precious stolen and is certain whose hands it ended up in.

I sigh. Of course she feels like that. I suppose any mother would feel that way. But the itch under my forearms warns me of the other reason she blames me. It's not because I married him but because she thinks there's some evil lurking about. I wonder if she thinks I'm somehow doing Djevelen's deeds. When did magic become associated with Djevelen? The magic I know is benevolent, protective, healing. It makes the world stronger, brings us together. Djevelen only wants to tear us apart. I wish I could assure Mari that not all witches are like that. Even my sister has softened, I realize. She came to find me after all.

Despite what Tante Tilde says, I cannot see Mari jumping to that conclusion, wondering about me. Lately, I've been trying to play my part as the reticent daughter, helping prepare meals as much as I can. Though now that there seem to be no more fish in the sea—except those that turn up under Olen Bren's boat—the meals have been easier and easier to prepare, and she hasn't needed my assistance. Or so she has said.

"They have magic all wrong." I say it to Jon, but then I remember I'm supposed to be speaking to God. Something inside me bubbles up. It's a laugh. I came here to do one thing, and I can't even do it right. I wish Jon were here for me to lay my head on. I wish he were here to tell me a funny story about his pappa. I miss his hands tangled in my hair and his salty skin so close to mine when we slept.

I look around me. No one is out, and it's quite far back to the village. If anyone sees me here, I'll simply look like a mourning widow. And I am. But this matters to me, the fact I'm alone out here in the cemetery, because if I can't pray right, magic will have to do. Luckily, I came prepared, just in case.

I reach under my skirt and pull out the rune stone, the knife, and the feather from the band of cloth tied tight around my thigh. Even though I never told him who I was or why I might be pulling such things out of there, I think Jon would enjoy the sight of it.

I place the rune stone on the earth, over his head, and lay the feather next to it. The mound reminds me of Mormor's for a moment, especially with the stone perched on top of it. This time, though, it's not Minna who's going to do the blood sacrifice but me. I've brought Jon's fishing knife, which is sharper than anything we would have used in the woods, but I'm still hesitant. To make myself feel better, I have also brought a bit of my favorite kind of magic—the kind that blooms in spring and summer and lasts all year if you dry it correctly. It's fresh today, picked on the way over. Bright yellow petals, a tall and sturdy stem. This is the right flower for Jon. I place it next to the stone. I take a deep breath and slide my wet skirt up until my right thigh is exposed to the rain. I think Jon would probably enjoy this, too. I place the sharp edge of the knife on a soft part just on the inside of the muscle. I'm aiming for a poke rather than a swipe, a luxury that is only available to me because the blade on this knife was just recently sharpened. I can remember Jon scraping the stone along it, back and forth, a shrill ring echoing throughout the house while he told me how beautiful I looked with my hair the way it was that day.

Closing my eyes, I push the point of the knife into my leg, and I can feel my body reacting. It's wondering why I would do such a thing to myself, sending a stinging response. But the magic responds quickly, too, and they seem to balance each other out. In just a quick moment, blood spills out from my skin and onto the knife's edge. I grab the rune stone, which I carved just before coming out here, and I can feel the rough scrape of my handiwork beneath my finger as I smear my own blood over it and watch its white shapes darken. Then I replace my skirt, apologizing to my husband for not offering him more, and then I pinch the buttercup between my left fingers. The feather, I pinch with my right.

"Rise now and fly, soul to meet sky." I lay both the flower and the feather down on the earth, and then dig two shallow graves. "Ride Odin's flight in spellfire light."

With the feather and flower snug in the earth, I place the rune stone in and bury them as gently as the mud will allow. I realize the galdr sounds incomplete, and so I pause to think, but the words come without any bidding from me. "Till we join thee, always, your family of three."

The mud ends up coming out of my fingers in clumps rather than sprinkles, but in the end, everything is covered, the ritual is complete, and the galdr has been sung. That's all that matters. The simple yet powerful spell is cast.

When I walk home again through the rain, I think, for some reason, of Minna. I suppose I feel a little bit now what she felt after Mormor. I feel awake—the kind of awake you can only feel when you've helped a beloved soul find its eternal home.

Minna

When I'm angry, I can go without speaking to someone for as long as it takes for them to realize the error of their ways and beg me back. I can hold out for months if that's what it takes. I did it to Mormor once, and she tried to break me by doing the same back, but I wouldn't give in until she finally called a truce.

Eventually, she did, and the funny thing is that I don't even remember now what I was so mad about. But I made my point.

Olen isn't me, though.

He was clearly annoyed by my lack of compassion, even my lack of memory, but it wasn't my fault. The memory may not have been unwelcome, but it brought with it the possibility of so much more, and I'm not interested in remembering.

Olen, as I said, isn't me, which means he's back the very next day. I'm carving a rune into a small stone when I hear him call my name. I lean out to see his arms swinging easily at his sides as he marches through the rain. I place the rune stone atop a gull feather sitting on a damp rock next to me. He slides inside the tent. He says he has no fish today. He has given his latest haul to the people in the village. "They can't go out in weather like this."

For a moment, I think he knows what I've done, but then he sits down and pulls out his own stones, unaware that the weather around this tiny ramshackle tent has been called up by a witch, and that witch is sitting right next to him, tingling in anticipation of her next spell.

I can't take another day like yesterday, but I've decided he's not so bad to have around. At least he's someone to talk to, and even though I don't want to remember, the sound of his voice, his gait, his laugh—they're all familiar to me now.

I'm not even angry that he saved me, not anymore. Now that I have Olen to exchange stories with, I don't mind so much that I didn't die.

Suddenly, I'm standing. I pull him up and make him walk with me. We give the waves a wide berth, staying up on the rocks, still out of sight of the village and out the sea's reach.

"That water is brutal," I say, wanting to bring up the incident but taking the emphasis off the near drowning.

"It's always been unpredictable."

"But not for you?"

"My family has been fishing these waters forever." He shrugs, smiling a little to himself. I know that smile, I think. I don't know what's behind it, but there is only one reason a person wears a smile like that. Olen has a secret.

I tell him about the memory that came to me—the one with the stones and the man's hands. He tells me the hands I'm remembering are his father's and that he recalls that day, too. It was the last day we spent together before they took my Mamma and locked her in some castle miles away and then brought her back to the lane outside our houses so she could burn where she was born.

It's nice, in a dark and twisted way, that we share the same story. We both had a parent who felt the hot fear of burning alive. I don't say this to him, of course. Most people don't have skin as thick as mine, and I'm afraid he'll take it the wrong way.

Instead, I say, "So your pappa wasn't magical, then?" I've been wondering this ever since Olen told me his father wasn't a witch. But was he a sorcerer?

"Were any of them?"

"Yes."

He laughs, and I'm comforted a little bit because at least I know where I've heard that laugh before. But I'm also annoyed. I can sense that he doesn't think I'm serious. I stop, holding out my arm and grabbing his.

"Were we friends when we were young?" I want to dig a little deeper into him, but carefully. I want to know our story, but I don't want to dig up anything too raw. He's not giving me much to work with anyway. I guess I could have reacted better when he started to open up yesterday.

"Yes," he says.

"I don't remember very much."

"Well, a lot happened right around then, for you anyway. So it makes sense you don't remember." He says it with such kindness, it takes me a moment to understand he's not trying to goad me. "We played together all the time," he continues. "Your mamma and pappa are some of the few people I remember from before—well, before those women burned. Everything changed then. You left, your mamma was"—he looks away—"gone. Pappa and I were all alone. Then, once they named him a sorcerer, that was it. I've been sort of feared and avoided by the village ever since." He pauses for a moment, and I know this kind of silence. He's thinking of his pappa. "Anyway, yes, you and I were friends."

I'm fighting back flashes of memories as he's talking, memories I don't want: Mamma's dark hair draped over me like a curtain while she tucks me into bed, me playing in the sand with a small boy, being caught with Mamma's rune stones and crying as she whispers sternly into my ear. Olen has awoken some deeply buried memories, that much even I can see, and I'm not sure how I feel about it all yet. It's so fresh. Part of me doesn't want to remember because sweetness like that never lasts. It always fades into the present, or else it catches fire so quickly I can't stop it. But another part of me doesn't want the memories to stop.

"My mamma was a witch." I say it without shame, though my heart is thundering. I'm not sure what makes me do it, but it must be said. She should be remembered for the powerful woman she was, and Olen is the only person I can tell. At least I think I can trust him.

He laughs again, and I'm expecting it, but I square up. "So am I."

His laugh fades into a sort of squint. I can tell he's trying to figure out what to make of me. He trusts me because I'm an outcast like him, and he remembers me as the daughter of a woman accused of witchcraft.

But he hasn't yet put the two together.

I wait for the fear to cross like a shadow over his face. I anticipate he'll make up some excuse, some reason he just remembered he has to be somewhere. The rain is lightening up now, but the seas are still raging. I turn to them.

"You did this," he says, and I feel the smile spread over me. He's not afraid. He's in awe.

I bend over and tear ruthlessly at the hem of my dress. There's not much of a hem there anymore, and I can almost hear Kaija's disapproval. I hold out my palm. "Stone."

He hesitates a moment before reaching into his pocket. The black stone is light in my hand, smaller than the one I used before. This is makeshift, but it doesn't matter. I've practiced so many times, I know it will still work.

I knot the wool once, then twice, fitting the stone snugly in between. Then, I run toward the sea and hurl it into the next receding wave. "Wave, hear my song. I call thee now. Out of the sea, rise, tall and strong."

I turn to him and show him my smile. The tingling is young and excited in my veins. It likes this kind of quick witching, I think. So do I.

Before either of us can say another word, a far-out swell grows ominous. It rolls toward us, growing in height and not losing strength. It gets taller and taller until it's too tall for us to stand where we are, and we run backward. The wave peaks at a height above any house, any treetop I've ever seen, and we barely make it out of its reach before it comes crashing down in a chaotic explosion of white and black and green. The spray catches us, but we're still backpedaling so we don't get caught in its current. It floods the rocks, engulfs my tent, and comes up to hug our ankles. Only then does it relax and slide back into the sea where it came from.

The next waves are much smaller in comparison, though they still crash ominously against the shore. I only conjured one this time, but it was enough. The itch is dancing inside me now, celebrating our accomplishment, the speed and the accuracy of it. And Olen is staring at me, his mouth slightly open.

"Dritt," he curses, turning to the wave that disappeared as quickly as it arrived. But I don't see fear on his face. In fact, it's the opposite. There's a smile growing there to match mine.

And then he laughs that familiar laugh, and we're two children looking out over the sea, both amazed at how powerful a stone and a simple rhyme can be in the right hands.

Kaija

Gray light peeks through the window and fills the room with the obstinance of a child.

I only notice because I can't fall back asleep, and then, once I wake fully, I sit up, squinting into it. This is usually my favorite time of year, when I get my days and nights mixed up, when I can go for a stroll or find fresh flowers waving up at me during some confused hour when no person should be awake. There's magic in these times, and not just the itchy under-my-skin magic—though that's ripe in the wee hours as well. The magic this time of the year is usually more of a peacefulness, a quiet. Everything alive is both stunned and thrilled to have more time under the sun, to keep night at bay. Winter is for resting. Summer is for celebrating.

And yet the storm that's pressed down on the village has prevented any jovial summer feelings. I will admit the tumultuous gray fits my particular mood much better than the brilliant shine of sun. I wiggle my feet out from under the blanket. The drab light gives them an aura, and the magic inside me wakes up, starting at the toes, bubbling all the way to the top of my head. I'm full of magic now, and I'm not afraid of it. I'm not trying to push it down. I know this feeling can't last all day. Soon, I'll have to make my way over to help a reluctant Mari with some mending and prepare some of Olen Bren's latest catch. I swear that man has a knack for finding fish in the toughest times. No one else has even dared venture out in the treacherous waves, and yet Olen Bren seems to come home almost every day with a pile of food. He may well be feeding this whole village right now.

My stomach rolls at the thought of food, and I reluctantly sweep my feet onto the floor. I place my hands on my belly. Finally, I think I may be able to feel a swell there, a lifting where there was flatness before. I peer down at my hands. I can clearly see that I have grown, and though I should be weeping with joy, I'm suddenly awash in cold despair. Why could this not have happened with Jon still alive? What will happen to this child now with no father? What if he is a little boy, blond like Jon, and it's too much to bear to look at him? Or what if, so help me, it's a daughter? She'll be born with my magic bubbling through her, I realize. That would only mean more secrets for us. More lies.

There's a solid knock at the door. A man's knock. For a flash, I imagine Jon returning home with too many fish to open it himself and wearing a bright smile. But as I carelessly whip my hair into a long braid and slide my dress over my shoulders, I remember that, of course, it can't be Jon, and the thorns in my heart prick me again. Jon is dead. The only slight consolation I have is that his soul is up in the sky waiting to dance with the spellfire, and somehow that makes it better, and at the same time, the finality of it makes it so much more painful.

Outside my door, I'm surprised to see a woman there. It's Astrid Olsdatter, and she has an expression on her face that I can't pinpoint, but she seems to always be wearing that expression, doesn't she? It's like the frown of a lifeless fish. Sometimes Tante Tilde and I have laughed about it at her table, speaking low and conspiratorially into our cups. But here Astrid is now, nose raised higher than it needs to be, and though we are the same height, she's trying her best to look down on me.

"Ah, Kirsti." She says my name with a forced smile. She wants to seem like she's come for a friendly chat, I think, but there's something not right about her being here. Not at all. Then the woman raises a small basket in her hands. "Fresh lefse?" She isn't the kind of neighbor to do such a thing, and yet here she is. I can't smell the lefse in the basket, but I wonder how fresh it is and if it might still be warm.

"Please," I say, moving to the side for her, instinctually adjusting my apron so she won't see my swollen belly. She looks pleased, if haughty, and she limps inside and places the basket on the table. Once the cloth is unwrapped and the lefse are exposed, I look for steam and don't see any. So they're not warm. Astrid is expectant, and I invite her to sit. I'm adjusting my dress and my hair as she does this, hoping she doesn't notice I've been in bed until…what time is it anyway?

"Takk Gud that storm has finally passed," she says, groaning with effort and pulling something else from the basket and placing it on the cloth.

"Takk Gud," I agree, watching her. I see she has brought her own gjetost cheese, and I understand. She means to eat with me. My repayment for letting her in with her cold food is to converse with her. My heart pounds a bit. This is something Tante Tilde told me never to do. *Let me deal with that woman*, she said. *Astrid Olsdatter has the tongue of a troll.*

Sitting at my table, Astrid looks around my house, and I realize I have a choice. I can fear this troll of a woman in my own home, or I can stand firm and be Kirsti, wife of Jon Erichsen. "Takk for the lefse. Shall we try some?" I keep it sweet but stern, trying to channel some of Mormor and Tante Tilde's tones.

Astrid eyes me but she acquiesces, and we begin to eat. I search my mind for things to talk about, but everywhere I turn, there are warnings firing. I can't talk about the weather. Too unusual for this time of year, might raise suspicion. I can't speak of the fish the men have brought in because there are none, and I'm not sure she knows how much Olen Bren has contributed to keeping me and the rest of this village from going hungry. What is left?

But, of course, Astrid Olsdatter finds the one topic that won't raise any eyebrows, and yet it's the thing I want to keep safe from her most of all.

"Jon was a good boy," she says to me, a mouth full of lefse and cheese. "Raised well by his mor."

I feel sick, and I want to stuff this stale bread into her basket and demand she leave, but I know I can't. I know I must play my role. And so I nod politely. "Ja."

"And the two of you never spoke of children?"

I widen my eyes in surprise but am careful not to inhale too sharply. She certainly isn't one for idle talk. "We did, but…" It comes out gently because it has to, but I have a sudden surprising urge to stab this cheese knife into her hand.

She nods in understanding. "Ah, yes. His death was so sudden, was it not?"

"Yes, very sudden."

"He was so young. Too young, wouldn't you say?"

She doesn't wait for my response, which is perfectly fine since I can't think of a single thing to say to her.

"And your friend Anne. Sweet girl. Did you know she was betrothed?" she says, as if she's discussing the inconvenience of mud inside the house. I can hear something slithering beneath her words.

I nod stiffly.

"Shame she never had her wedding," she says. "But you did."

She's trying to pry me open. I can feel it. But I remain closed, with my hands resting on the table. What was the word Tante Tilde used? *Demure.*

"The young simply shouldn't die like that." She is waving a finger at me as she speaks. The motion is mesmerizing, her hand resembling something between a point and a carelessly wielded runestave. "The will of God wouldn't allow it." Her voice is growing more resolute with every syllable, and I can tell she's getting closer to her point now. She's almost arrived at what she has come here to say. I grip the wooden seat beneath me, holding myself there. "It's all Djevelen's work; of that, I'm sure."

And there it is. I'm careful not to flinch, but I feel her directness as sharply as if she's put down her stern finger and grabbed the cheese knife to brandish in my direction instead, daring me to make the next move.

"Djevelen must be very busy, then." The words tumble out before I can stop them. I sound just like Minna, and I know instantly that I've gone too far. Astrid's eyes narrow. I'm not sure she's used to insolence. It certainly won't soften her to me, that I know.

She's looking so hard into my eyes that I think for a moment she can see the magic swirling within me. Then she says, "I think he is."

I must keep my composure. I must be careful. I imagine Tante Tilde at my shoulder, coaching me through my every movement, and I am happy to see her there. I'm strengthened by the normalcy of her voice, the familiarity of her cup of beer sloshing to and fro.

"As a matter of fact," I say, "I'm due at Mari's this morning. We are mending some breeches for Nils and the boys." I think of the mending I did the night of my wedding, and I feel the itch slither through me. Someone saw me that night, I remember. My blood feels like ice, and I am frozen to the chair. She is standing now, still scanning my home. I'm aware of the dust in the corners and the untidy bed, but she won't find anything in here, at least not what she's looking for. I've been far too careful for that.

"I'll see you at kirke, then," she says, taking her basket but leaving the lefse and the cloth behind. I am still hungry, but the look of it—a stack the color of a wind-worn brygge—it makes me feel ill again. Once she's out of sight, I gather the cloth, making sure to wrap the food in a tight knot. I'm queasy, but I'm not stupid enough to turn down food. Maybe it will appeal later. As I lift the cloth from where Astrid placed it, I see something there.

It's a feather, gray and white, and next to it, a small rune stone with an etching I know so well. It takes me a moment to understand. Before long, the dizziness is back, and I'm overwhelmed with it as I take the feather in my hands. I suddenly run outside, to the back of the house, and I heave into the grass.

But I was so careful the day I buried this feather and that stone in the cemetery. No one could have seen me. There was no one nearby, I know it. I wonder if she discovered it later, and then I think it could have been Mari, the only other person who would be so close to Jon's grave that she might see something like a feather buried in the earth. But even if it was Mari, it would be impossible for her to know who did it. It could have been anyone. That's the only bit of solace I have, and I wipe my chin with it and walk back into the house. I stop myself at the door. The magic in me is boiling with something now, but it's not excitement anymore.

Just below me are my shoes, still muddy from my traipse in the graveyard, their soles lined with white flower petals, and it's just about the witchiest thing I've ever seen. I slump, leaning against the house. I don't know what will become of me now. She may well bring the throngs of angry villagers, the chains, and the pyre itself. I sit for too long, and by the time I stand, I still don't have a plan, but I'm tingling all over.

That's when look out into the distance. The storm has broken now, and the sun is out. Astrid strides quickly away from another person toward the kirke, a determination in her uneven limp, in the way she clutches her skirt. I know what she's going to do, whose name she's going to speak. I can almost hear the acidic spray of the way she'll say *witch*. But there's something odd happening now. She stops before she gets too close and throws her hands up to her face. The kirke stands before her as it always does, but I notice it's different now. Angry golden flames pour out its windows, trying to climb to its roof, and I watch with my own hands cupped over my mouth as those wretched flames swallow the cross that stands atop the building.

And now the witch inside me is snapping at me, trying to get my attention, but I can't think of what to do. I can't think of anything but hot consuming fire.

Minna

I know I can't stay here much longer. What's here for me?

I can't just sit on the beach and make waves for the rest of my life. Kaija is not coming. She doesn't want to be saved. How can I help her? Being here any longer is exhausting and pointless. I need to go back to the birchwood and find a purpose for my witching. Maybe I can do more trading with the Sami along the coast. I have come to really enjoy the taste of sea fish. It would be hard to give that up forever just because I leave here.

I'm walking up and down the shore, watching the rise and fall of the swells, but they're nothing like what I made. They're low and content with the calm. They're part of the reason I feel such a pull to leave here. They're beautiful, these waves, and yet they're someone else's beauty. They're not mine. My world is snow and fire and arrows piercing the hearts of beasts and tearing their skin from their meat before I roast and wear them.

It sounds brutal, but it's life, isn't it?

I'm a girl of the woods above all else, even above being a witch, I think. But the tingle in my skin rises to the challenge, and I give her a good itch. *Soon*, I say to the witching that runs through me. *Soon we'll be alone again, and we can do all the spells we want. No one will ever bother us.*

I think for a moment of leaving Olen, and it makes me stop in my tracks. He's become familiar to me—the way he walks up along the shoreline around the bluff and out of sight of the village to get to me, or how he rows up onto the sand and gives me a smile, the intensity of which tells me exactly how many fish he's got in there. We stroll and talk and eat the tender flakes of pollack or the hearty, salted char of mackerel as we watch the waves roll in and out.

He told me about his father, who showed him exactly how to find the perfect pockets of fish. The knowledge he has of the sea has come from many, many, many generations of fathers teaching their sons—stretching back to a time that existed before Norwegians even set foot in these arctic lands.

He was the one who convinced me to stop the storm. I knew he could navigate the waves well enough, but the last time he went out, I watched the wind tear the sail of his boat and damage part of the hull. Without panicking, without even a moment of hesitation, he grabbed his oars and began to row. His arms moved quickly as he sliced his way through the swells. I was surprised to see him grow closer and eventually shove the damaged boat up on a flat rock nearby. I waited for him to spit anger at me as he strode up the uneven beach in my direction. But he just stuck his oars between two rocks—they were sharp-edged and carved precisely—and dropped next to me, exhausted. "Why are you still doing this?" he asked.

And I didn't have an answer, not really.

It was taking almost as much energy to keep the storm brewing as it would to scour the shoreline for sea kelp, which Olen showed me how to roast so it peels off the coals every time as a sweet and salty wonder. I don't know how well it will travel with me should I try to take some of it back to the birchwood, but it suddenly seems essential.

But Olen. I can't take him back with me, can I?

The sea, as it rolls up to the shore at my feet now, is placid and the color of his eyes. I know Kaija and I were close all those years, but there is something different about Olen. I think he is my first friend. That's why I hold his sail in my hands, balled up and well clear of the ground.

I have the security of my memories, at least enough to know he was a very early friend, defining so many of the good feelings I must have had as a young child. But he's also the first person I can truly say is my friend now that I am old enough to know the difference.

And the way he is. He's just free from anger. Despite what has happened to him, what they did to him, he doesn't let it control him. That is foreign to me. But seeing it has done something to me. It's at least changed the way I see myself.

I used to look to Kaija to help me control my witching. But Olen has shown me that I can control it on my own. The thought of leaving him lingers heavily in my muscles, weighing me down more than I'm used to.

I expect the tingle to grow and pinch the sensitive skin at my wrists with this new feeling crowding around her, but she remains vague, almost like a tickle.

I take another step and realize there has been less excitement in me for the power of witching. Sure, it's there—the need will never go away—but it's not a need to break or burn things anymore. It's not a need to make things go my way in a hurricane of fury and might.

It's more of a practicality.

I do witching because I am a witch, and it's what we do. I'm proud that I was able to mend the tear in his sail. It wasn't the magic I'm used to, but I think spending all this time with Olen has quieted some of my rage. I don't need big witching quite like I used to.

It's a little sad, this lack of excitement, but it's also a relief. It's like I've been running all my life and now I'm just walking calmly along the rocky beach. I'll still get where I need to go, but it just takes a hell of a lot less energy. And I can do something helpful for my friend as a result.

Soon, I'm making my way up the bluff, toward the back of the village, and I remember again where I'm going. He didn't come to see me yesterday, and I can't wait any longer. I didn't want to present the mended sail like this, hidden from the rest of the village. I wanted to lay it out flat on the rocks and wait for his face to stretch into joy, touched that I would take the time to help. *It's the least I can do. You bring me fish every day.* I had it all planned, so when he didn't come, I was thrown.

I wonder what he'll say when he sees it, and I feel a wave of pride. But then, the sadness comes back for a second. Maybe I'll ask if he wants to come with me. No matter what, I can't sulk or become too soft when I see him. Then I'd be too much like Kaija.

I kick a stone in my path for good measure, and it feels better, but only slightly.

I can see the village now. I try to spot Kaija's house. I gave Olen a gull feather and a small rune stone to hide outside her door when he left me last. It was a symbol I knew she'd recognize, my final plea to get her to come home with me. Or maybe it was a surrender. I hate that idea, but I can't shake it.

But, feather or no, my sister still hasn't come. She does not want to leave.

I know I must be careful. I can't be seen by anyone, of course, but I don't intend to be. I should learn how to do the kind of witching some of the burned women admitted to. Maybe there's some truth to it, though I'm not sure. Women transforming into ravens? It may be possible, though, and part of me wishes I had thought of that before walking all the way up here, but I don't know any spells that will turn me into anything other than who I already am. But who I am has gotten me this far, so it's not so bad.

Still, becoming a bird would be freeing, wouldn't it? That's something to practice when I'm back in the birchwood.

I stay as low as I can, but I know they're all at kirke today, so it doesn't really matter.

His house is situated at the far end near the expansive beach, just where I remember him coming out of weeks before. I glance behind me, at my sister's house, and there's no sign she's there either, no feather from what I can see, not even a pair of shoes outside her door.

She must be at kirke, too, playing Kirsti. The itch inside me grows slightly when I think of her, and it makes sense. I long for my sister's magic a little bit. It's like when we're together, our magic dances and plays, but when we're apart, it becomes confused and wrong and dark. I guess that's my fault, I realize as I approach Olen's window. I bring the dark. She's the one who brings the light.

It's darker inside than it should be with the sun bursting through the clouds now, and it takes my eyes a moment to adjust. I can see from here that it's sparsely furnished, and I'm at the only window, which would explain the lack of sunlight. There's a table with two chairs and a tub for bathing that has some remnants of dark water in it. There's a clean hearth at the center of the house, and behind it, I can make out the arms and legs of a bed.

And then I see a person's foot dangling lazily over the side.

I stare at the foot. It's midday. Surely, he's not still asleep? I feel a giggle rising in me, but I clap my hand over my mouth. Maybe he spent an exhausting day out on the water yesterday with just his oars and no sail, or maybe he just has his days and nights mixed up. It's easy enough to do when the sun doesn't ever set.

I stand on my toes and scan the rest of the bed.

I can't see his face, but I see something else up near his chest. It takes me a minute, but only a minute because I know what I see. I've seen it so many times before.

It's blood.

Now that I look, really look, I see there's blood everywhere, and I can't believe I didn't see it before. It's in a puddle underneath him, and it's dripping onto the floor. I notice, searching the rest of the house, that it's blood, not seawater in his tub. It isn't a clear blue or even a busy gray but a putrid, rotting, blood brown. His skin is pale and wet. There is a blanket pulled over him, covering everything but that foot, though I still can't see his face. I'm afraid of what I'd see if I could, so I just focus on the foot, which hangs there like he doesn't need it anymore. It looks so thin and almost transparent, like his blood isn't on the inside of him where it should be, running alive through his veins, but it's on the outside of him, exactly where it shouldn't be. From here, I can't even see his chest rising or falling.

If he's taking breaths at all, I can't tell.

I sink back down onto my heels. I need to get in there. Maybe he's not gone yet, and I can come up with a quick spell to heal him. I can try to remember one of Mormor's. But if he's dead already, I can't help him. Bile swirls in my stomach.

Before I can move toward the door, I hear a voice. Someone is here. Right around the corner.

"Astrid, oh." There's urgency in the woman's voice, but it's mixed with irritation.

"You're helping him, Tilde?" The second voice also belongs to a woman, but this one is sharp, suspicious. It, too, is urgent but in an entirely different way.

"I would like to, but I don't think his chances of surviving are very good."

"But why help him?"

A snort. "He's had an accident. He's dying. And he's a member of this village, just as you are."

The second woman scoffs.

"Not to mention he has been feeding you, feeding us all, for the past two weeks."

"And how has he been doing that? What sorcery has he been using?"

"Sorcery? Since when is kindness sorcery?"

"His father was a sorcerer."

"He was not. And Olen has no drums. He's done no spells. He is one of us."

"Not fully. Sorcery is in his blood, Tilde."

"You really speak of sorcery? Where's your proof?"

"We've eaten the proof—we've fed on Djevelen's fish these past weeks, cursed fish caught by his servant."

"Well, Djevelen's fish or no, you have been going to sleep full, have you not? You've not had to survive solely on your terrible lefse."

"How dare you? That's heathenish talk."

"Oh, Astrid, you don't truly believe this young man is colluding with Djevelen himself? If he is, then why would he have had this accident? You don't think pure evil would have wanted to keep him alive to do his bidding?"

My knees shake, and I lower myself into the grass.

"It was God's will."

"Are you saying someone did this to him?"

"I'm saying the man's a sorcerer, and I saw him pay for it by the hand of God."

"Did you see him hurt and do nothing to help?"

Astrid huffs. "Who am I to intervene with what God himself wants?"

When Tilde speaks again, her voice billows like smoke through the air. "You evil woman. You wretched, evil troll."

Astrid's response begins with a slight quiver, then gains strength. "You know he's the only one who could find fish. He was the only one who could sail those seas. He cursed them, Tilde. Even the men swear there's sorcery in it."

"Sorcery? To bring his friends and neighbors a few herring?"

"And trolldom."

Witchcraft. My blood races at the word, and the sail crinkles in my arms. I freeze, making sure I'm well hidden behind the house. Not a toe visible to these women. The one I think may be Tante Tilde—the woman from Mormor's stories—she doesn't respond. I don't know who her companion is, but I understand enough. The woman called Astrid speaks with temporary authority now and with acid on her tongue, the tone of someone who's won.

"Tilde, I have just been to see your niece."

A long silence stills the air. "Have you?"

"Again, the truth is before you, and you remain blind. Kirsti's friend Anne dies of a bloody cough while your niece is busy stealing her young man for herself. Then, once she's gotten what she wants, her own husband dies of the same mysterious cough. Even poor Johanne Henningsen died of this same illness, not long after the day your niece arrived. Who will be next? Will it be me?"

Kaija's husband is dead? I'm trying to take in what the woman has said during another long pause, and then Tilde says something that singes the skin at my wrists. "Maybe you're right. Maybe it is witches, as you say. You are right. This illness is cunning and unlike anything we've seen. And it certainly does look like Olen Bren was struck down by a curse." Her voice is dark now, threatening. "But how do I know it wasn't you?"

Astrid inhales sharply. "How dare you."

"Astrid, when these things happen, it's either none of us are witches, or we all are."

"Well, I certainly am not."

"Prove it."

If this is meant to quell this Astrid woman's temper, I'm pretty sure it hasn't worked because she makes a sound like a growling animal. It sounds like there is more to be said, and she can't wait to get it out. I can even hear her inhaling a breath to prepare for such a sermon. But she must think better of it and says simply, "You have made me late for kirke," and then there's the disappearing of stomping feet.

I think they're gone because there's only silence in their wake, and I think about rounding the corner, but before I do, I hear a grunt. The door creaks open and slams shut again. I move to the window, trying to see inside, but I can't make out much. Tante Tilde is there, hunched over Olen's bed, leaning him up and then down again. She's cleaning the bed linens, moving swiftly from one task to another, a bit nervously.

A corner of the bloody linen dips into the tub of bloody water on the floor. She tugs a fresh tub over toward him and dabs at his face. I can't see what she's doing exactly, but I can see clearly that Olen doesn't move. He doesn't flinch at the cold water or move his legs to reposition himself. I don't hear a single moan or cry of pain.

How could he do this? How could he be taken already? The man who saved me from drowning, who remembered me as a girl—he's all I really have. The idea stings, and I drop the sail to clutch at my side, trying to draw deep breaths but failing.

Olen Bren was struck down by a curse. Tante Tilde's words burn; they sear my flesh like they're being branded into me.

I have been to see your niece.

The clothes I'm wearing—that I've always worn—suddenly feel too tight, and I'm tearing at the collar, ripping at the belt at my waist, which stays firmly in place. I consider the tip of the knife, think about how satisfying it would feel to slide it across my skin, then dig it inside, to get at the itch properly.

I know why the witch is clawing at me. I know the thing she knows. This is witching at work.

This is my witching at work.

I begin to understand. My curse did not fail after all. My magic seeped into this village like blood from a wound.

But this is all wrong. I don't want pain for my sister. I don't want pain for Olen. They have had enough in their lives.

I don't unsheathe the knife. Instead, I realize suddenly what I have to do. It's not a healing spell, not now anyway. I turn from the window and run. It hurts to leave Olen like this, but if there's any chance he'll live, I must go. It's all connected. The vision I had of my sister, the pyre, the pleas. I am the one who brought the accusations. It was my witching that did it. It must have been my reckless curse that killed her husband—the father of her baby. It was my reckless curse that killed those people, that made women like Astrid use their voices like kindling.

If I don't do something, they will name her a witch. My sister will burn. And Olen. Olen will surely die.

I run faster than I ever have before, and the strands of sea kelp I tucked into my belt slam into my thigh with every step, a reminder of how simple I thought things could be. Faster than when I hunted with Kaija, who is always too slow to keep up, faster than when I heard the call from my sister that Mormor was dying. But still it's not as fast as I want, and for the second time today, I understand why a witch would want to become a bird.

A new smell—smoke, maybe—follows me as I climb the craggy bluff, and I think I can hear the yell of men and the cries of women rising behind me in the distance. But I don't turn to look. I don't need to see any of it anymore.

Kaija

The first flame ignites with just a spark and a breath. It's so small, I find myself wondering what is going to happen next, what all these people standing around are hoping to see. And then the small beginning grows into two flames, then three. They dance around Mamma's feet, and I notice she looks so tired. Her head is tipped forward, and I think she may be asleep. All I want is for her to wake up and jump down. I almost shout this to her, tell her to stop it because she's scaring me, but then the flame catches her dress and doesn't let go, and I see her wake with a scream that sounds like it comes from the center of the earth. In just another second, I can barely see her anymore, and I don't know if it's because I've hidden my face behind my hands or if the flames have eaten her completely. Maybe it's both. Between my fingers, I catch a flash of white, and my sister is racing toward the pyre, one small hand outstretched. The screams seem to be coming from everywhere now. They're behind me, above me, within me.

A bang on the door startles me upright. I'm clutching the blanket to my chest, and I can feel sweat sticking my nightclothes to me, as if the memory happened now, as if the fire were real, right here in this room. And then I remember yesterday. The torrent of flames that devoured the kirke as men crawled along the grass and women screamed for their children. How very real it was.

Apparently, the fire began just as the sermon did. The men smelled it first, since they sat in the front, but even by then, it was too late. I was told there were some who believed it was a candle that tipped over, nibbled at the corner hidden behind the pastor. No one could have seen it in time. There was a panic filing out. The smoke made it impossible to see almost straightaway, Erich told me, as soon as I arrived with Tante Tilde and Astrid Olsdatter panting beside me. The two of them hadn't made it to kirke yet, either, but even my encounter with Astrid just minutes before was already a distant memory. From where we stood, the kirke was blackening helplessly, and the flames reached higher than they should. People called frantically, Erich among them, attempting to reenter the doors, but they were blocked by walls of smoke. "There are people still inside," someone shouted, and I scanned the crowd for faces I knew. Erich was sooty and hunched over coughing, but alive and too close to the flames, almost as if he were contemplating diving back in again. Behind him was Peder, who looked unscathed and was dragging an inconsolable Ellen, wiping her face with charcoal, away from the fire. I searched for Mari and Nils, but I didn't see them. Nils wasn't tending to his sister or helping his father. Mari wasn't huddled near the other women who were gathered motionless with their hands over their mouths.

There's another knock at my door, and I'm startled again. "Kirsti?"

It's a small muffled voice that comes through the crack under the door where the light and sea air have found space, too. The sound of it throws me back into a memory from earlier: Mari running over to her husband, looking as if she'd barely escaped, her eyes mad with fear. She was screaming something at him. She wanted to know where Nils was. She wanted to know why he wasn't here. But Erich never turned to her. He had fire reflected in his eyes, and he saw nothing else. She stumbled back as he shoved her away, and I understood at that moment why he was darting in and out of the thick black smoke. He *was* trying to find a way back in. There were others, too, I noticed then, shuffling like Erich was, screaming at the flames that dared them to try to enter while they consumed the walls and the rows of seats and the crosses.

The fire burned all day and into the evening, until there was nothing left for it to feed on, until it was satiated. Among the dead: Nils and Pastor Thorkild, a boy of five, a girl of thirteen, and ten others. Erich trampled the still-smoking coals to look for his son, and I did not ask if there was anything left for him to find. The pastor was probably the first to go, being so close to the source of the fire, though no one had discovered his body among the black dust either. For a long while, I could not find Lisebet and imagined her, too, unrecoverable. I sobbed into my apron with more raw pain than I had felt since Jon. There were others doing the same, though, and so it felt almost like we were a community of grievers, even though we were crying only for what we had each lost. They cried for their son or sister who didn't make it out of the flames, while I cried for a friendship that barely kindled, a family that never was. A life that could have been. I eventually saw Lisebet, on her knees, scrubbing her hands and face in the sea, trying to wash the fire from her skin, and I ran to her, relieved to see the wholeness of her, the aliveness of her movements. But when I knelt beside her, she looked right through me.

"Kirsti, please." The voice outside my door is steeped in urgency now, and I know who it belongs to.

I drop the blanket onto the bed and straighten my nightclothes. I should have managed to get some sleep, but I know there are others who need it more than me, and I felt I was doing them a service by sacrificing it for them. But I did not do a ritual. I did no magic, even though my heart was breaking for it. I yearned to mend it all with a simple spell, but I felt that was the only thing I could not do.

I open the door a sliver, and I see Ellen there, small and still covered in the proof that the fire was real, that the second of her three brothers had so recently perished. Her eyes are an irritated red, and she's bouncing on her toes.

"Please, let me in."

I obey, wanting to grab her and hold her tightly. She comes in, and I can see she's shaking. I guide her to a chair and sit her down, placing the blanket around her shoulders, then tucking it over her chest and around her neck. She nods a thanks at me, and I'm touched that she can even see me after what has just happened.

"They said—" She doesn't finish. The hand I'm reaching for her with pauses in midair, waiting for her to complete her thought. She looks at me dead in the eye. "Um." There's a quiver in her voice, but she doesn't move her gaze. I let her go on without speaking. She takes a deep breath, and that's all she needs before it all pours out of her like water spilling from a kicked-over pot. "They think you started the fire at kirke. That you set fire to it with a stone and a feather you put outside your doorstep because you are a witch. They said—they said you killed Jon, too. And that woman Anne, who was supposed to marry him. They were betrothed before you came here, and they said—Mamma and Tante Astrid—that you murdered her so you could have Jon for yourself, and then you bewitched him with some awful love spell." She pauses for a breath, though her inhales are interrupted by tears. I can't stand anymore, and so I lower myself onto a chair across from her. I want to respond, but I have no idea where to begin.

And that's when I feel it—the sharp biting at my skin, beginning at the wrists and pulsing through my body. I nearly convulse at the suddenness of it, and I wonder only for a moment what it means because I must already know.

This is a warning. They are coming for me.

I step toward the window and look out. I see no one.

"You didn't do it, did you?" The question is as delicate and careful as she is. Her eyes have filled with tears, and in another moment, she's heaving sobs into the blanket.

I'm away from the window in a snap and rounding the table again. "Shh," I say, wrapping her in all the love I've ever felt, willing it to seep out through my skin and comfort her. "No, lillesøster, no. Of course not. Shh, now."

She sobs into me, lets me hold her. We rock back and forth like that, stuck together for a few moments—I can feel the warning stinging me with every heartbeat—but in my arms, Ellen feels so tiny, something between a sister and a daughter. She's so helpless. She only has one brother now and a lifetime of flames for memories. I don't want it for her. I don't want it for anyone. It's a lonely thing to see when you close your eyes at night.

Ellen pulls away, not looking at me but gathering strength. She bites her lower lip. "They're coming here. Soon. To take you away. Mamma was screaming about it to Pappa just now before I ran over. Tante Lisebet and the other women, too. I could hear what they were saying about you, and I was so scared. They said such horrible things. But I didn't believe them. I didn't think you were a witch. But I just had to come and find you. I had to…check." She sniffles, and she looks so young.

Lisebet? I'm nodding along with her story, doing my best to hide the panic rising in my chest. *They'll be looking for someone to blame.* Suddenly, I can picture them: their pale faces bent and mangled with rage, sticks aflame in their hands, ready to toss them onto my house, to catch a witch asleep. I'm not certain, but I think I can make out the faint slam of a door in the distance. In my mind, and without looking away from her fawn's eyes, I'm quickly locating the most important of my belongings around the house: the rune-carved box of Mamma's under my pillow, the unused spinning stave that sits near the hearth, my baskets from the birchwood, and scraps of flower petals inside the chest, just next to Jon's fishing knife. "Thank you," I manage to say. "Thank you for coming to tell me." The words are a squeak, and they're not enough. "How much time—? When—?"

"I don't know," she says. "Soon."

I can't tell if I am imagining it, but I think I hear another door slam and a shout from down the lane. The magic under my skin is now boiling with warning.

"Listen to me, Ellen." And I sound like Tante Tilde now. I wish I could say goodbye to her, too. "I have to go now. Do you understand? I don't want to leave you. I love you like a sister. But I must leave. I don't want you to worry, all right?"

She nods but doesn't seem to be taking my advice. Worry is scrawled across her tiny features.

"That's good," I say. "I will always think of you, I promise. Be good for your mamma and pappa, now. That's very important."

"Yes," she says.

"I need you to do me another favor, Ellen. Can you do that?" I'm holding her by the shoulders, trying to be as gentle as I can be. I can almost see them again, marching down the lane in my direction, faces gaunt and mangled with terror, fresh with loss. Could they not sleep on it? Could they not wait one full day before casting their net of accusation? Tante Tilde will try to stall them, I know, but there's only so much she can do. "Good girl. I want you to close your eyes as tightly as you can. Can you do that? Let me see."

She slams her eyes shut, squeezes down hard.

"That's wonderful. Good girl. Now I want you to cover your ears with your hands." She hesitates. "It's very important, all right? And I want you to stay like that."

"How long?" she asks, her eyes still closed.

"As long as it takes to say the Pater Noster ten times." It's all I can think of, but she nods, accepting the challenge. "That's good. Go on now." I watch her obey me, slipping her little hands out from under the blanket and pressing them to the sides of her head. She begins to speak the Latin slowly, carefully, as if she's just learned it. She probably has. *"Pater Noster, qui es in caelis…"*

I don't wait another second. I rush around the house, gathering what I can, stuffing what little there is into baskets and into my bag. I don't have many possessions, thankfully, so I make quick work of it. But I must hurry up with the next part.

I run to the window and look out. I don't see anyone yet, but Mari and Erich's house sits there with the door wide open. A warning. *They're coming for you. They've always been coming for you. You're a witch, Kaija.*

I glance back at Ellen, who's running through the words. They're choppy, taking her some time, and I'm glad for it because I have more to do. I close my own eyes and set a witching candle on the sill of the window. It lights quickly, and I'm ready to begin the galdr.

"Of smoke and sea. Clouds surround me," I say into the window.

I am quiet so I don't disturb Ellen, but I can hear her chanting right alongside me. *"…et dimitte nobis debita nostra…"* Our words tangle in the space between us.

"I call thee shine, god Niflheim."

"…sicut et nos dimittimus debitoribus nostris…"

"Hide me with your veil."

"…sed libera nos a malo…"

"And their chase will fail."

"Amen."

I breathe heavily onto the glass, and it becomes fuzzy and unclear.

"Pater Noster," Ellen begins again, but I'm already slipping out

the door into the magnificent shroud of fog—the first fog I've ever conjured—that will hide me as I run from this place.

I never imagined such a spell would feel so powerful. I had to become Minna for a small moment, just so I could conjure the passion I needed, but it came, and it felt wonderful. The magic moved underneath my skin in a way it never has before. I was doing big, earth-moving magic, and I will be doing it again because it's absolutely thrilling. I left poor Ellen alone in my home, but I left her just in time because I saw them leaving Mari's house just as the thick mist swallowed me. They were coming for me, just as she told me they were, brandishing torches and vehement expressions, I have no doubt. I know they will find her there, saying her prayers with her eyes closed tightly, before they light the place aflame. I was careful to leave the front door open for that very reason. I will miss that sweet little girl, and I know she will miss me.

I realize now, as I look back at the village that's cloaked in a viscous cloud of fog, a fog that came from my magic, that this is like the last time I ran away. Only, this time, I don't have to contend with lightning or the rush of overflowing streams. I contend only with a wet mist tickling my nose, settling on my skin, and mingling with the smell of the sea. It's a reminder of how much I never belonged here, of how simple I thought things could be, of how stupid I was.

My shoes feel heavy beneath me. I know I shouldn't, but I run first to the graveyard, my path illuminated by a witch's candle they can't see. When I get to the mound of earth, I slide to my knees and let my forehead rest against the dirt. I can only stay for a few moments, I know, though the mist makes me feel protected. I dig, and it doesn't take long before the dirt-covered petals of a summer flower emerge, yellow and bright. I dig next to it, and again, my fingers soon meet something that's not dirt. I brush at it, and soon, the feather is visible. It's the same feather I buried here just days ago, solid gray. I should have known the striped feather Astrid left on my table for me to fret over was different.

But how could I have remembered a detail like that? Maybe that's what she was counting on—Ellen did say the woman found it outside my door, not here—and the wet sea breeze in my nose seems to agree with me. More importantly, my rune stone is still here, too. I'm not sure how she got her hands on that rune stone either, but I know it wasn't mine.

I can almost hear Tante Tilde scolding me. *I told you. It doesn't matter who you are. It matters how well you get along with your neighbors.* The unfairness of it makes me grab at the dirt with both hands. There's no escape for a woman or a witch, is there? Your fate is decided by the woman next door whether you're practicing dark magic or using everything you have to be polite and blend in. It doesn't matter to them who you really are. Not one bit. They'll see you how they want to see you, and the worst of them will make others believe it's the truth. And now that the fire has come to the kirke in their village, there will be hell to pay. A horrible thought strikes me: I hope they don't discover me gone only to turn their hate on some other woman.

I cover the feather and the flower and the rune stone once again, happy for one thing, at least: Jon's soul will make its way up to the spellfire in the sky. He will dance for eternity with my ancestors. But that's all I have time to feel before I'm back on my feet and running toward the bluff.

I emerge from the fog into the glinting sun only once I've climbed the bluff.

It's quite a journey to the other side of these rocks, and I follow the same trail I did on the full moon when I spotted that reindeer—when I first saw Minna. Her little hidden camp hadn't seemed so far away then, but now, it feels like I'm traveling to the other side of the earth.

I clamber up and over, feeling the sea wind toss my hair in spirals around me as I near the top. Though I'm not sure I'm going to make it, I know I don't have much farther now. In fact, I think I can see Minna. Or at least I can see something. I'm reminded of that night of the full moon ceremony when we danced together around the fire. The thrill that raced through me. The magic inside me was delighted to be given freedom. Maybe that was the freedom I've needed all along.

Minna's so solitary on the great rocky beach, it's a powerful sight. Her form is crouched low, and she's hovering over something. The way her hands are placed, I can tell it's a witch's candle, and she's trying to light it with magic. The wind has picked up even more now, slapping my dress against my leg and my hair against my face. Strangely, I miss the birch trees at this moment. They, at least, would offer some protection. Out here, I'm so exposed, and my eyes are watering not from sadness but from the relentless northern wind. I sidestep to keep moving forward unimpeded, and I must be careful where I place my feet. More than once I slide down, and my skirt tears. I bump my bottom on the rocks. But still, I press on, glancing at Minna when I can afford to. She doesn't see me approach, that much is obvious. She's concentrating hard on her candle.

My skin tingles pleasantly as I touch sand. I suppose it's because I'm growing near my sister and whatever magic she's doing. It seems to be telling me I've rediscovered something that fits. That village, even my own house, felt as tight as a child's shoe, but in the span of an afternoon, I've been squeezed all the way out of that shoe, and if I even think about fitting back into it, I may as well lash my arms to the stake myself.

It's ironic, this image. My sister is here, doing her magic so freely, so openly, while the village just beyond this unfaltering bluff is likely tearing apart my bed at this very moment, turning over chairs to look for runes, as though proof of my pact with Djevelen might somehow be scrawled there. I see Minna holding her finger to a birch stave, every inch of which is carved in one rune or another. I'm still running but

I've slowed. I'm near enough now. I can rest a bit. She's started to say something, and I can just barely make out her words between my own heavy breathing.

"Dark spell of mine, go back in time."

A step, a breath. Another step, another breath. I feel in rhythm with my sister's chant, but there's an odd pain, a desperation in her voice that makes me slow down even more, makes me listen instead of run. Her words are heavy with magic.

"That cursed curse: reverse, reverse."

Another step, a slower breath. She's breaking a curse. I'm listening now with my entire being. What curse is she reversing? It must be a horrible one because I can see her face now, and the expression she wears is wrenched tight with emotion, but it's not anger or vitriol like it usually is. It's not even passion, like she would wear to call up the wind. It's something that looks foreign on her face, even at this upward angle.

"The words I sent to hex, to kill, I take them back, reverse my will."

She is shaking and maybe crying, and a shadow moves through me. Everything suddenly becomes still. I've stopped running. I don't even think I'm breathing. *Hex. Kill. My will.*

I'm transported to the night in the birchwood when I let her disappear beyond the warm ring of the fire's glow. I had other things on my mind, a life to begin anew.

"My dark magic, now, disappear. Bring no more death and no more fear."

I'm on my knees when she finally finishes, and I'm gasping for breath. She turns to me, violently, and the flames of her witching candle splash guilt all over her face.

I'm still back in the birchwood. Minna was busy that night, wasn't she? Now I understand it. She went to the clearing to cast her hot flames on this village. Long before I had any of it, she had already cast a spell to tear it from my heart.

"Kaija."

She says my name, but it's so distant now, the sound of her voice. It's drowned out by the drunken chatter of Tante Tilde, by the ache of Jon's sweet whisper as he calls me *min brud*, by the meek crying of a baby in his arms. It's drowned out by all the things she took from me. I shake my head, trying to think clearly, but the voices won't go away. I understand now who she is. I understand now what she did. I think I see her coming toward me, but I'm already back on my feet, using the last of my strength. I turn and head south as fast as I can manage, falling and scraping my knees on unforgiving rocks, and as I muscle my way over them and find my footing on the grass beyond, I don't think about where I'm going. I don't know if this is the beginning of my journey or the end of it. I'm only certain of one thing.

My sister is a wicked, wicked witch.

ᚾ
Minna

She's gone before I can get to her.

I never realized how fast she was. She always lagged when we were on the hunt, always came home last when we were young and Mormor called us for supper. I want to chase her, but I stumble. I stumble not once but three times. First over the candle, which thankfully stays strong and still. Then over an ill-placed rock. Then over my own damn feet.

She disappears into the distance, up the rocky bluff and over, well beyond my reach before I can get any surety in my step. By then, it's too late.

I wonder what her face looks like now as she tears away from this place. Hers was the face of a scorned witch, and I'd not like to be on the receiving end of it.

Except I am on the receiving end of it. It's me who's scorned her. It's me she looked at with those unforgiving eyes. Why the hell did she have to come down here now? Why did she have to see me doing this reversal spell? One minute later, and I would have been done. The curse would have been broken, and this all would have been in the past—a history not worth repeating. In response, the witch streams through my veins, stopping at each of my fingers to set them alight, stopping at the crest of my scalp to remind me of our combined power and what we were able to achieve—what this spell accomplished.

Seeing my sister's face, though, the way she slowed as she neared me, the way she listened as if what I said stabbed her very soul, the way she swayed on her knees like she had an arrow in her heart—I can't unsee it.

They'll be hunting her soon. That Astrid woman all but named her a witch. And it's my fault.

I pick up a rock—it's jagged and small—and throw it in the direction she ran. Pain is sharp, and this is why I never want to feel it, not like this. It's all-consuming. I was so absorbed by my own fear and pain that I didn't think about hers. That's not a very nice thing to know about yourself, but there you have it.

And I know people say, *I would take it all back if I could*, but I really would. I have, in a way. I'll at least save this village from any future heartache. I don't know if they deserve it. There are some who do, maybe, but not all of them. Olen and my sister, neither of them was meant to feel the curse in their own life. I wanted to hurt, but I never would have imagined someone I cared about getting caught up in my fury.

I toss another rock and shout for good measure, cursing the witch's cloth and the storm that started it all. Then I melt to my knees again, and I can almost hear Mormor saying I should have listened to her. I can almost feel her hands on my back, rubbing me with compassion I don't deserve.

A wave slides up and over my feet, and all I can feel is the heaviness of my own pain and the thing I took from myself.

I don't know if he was already dead before I finished the ritual, but I don't want to wait any longer to find out. My sister will survive. She will hate me for eternity, never want to see my face again, but she will run. Olen cannot.

When the candlelight finally flickers and dies, the wind dies with it. There's a silence around me. It's like the wind and the sky and the earth, they're all lingering to see if it worked. But I won't stay here.

The first thing I notice when I get to the top of the bluff is the smell. It's a char that isn't quite the same as a contained hearth fire or a fish-smoking fire. This is the scorched smell of a fire that has taken more than what was intended. There's something putrid in it, something that brings back a searing memory, and I stumble for a moment because I wonder if it's Kaija. Have they caught her?

The village is completely hidden under a thick pillowy fog.

When I come down off the bluff and start to make my way toward the direction I think is right, I find I can't see a thing. I can barely see my own hands in front of me.

I follow the smell through the fog, my feet racing against my heartbeat.

When the smell grows stronger, I realize it's not exactly the same as my memories. There's no heat behind it. It's cold, the smell of a burning that was.

Before I know what I'm doing, I'm at the source of the smell. There's a shadow of a building just steps from me. Its walls are black-ened. Its roof gone. But I know a fire that has taken life, and this reeks of it. I look behind one charred wall that still stands, and inside, the fog is thin, like mist. A woman sits on the ground, sobbing into the scorched earth, charcoal staining her hands and face. A man steps over piles of ash and wrinkled black wood, pauses, bends down to pick something up, examines it, and falls to his knees.

My cursed words come back to me, harsh and unbidden: *Till only ash and souls remain.*

My insides go hot.

I turn away and run again through the fog until my face is wet with it. I retch somewhere into the grass and keep running.

This fog feels too thick, I realize, and it feels like witching to me. My skin agrees since it sends up a responsive tingle as we cut our way through it.

I wonder if this is Kaija's work.

And then I know it is. It's hers; I can feel it. But it's so strong. She's outdone herself. I didn't think she had it in her to do weather-changing spells, but I was dead wrong. Suddenly, I know what this fog means. It means she's gone. She hasn't burned. She will not burn.

The witch within me must already know that because she is guiding me somewhere else. She knows where I'm going, and we help each other out when we need to now. I can hear nothing but the scratch of my own breath, but I can still smell smoldering wood. It sits thickly, that smell, trapped underneath the witch's weather.

When I reach the window, I can see Olen's house is even darker than it was earlier, and there is no one here with him now. His foot is covered by the blanket, but I don't know if Tante Tilde put it that way or if he managed to move it himself. *Please let him have managed to do it himself.* Before I allow the panic to crash back down on me, I take a deep breath and step away from the window.

It can only be for a few moments, but I must see him. I have to see the proof that the curse is broken. And, I guess, to face what I had to reverse in the first place. To look my murderous negligence in the eye.

He was just starting to feel familiar, fitting into my life like a well-worn pelt. My only friend. He jumped into the sea to save me. He could have died himself doing that. And he brought me fish every day. Every day.

I don't like the sensation coursing through me right now. It feels like the life is being sucked out of me, witch first. Thinking back on my blind rage the day Mormor died exhausts me now. How stupid was I? Stupid and young. I was a girl who refused to heed her warnings. I refused to get my witching under control and look what it cost. Look at what I've done.

Olen is innocent. He is kind, and he is innocent. And yet I carelessly blew a death curse right through his front door.

I still can't help the bitterness that lands on my tongue, and the smoldering air reminds me that the haunting feeling inside me is guilt. No one deserves a fate like this.

Kaija managed to escape, I'm sure of it. But she is probably finding a hole to dig for me right now, ready to bury me since she can't bear to be near me anymore. And I don't blame her. She has nothing left. I took it all.

As for me, all I have left is Olen. I hope I have him left, at least. I clasp my hands to keep them from shaking.

The old me would have been thrilled at the events thus far, I think as I push open the door with my hip. I would have reveled in the pain and suffering I caused.

Death, starvation, accidents, storms, fire. That's witching; that's power. I wanted to make them pay, and they were paying for it. But that was back before those light-blue eyes asked me if I remembered, before I became the little girl who learned to stack stones on the shores of this forsaken village.

That's all it is. Distance. Distance can make the heart grow fonder, as they say, or it can make your hate grow stronger. Unconsciously, I make a note to remember those words for a future spell.

The house is so dark, and there is not a single sound. If Olen is breathing, it's too soft to hear. I step carefully toward him, seeing his round face, his brown hair as if for the first time. He is pale. That's my first thought. Too pale. And his hair is wet and slicked to his head. He looks so stern, so unlike himself. I wonder if this is what his father looked like. Olen's pappa, I only remember as a pair of hands, a pair of breeches. It's just like Olen said once: There's nothing concrete for children about the adults around them. They all seem to fade into the scenery.

I lean in, hover my hand over his body, trying to feel his warmth without touching him. He wasn't even one of them, and yet my magic, my anger…they're both so erratic and out of control that I'm not surprised he was caught in my storm.

I was always going to wind up on the wrong end of a spell.

Mormor used to tell me that when she was angry or when I was being too stubborn. But when she said it, I didn't think she meant this end. I thought she meant the other end, where I would be the victim. Not this end. This end is so much worse. It's too much to bear, the guilt, and yet I must bear it because there's nothing else to do with it, and there's a sick pleasure in torturing yourself.

Even I know that.

He is so still when I begin that it almost doesn't feel real. I haven't brought anything with me because I imagined him, at the very least, sitting up in his bed and giving me a little smirk.

I thought when I broke the curse, it would break the damn curse completely.

And yet here he is, unmoving. I have to try something else, I know. That's why I close my eyes, feel the tingle racing through me. The witch inside is prepared. She's ready to help however she can. She should be. This is as much her fault as it is mine.

I breathe in fully and lean over, right up to his face. His mouth is still a closed line—what I would give to see that smile again—and so I find his nose. My own lips nearly touch him, but they don't. And then, slowly, I exhale. My breath travels out of my lungs, through my cheeks and up over my tongue. I form a small O with my lips, and it comes out in a stream, aimed at his nostrils.

I keep up the breath as long as I can, and since I can't say any rhyme while I do it, I just think about his eyes opening, his face brightening, his blood seeping back into his body. Once my lungs are empty, I draw another breath and pour my life into him through his nose. This isn't working. But it shouldn't be necessary. I already broke the curse, so why isn't he waking up?

"I already tried that one."

It's a woman's voice, familiar, coming from behind me. I cut my breath short, more out of surprise than on purpose, and I turn to look. She's stout and stern, but her face is knowing, and she reminds me of Mormor so much, I'm taken aback for a moment. She's familiar, but I don't know her. She seems to know me, however, because she says simply, "Time is the spell we always think of last, isn't it?"

Kaija

W hat is death, really? Isn't it just life looked at from another angle?

I'm thinking this, not saying it aloud—that would be madness—while I slice off a hare's head.

I didn't look into his eyes. I couldn't. Even after I knew he was dead and not just unconscious, neck caught on my husband's fishing line hidden in the underbrush, I struggled with it. And yet I have never been hungrier in my entire life, so I had to. I approached him gently, trying not to hear in case there was a whimper, and I had to look at him for a second, but I was careful not to catch sight of his eyes. I couldn't handle that much just then, not with everything that's happened. I was happy to discover he died a relatively painless death, and I could get on with the cooking.

I wipe my bloody knife on my apron, just as Minna would have done, and I realize, now that I'm prepping the hare, that it's larger than I originally thought. It will feed me well tonight and should last for several days. I'm still very far from the birchwood, I know, but I'm close enough that I can't smell the smoke anymore, nor can I smell the sea, and that's something. I don't know if I'll ever be able to smell the sea again, at least not without retching. My sister's pitiful face glows in my mind. It's her doing, all this. I wonder what she thought when she saw me at that beach. I could tell she did not expect to see me, not there, not then. She was feeling something too strongly to launch some angry excuse at me. But whatever the feeling was that drove her to take back such an abhorrent curse wouldn't be guilt. My sister isn't capable of guilt.

I'm not angry. That's an emotion she claimed for herself long ago and used up until it became nothing but dry bones. I'm not about to take her scraps. So, no, I'm not angry. But I certainly don't forgive her. I will never forgive her. What she did is distinctly unforgivable, even between sisters. Especially between sisters.

Jon's blade is sharp, and it takes almost no strength to pull it through the hare's fur. I wasn't sure the fishing net would work. I didn't think I would catch something this substantial at least. Witching be damned, I feel alight just having this blood on my hands because it's blood that will give me life, isn't it? It will help get me back to those cursed woods where I can live out the rest of my days like the old hag in the witch tales we always thought weren't true. Living alone, growing uglier and eviler over time—that's what they expect to happen to a witch if she doesn't burn. Sometimes a young fool will even venture out into the woods in search of a hag, and he'll usually find her. At least he does in the stories. But it's his loss and her gain because she has no problem eating lost strangers who threaten to take away her livelihood. She won't go easily with witch hunters who just want to put her on a spit.

But I won't be on my own, will I? This morning, though, the hunger overcame me, suddenly, without warning. I was forced to stop, set my snares, and wait. That was when I put my hands to my belly for the first time in days, since that horrid woman sat at my table. I felt the bump there and could hardly believe it. When did the baby get so big? It felt as big as a man's cap. No, not a cap. It was bigger, so swollen and sure, and so natural, it seemed to be built right into me, like a fell in the woods. Instinctively, I unhooked the buttons and looked down. Below my breasts was the bump, round and shining.

It's been three months now since Jon died. But I am much further along than I should be, than I am prepared for, especially because I'm on my own and headed for an enchanted, abandoned wood. I'm amazed the bump is as large as it is. It's like we're finally gone from that stifling village and neighbors hovering like vultures, and now I am free to grow, and isn't that the strangest thing? I may be a witch, but I didn't see this coming. And a baby—that's a different kind of magic altogether.

But a memory blossoms. *Childbearing can be fickle for a witch.* That's what Tante Tilde said, wasn't it? I suddenly wish for my rune stones again and am eager to get to the birchwood so I can practice the right spells, make sure everything will be all right.

I pull the fur away from the hare's body, starting in the middle of the belly, and it peels apart with more ease than I expect, all the way down to the feet and neck, and I'm almost ready to have my supper. If it weren't for the rolling wave of nausea that makes me stumble backward, I think I might feel like Minna again. I realize now that I had it all wrong with her. It's not rage that drives a good hunt. It's not even desire. It's simple practicality. We needed to eat, and my sister delivered. I was just too squeamish to do it myself. I'm still squeamish now—look at me—and I'm surprised, but I suppose there's still a little bit of the village in me. I was there until I was ten, after all, and then this past year has felt like a lifetime, so perhaps it will always be there. I always wondered what it would be like to be a woman in that village. What I didn't imagine—stupid, stupid me—was what it would be like to be a witch.

I make a few careful butchering cuts so I don't have to tear at it with my teeth. It's delicious and tender and well worth the wait. I didn't eat for the first few days mostly because I couldn't find the strength to find food, other than nibbling on plump cloudberries that crossed my path. That, and I wasn't hungry. Every time I thought about eating,

I'd release the contents of my insides onto the green fellsides until the fiery cloudberry juice was expelled completely and the bile turned to strings of yellow.

I am starving, and this is worth the wait.

⌖⌖⌖

I know I'm getting close when I feel my thighs burn. I'm carrying extra weight, but this burn is welcome. It's part of coming home. It means I've reached the fells, and I can see the shadows of the forest beginning just ahead of me. Only a few more days, I suspect. I decided not to stop at the Sami settlement on the way back, though I don't plan to make Riiga a stranger. There will be rare wildflowers and herbs from these parts that I think some of the Pomor traders who grace the coast with their timber may be willing to trade for. Also, she was so kind to check on Minna for me, even though Minna didn't appreciate it. A woman took time and energy to come all the way up here, away from her family, away from her life, to look in on my sister, just to make sure she was alive. Minna doesn't see the work that goes into kindness, does she? She barely sees kindness at all. A coldness wraps itself around my shoulders for a moment, and I wonder when she'll show her face again. I'm sure she has some more villages to burn and husbands to murder before she comes back here. She always said she loved this place, but I knew she had something bigger in her heart. She needed to see her power. Small delicate magic, the kind that gets you through the day—that was never enough for Minna. I shrug off the cold. I can't make room for that. I only have room for strength and preparation. There's a baby coming: another mouth to feed and another heart to tend to.

During the rest of my journey, I see a brown fox, a few deer, more birds than I can count, and hares, of course. I don't have an arrow, so I can't do proper hunting, but I have my makeshift snares, and I do all right. I have lots to carry and lots to prepare when I get home. I'm not sure I know what this timing has to do with anything, but I am certain I'll be giving birth to a witch—a powerful one at that. I will protect her. I will keep her safe. I will need to be more ruthless, more stalwart than I ever was if I am to keep this baby alive.

⸺⸱⟩⟨⸱⸺

In a few days, I reach the birchwood. It's a homecoming in a way I never expected. I thought, for all those years, that coming home would mean sitting at a table or around a hearth with some knitting in my lap and a baby in the corner. Well, I won't have the knitting, but at least I'll have the baby. My heart pounds at the thought, stirring the magic inside me. I'm still moving fast. There's not much time left, and I have to prepare.

I hear the chatter and whistles of mamma birds around me, keeping track of their young, and I pick up my pace. I must hurry to make this little fell a safe, protected home before I become a mother.

As the birchwoods grow denser, some of the trees growing from the same set of roots, I imagine what would be happening if I had stayed in the village. Astrid Olsdatter would tell the world about a witching feather she found. Maybe one day she would even find the real one I placed at Jon's grave. I think of Tante Tilde, wonder how she is faring. In a particularly terrifying image, I am sitting inside my cold house, waiting for the religious men to come, waiting for them to arrive with their chains and set up the pyre before I'm even tried. In another, I'm tossed into the sea with my baby yet unborn, destined to either sink or swim. That village is no life. I wish I could tell my old self that. It's what I will tell this child. There's only death there for a woman like me.

And yet it gave me something I never would have gotten out here all alone with my sister.

The birchwood smells fresh. Has it always smelled this way, or is it that the smell of the sea and briny fish has lived in my nose for a year? And, now that it's cleared, am I free to sense the world anew? There's no answer to this, I know. There are few answers to any of it, I'm learning. That's why I'm going to teach my baby not to worry about asking as many questions as her mamma.

I can feel the soft, spongy earth between my toes because I have long since taken off those impractical shoes. I left them back somewhere before the tree line began and the air thinned until my breaths were crisp and light, just like I remembered. With my bare feet on the ground and the wind in my lungs, I can feel the magic in me stirring in rhythm with my footfalls. The witch inside has been content so far on this journey, lulled by the beat of walking, the warmth of motherhood calling us both. But she's awake now, and I can't tell if it's because she recognizes where we are and longs for it, or if she's anxious to stretch her legs. Either way is fine. I plan to do a new protective enchantment on this little birchwood every day for the next few weeks. She'll get her fill then.

And then it's here. The tip of the hut sticks up, gray and unyielding, and as I get closer, I can even see the ring where we used to light supper fires and the rack that held our catches as they dried in the afternoon sun. It's all there, just as it was, just as if we never left it. I stand back for a while before immersing myself fully. Once I step onto this well-trodden earth, it will all become a choice. Up until now, it's felt like a choice, but it hasn't been, has it? I've simply been running away in one way or another. My work is clear now: I must be a strong and willful mother.

⫘⋉⫗

This baby is growing fast. Fickle, I think. Magic rumbles inside me.

My sister has left an enormous bear pelt in the hut. I've never touched a bear, and it frightens me a little, but as the nights have cooled now, its warmth is welcome. I find the rune stones I left behind stuffed underneath my own pelts along with a crumbling crown of decaying flowers and some other flowers I had forgotten about in a basket in the corner—wormwood, posies, buttercups. Some of the things that are different: Minna is not here to do the hunting for me, so I must make new arrows, because Minna must have taken a few for her journey, and the rest seem to have been ruined by months of unpredictable weather. Also, Mormor is not here. I can't rely on her for stories and wisdom, so I must find those things inside myself. I speak aloud in front of the fire every night, telling the baby my story and my mother's story and her mother's. I don't tell her my sister's story, since I can't bring myself to say her name. I can still see her there, on the beach, chanting into her candle like she was putting everything right. But it's like Mormor used to tell us: some things just can't be put right.

By day, I forage for cloudberries and mushrooms. The more days I spend here and fall into my own rhythm, the more I realize I need this to be our home. Not Minna's—just mine and the baby's. It starts to feel comfortable soon, life without my sister here, though I can feel another worry creeping at my back and itching under my skin. What will I do when she does come? How can I look her in the face? I won't want to share this space with her, but I'm not leaving. She'll have to pry me from here, dead and cold, if she wants me to go. Thinking these things is fine, but the more I worry about it, the more I know I need protection. I'm suddenly shaking. What if she brings harm to the little one? I can't bear the thought of something happening. My sister cannot come here. She can't bring her evil witching to these birchwoods, not now. I don't know a spell strong enough to keep another witch away, but I wish I did. A simple enchantment or protective spell won't do a thing to stop Minna, and knowing that reminds me of the thorns that continue to prick my heart. I need to close her out in a way that she wouldn't expect. I need to think like her. I know what I want to do, and I hesitate because it means

I'll be just like her. Only, I realize quickly, she would do it without a second thought, and that is the sick truth. But I need to think about the baby now, so there's nothing I can do about becoming more like Minna. However I end up, this home cannot be a place of darkness. It must be a place of light. To keep out other unwanted guests, I hurry to work on my regular enchantments by moonlight—that bear did not look like a fair opponent.

And when my gentle enchantments go as far as they can, I do what needs to be done and slip the small dark bag underneath my sister's pelts.

Minna

Y ou look more like your sister than your sister does, you know."

Tante Tilde is sitting across from me at Olen's table, sizing me up. I didn't run when she came into the house and started talking to me like she knew everything about me. That would have been smart, but I have nowhere to go, and I can't leave Olen. Not yet.

The more I sit here, the more I realize how much she actually does seem to know me. I guess Kaija's told her plenty over this last year. There's a wholeness in meeting someone who already understands you, especially someone who reminds you of your mormor without even trying.

Tante Tilde is short and watchful, like a perched eagle. But her voice sounds so familiar, the way it soothes and sets firm boundaries at the same time. I know exactly where I stand with this woman, and I've known her less than a day.

Tilde left once to stop at her house and pick up supplies. That, and she had to pay her respects to the rubble that was once the kirke. I don't think she knows it was me, and I'm fine with keeping the secret to myself. I don't like thinking about it. Even the witch doesn't play at my skin or my scar anymore. She is quiet, maybe feeling some of what I am feeling.

Tante Tilde came back with a kerchief of salted cod, burnt lefse, and an entire jug of beer. Then she barred the door and put a cloak up over the window in case a curious onlooker got too close. "The villagers are restless," she said. "You and Olen must leave before the day is through, before this fog lets up."

So now we wait for Olen to wake. He is as still as he was earlier, but he doesn't look as much like a corpse. Some of the blood has returned to his face at least.

"It was his arm," Tante Tilde tells me as she recounts the healing charm she used to close the wound. She isn't sure, but it looked like he got the brunt of it during a major gust of wind when the boat tipped back and an oar sliced through him. The worst of it was that he lay there for hours without anyone noticing. But I know that's not entirely true. That Astrid woman noticed, and yet she did nothing to help.

Her story makes me flinch. I am not afraid of a little blood and guts, but this was different. I think of Olen and how he believed he was meeting a new friend, someone who was an outsider just like him, and I thought of the fish he brought me, wide-eyed and flaky and filled with the juice of the sea.

And then I think of what he didn't know—that he was caught up in a curse cast by a witch he barely knew. I couldn't be sure, but Olen's fate, the state of him now, it was because of me. Even if my curse didn't kill him, it is the reason that old hag didn't save him right away. Suspicion made her hateful. That is a consequence I never foresaw.

I bet Olen will be sorry for knowing me now.

The state of his arm is the one thing Tante Tilde doesn't need to tell me. I can see it in the depression of the blanket next to him. It was obvious, right away, what I cost him. But at least he's still breathing. At least Tante Tilde was there to help him, and now the curse is broken.

"She's not naturally blond," I say, turning the conversation back to Kaija and trying the beer again. It's bitter. I like it.

"Of course she's not. Anyone who knows a simple hair charm would see how obvious it was."

I laugh, soothed to be in the presence of someone who can talk about witching like it's not foreign, happy to be in the presence of Olen's breathing, even if his eyes aren't yet open. "She's gone," I say, and it's more a question even though it comes out as a statement.

Tante Tilde nods. "I tried to tell her something like this was brewing, but she kept wanting to stay."

"She's always loved this place. The idea of it anyway."

"You sound disappointed."

I don't know what to say to that. I've never put a name to how I feel about Kaija's obsession with the village. *Disappointed* seems weak, like a child's reaction to a world that's so much bigger than she could have imagined.

"Age makes a difference, you know. You may think your sister and you have experienced the same things in this life, but it's different for her. Always will be." She pours herself some more beer and sits again.

"How long will we have to wait?"

She sighs. "I hope not much longer."

I don't tell her about the curse. It's right there, hovering over us in this room, ready to become a part of the conversation, but I can't do it. She thinks I'm like Kaija, more innocent than that, and I don't want that feeling to go away. Not yet anyway.

Our beers are nearly touching on the table between us, their rings of sweat conjoining beneath them. Tante Tilde leans toward me. I can see the candlelight dancing there in her eyes, and I know she needs to tell me something serious, but I'm still reveling in the idea that she's a witch. Another witch. Our talk has been about spells and charms and curses—well, not curses—and I feel like I'm back in the hut, surrounded by snow and speaking with Mormor about how to make my way in this world with all this magic building inside me.

"Once he wakes up—Minna, please listen carefully. Once he wakes up, you will not have much time. They are enraged, just like they were last time, especially now that your sister is gone. They want to know why she left, and so suddenly. All I could tell them was that she ran away, that her grief overcame her. But make no mistake, this village is still thirsty for blood. Astrid smells something, but I can handle her. It's Mari, Jon's mother. She's relentless in her pursuit to kill magic and those who wield it."

She hesitates, and there's something waiting to be said, but I can tell she pushes past it, diverting the conversation slightly, like a bird changing course in midair.

"Anyway, this goes back to whatever it was that killed her son. And now another son has been taken. She wants someone to burn for it all. And she is not the only one. I know with certainty they will try Olen for sorcery."

My mind stops racing, and I'm suddenly alert to her every sound.

"His father was a Sami shaman," she says.

"He wasn't a shaman," I say quickly. "He just had that drum because he liked the music." Again, I sound like a child.

"Well, either way, it won't matter to them. Whether Olen is the son of a shaman or the son of a reindeer herder, they won't care. They will burn him, and they won't need much proof either. An accusation, just one, will be enough to put him on trial."

"But he's not a woman." This is something I've been wondering since Olen told me about his father. I thought this village had it out for women. I thought we were the only ones doomed for the red-hot flames of a scorned neighbor's accusation.

"He's not," she concedes. "But he's a Sami."

It hurts, knowing this. It feels unfair. Why should Norwegian men be exempt from all this burning? Why should a Sami be accused because he plays a drum or speaks a different language or holds a deep understanding of the sea from his father?

I don't know the answer, but I know it has something to do with this god they're always talking about. The way I see it, they can't see past him. He's all they obey, and everything else, every other way of seeing the world—even the ancient ways that run in my blood and those that run in Olen's blood—it's all a threat. They have to get rid of every threat to this god at every turn. Why? Their prayers at kirke—I guess they must be pretty fragile. If a whiff of ancient ways is enough to turn a godly village into a pit of hell, then they must not think their god can withstand very much. Not really.

I take a swig from my bitter beer, cut it with a strip of salty fish. I find Tante Tilde's eyes. She looks sad, and I'm reminded of Mormor.

"Okay," I say, and it's not, but of course I know what I need to do. Of course, I will hide just out of their reach because that's what I've always done. "What about you?"

She laughs, but there's no mirth in it. "I'm a witch, remember?"

"You'll stay here? If they want someone to burn that badly, you'll be the next obvious choice."

She looks touched that I should be this concerned for her. And I am as concerned for her as I am finished with this village. Plus, I enjoy her company. It would be a comfort to have another mormor type to spend days with and gift us with the stories from the old days. But when she speaks, it's final, like she's had a plan for a while, and I've just come at the right time to help her see it through.

"No, no," she says. "A strong, strong potion and a few of these should do the trick." Her cup is a shadow in her hand. I must look skeptical, and I am, because she puts it down and looks me straight in the eye. "I have no intention of burning, Barnebarn. Don't you worry."

⨳

I've never thought about what it would be like to lose a limb.

I guess that's a privilege of being a witch. A healing spell is just a moment away. But Olen isn't a witch, and now he doesn't have an arm.

"It's just a throbbing, really," he tells me as we row along the shoreline. Tante Tilde and the foggy village that never wanted either of us are just memories now. In his boat with us are two bags, filled with plenty of warm and dry things. The weather and the water, as I now know, can be fickle.

He was unconscious when we loaded into the boat. Now that he's awake, I want to ask him so many things: if he was sad to leave, if he hates them, if he is angry with me, if he misses his pappa. I'm curious, and talking would be the kind thing to do, even I know that. I just can't bring myself to dig it all up again. Instead, we mostly just row along in silence.

He's the one who brings up the feeling in his arm. "It's going to take some getting used to." He's rowing with his one remaining arm. First on one side, then on the other. It means I'm doing most of the work, but it feels good, the way my shoulder blades sing as the muscles around them make heat.

It also means we're cutting a sort of zigzag pattern through the swells, and we certainly aren't making good time.

Every now and again, the boat rocks too much, and I grip whatever's nearest to me. I still don't know how to swim, which is why Olen insists I wear a rope around my middle, keeping me inside the boat. It's pathetic, but he can't save me if I go over, and without me, he'd be out here rowing in circles for eternity.

"The oars," he reminds me. "You have to row through the wave."

It's not the same as being one-armed, but being on the water takes some getting used to as well. I'm at my best with two feet firmly planted on land, where it's still, not rocking from side to side. I wonder briefly if there's a spell to still the waves like there is one to call them up. I try to think of how it could be done. Maybe a flat stone skimmed along the top of the water, dragged behind the boat. But we didn't bring any stones. We brought almost nothing for witching. All I have is my knife. It doesn't matter too much, though, once we move close enough to the shore that the waves calm.

We weave in and out of inlets, and I can see villages as we pass, but to anyone who catches a glimpse of our boat from this distance, we are just two fishermen out for a short trip, not a witch and an accused sorcerer with one arm.

Olen loses his strength quickly, despite the healing charms I perform every few hours. I think it's because he refuses to put down that damn oar and just rest. Thankfully, my breath is enough to keep his pain from debilitating him, though it's not enough to heal his flesh as quickly as I'd like. The salt water has helped some, and I also do a spell without telling him, and it makes him sleep more than he's awake.

It's something.

We made plans to find the Sami settlement along the coast, where I know Riiga will be. I am nervous that I won't recognize it when we get there, but we'll stay close to the shore once we cross the fjord so we can keep an eye out. That's still quite a ways away. Olen doesn't know how far either, but we'll know we're there when we're there.

I feel myself being tentative around him, like he's fragile somehow. Maybe it's because I've done my fair share of breaking things for one lifetime. Or maybe it's because of his injury, which, again, is my fault.

I can tell he doesn't like it.

He snaps at me sometimes, tells me I'm coddling him. I think that's why we don't speak much, because I'm figuring out how to be around him, and he's figuring out how to be any of this: without a limb, without a home, without the solitude he loves so much.

He didn't want to come, but he had no choice in the matter. As Tante Tilde staunched the bleeding and healed his wound, she told him what the village was starting to say about him. She told him what they were getting ready to do.

He listened to the news, though I don't think he really understood, because he said something so childish then. He said, "But I'm not a sorcerer." And then Tante Tilde launched into her speech about how those who hate magic will see it not where it exists but where they want it to exist, and that she was sorry for it, but nothing good could come of him staying.

Olen sat there for too long trying to decide what he wanted to do. I hated to do it, but Tante Tilde and I agreed we had no other options, and so she did three little spells—one to conjure another fog, not as thick as Kaija's but still good enough to give us cover, one to put Olen to sleep, and one to lighten the weight of his body—and we carried him out to the boat. She pushed us away from the shore with such relief, I couldn't help but wave to her as she became a shrinking shadow on the shore. When he woke, he must have already known what we did, because he just sighed and skimmed a finger along the water, giving me an under-the-eyebrows look that was disappointed but resigned all the same.

One night, when I'm rowing us along as slowly as possible and Olen is drifting in and out of sleep, I try to find the stars in the twilight sky. It's clear, a new moon, and I feel the itch under my skin that wants to come out and play, but I force it down because I can't do that now. We have to get through this first.

A chill bursts into our pocket of freedom even though a reluctant sun levitates above the sea throughout the day and night. The boat bobs up and down, and the lick and bubble of my oars against the sea is rhythmic.

I could get used to this, a life at sea. Maybe Olen can teach me how to fish. He has already taught me a few things, since he needs help casting and pulling in the net, but the knowledge of the sea and reading the water, that's all him.

"Tired?" he asks me now, startling the quiet. "I can take over."

"No. I'm just enjoying the view," I say.

A few moments of silence go by, and I catch him looking at the sparks of sun that prick the sea like thorns. Finally, he says, "Minna, will you stay?"

"I'm right here." I reach out for him. Is he slipping into a fever dream? Does he need another quick spell for the pain? I crawl over to him so I can feel his forehead. The boat wobbles as I do.

"No, I mean, when we get there."

I freeze for a moment, then slide back into my seat and pick up the oars again. Before I start to row, I have to think. This is a decision I knew I'd have to make, but I pushed it to the back of my mind—there are a lot of things in the back of my mind now—and it feels strange to be facing the question so soon.

I search the sky for an answer, hoping it's written up there somewhere. But I'm on my own. The sky is empty of answers.

Do I want to stay in the settlement, fishing my days away with Olen and practicing how to do magic without killing anyone? It might be nice. We could fill our days with the practical preparations for our daily life and fill our evenings with juicy fish flesh and laughter. We could be part of a community—if they'll have us, of course. That would be something new.

My oars dip back into the gray sea, renewing their gentle rhythm, and I can feel the soft burn in my shoulders as I watch the scar on my hand catch the light of the sun, which hovers in the distance, steadfast and unblinking.

"I'm sorry," I say, and I don't know where it comes from. Something about the rocking of the boat, the soothing knowledge that we're all alone.

With my back to him, I hear him rustling, imagine him putting his hand to the round bulb where his shoulder would have met his arm.

When he doesn't answer, I keep going. "I didn't mean this. I hate that you had to leave. It was my fault."

Of course I know what I want to hear. I'm apologizing for what I've done, and the singsong comfort of *no, it's not* is too alluring not to long for. I think it's what I've longed for all this time.

I want someone to stand and shake me by the shoulders and say, *It's not your fault, Minna. You're just a witch with more power than you know what to do with.* I want to be six years old again, learning to light a witch's candle in the dark using only my hands, with the warm breath of Mormor at my shoulder. Back when nothing I did mattered. Back when the consequences were small. Back when witching was an exercise in my own strength, just like feeling my muscles stretch and contract while I'm on the hunt.

He never says the words.

He doesn't tell me it's not my fault. I will have to live with this on my own, I know.

I think I've always been too angry to avoid trouble. Too angry to be a good person.

Olen interrupts my thoughts with a soft voice. "It could be good for you. Being part of something."

It takes me a minute to remember what he means, what he thinks we're talking about. "As long as we can do this again," I say, feeling the tender side-to-side movement of the sea below us and meaning it as much as I have meant anything in my life.

Kaija

I am huge.

It takes nearly all my strength to check the snares in the morning, and sometimes I can't even bother with chopping the wood I need for the fire, though the nights are starting to sink into my bones, and I know it will be much harder to do this kind of work with a baby strapped to my back.

Today is one of those days when I have found strength to chop. I'm standing over the stump, panting as I prepare the next log. I keep them small because they burn better that way and because I'm not as strong as someone like Jon, who could probably chop down ten trees and make a pile of logs out of them within an hour. But then I remember that someone who grew up with the sea as his natural burden might not know what it feels like to put an axe between his hands and slice a dead tree into two. I'm sure it would otherwise be satisfying—and I'm even more sure there's a spell for this kind of work—but the exhaustion makes it too hard to think straight. It takes me all day, and I can't stop missing Jon.

I rest on the ground, letting the axe fall to my side. What would

I be doing right now if he were still alive? I laugh because I'm certain chopping wood is the last thing I would be doing. I'd be soaking my feet in a tub of warm water while my husband rested his hands on my belly, and Tante Tilde would bring us all beer to share just so she could find out how close the baby's arrival was.

I'm close, I know that. Not close enough that I've been feeling the pains, but close enough that the belly seems to have dropped lower than it's ever been, so low that it's more in my way than it needs to be. It's much too early, but I can sense a change. The baby will be here soon. It's been quite a time trying to do all this preparation alone, but I've managed to do more than I thought I would. Last week, I checked about a dozen well-placed snares and came up with five fresh hares. I couldn't believe my luck. The snow will be here soon. Winter is going to be long, and I feel much better knowing I can get through the dark months to come without having to venture too far.

I stand the axe up next to me and let it fall and then try again, wanting to balance it on its blade end, wanting to will some energy back into my muscles. Just a few more splits to go, and that will be it for today. This makes me think of Minna for some reason, the coaxing she always did to get me to keep going. When I wanted to leave her and watch birds swing low between the trees or weave crowns out of petals and birch leaves, she would always find a way to get me to stay. I'm glad she did, because I wouldn't know how to do half these tasks now if she hadn't. It's that spirit I'm trying to discover in myself right now—Minna's ever-energized spirit. It got me through the seasons back when we lived here together, and I want it to get me through winter now. But I struggle with this, too. I want the strength and the ability, yes, but I wonder if it will come with all the anger and fire Minna always brought. Does strength always have to be ruthless?

I feel for my pulse underneath the layers and catch its steady rhythm. At least I still have a heart.

I think of Mari, Jon's mother, and what she would think of this little hut in the middle of the snow-covered woods, and I'm tempted to spit. I have become defiant out here, I can feel it, and that woman was the definition of cold. If she had known I had her barnebarn growing inside me, would she have treated me differently? Would she have taken me in instead of branding me a woman worth burning, no better than a lump of peat, though hated more than Djevelen himself? How I miss Jon and his beautiful smile that always welcomed me. I can just about picture his sweet face if I close my eyes. But I don't linger on it for too long. I am so glad I am not there anymore. It's taken me time to realize it, despite my ache for Jon's touch, despite my longing to share a beer with Tante Tilde. But my child will be better off here. I'm glad I'm free of all the women who ever looked at me too long—and, I suppose, the women who never cared to look long enough.

⌿✕◇✕⧹

Over the fire inside the hut, Minna is suddenly everywhere. She's not truly here, I know, but the visions of her are so vivid, I feel a little bit afraid. Her stern face peers at me from the doorway because I left a scrap of meat out, and that's a waste and could attract wolves. Her face glows with passion as she sits next to me closely, on my own pelts, as she tells me of the latest spell she's pieced together—something she's created with bits of Mormor's incantations and bits of her own roiling witching. She's sleeping next to me, always a hard sleeper, not easy to wake. Not like me.

I'm enjoying the warmth from the flames and stretch my feet toward them. The fire responds with a small spark, which flies out and catches my dress on the knee. I don't flinch from it, even though there are holes there already, and it goes right through to the skin. I'm too tired to move. I close my eyes, and I'm trying to push away the visions of Minna with all my might, but she won't leave my side. She's watching me, but all I want to do is sleep. I let myself look into her eyes, big and icy blue with something, but it's not magic this time. She speaks, and it takes me by surprise to hear the depth of her voice when I've been alone for so long. "I'm coming," she says, and I feel the muscles in my arms and my legs and my chest tense at her words.

And then there's a twitch in my belly that I haven't felt before. I sit straight up, all alone in my birchwood hut, and I can't help it—all I want is my sister.

Minna

The three girls—Riiga's daughters—follow Olen and me around almost everywhere we go. They're behind us now, watching at a distance and giggling every time we turn around. They've grown bold over the weeks we've been here. They're especially interested in Olen, and I start to see him the way they might. I guess it's strange that I haven't before, but there were more critical things on my mind then.

He's handsome in a quiet way, always a moment away from a smile. There's something very likable about him, even though he keeps to himself, and I find two things hard to swallow about his life: one, that the village never accepted him fully as one of their own, and two, that he's not magical. Because he seems like he may be made of magic. The way he can tame the seas and find the fish exactly where he wants to, the way he can reach people who were previously unreachable—it's not sorcery, I know, which makes it somehow even more impressive.

There are a few places on Olen's boat that still need patching up. I've been busy assisting Riiga with her chores during the day, and Olen's spent weeks learning how to fish one-handed.

Now that we have finally found some time to examine our boat,

Olen points out where a piece of timber wasn't quite sealed tightly alongside another one or where a nail came loose during our journey.

"It's common," he tells me, running up the beach to ask the girls something in slow, intentional Norwegian. They seem to understand and go running away, pleased to do something that will help him.

"Nails, maybe some more timber," he says with a sigh.

It won't be enough, these materials he's asked for, even if they have them. From here, we can see one of the Sami men's boats. It's pointed at each end, expertly crafted to shave through the fjord waters as smoothly as a blade. Olen's, as sturdy as it once was, is taking on water, even in the shallows. It's surprising we made it all the way here, by the looks of it. I examine the runes I scratched on the side of the hull before Tante Tilde pushed us off. Those bindrunes, smeared with my blood, must have kept the water out. But even magic can fade over time if it's not given attention.

Even though he's sent the girls up for supplies, I know how I can help.

It's so strange, doing small magic like this, practical spells that don't require any great yearning, any passion at all. They simply require the right objects, a little rhyme, and a well-executed ritual—that's it.

I understand Kaija's obsession with this now. It doesn't quite have the same satisfaction as calling up the wind or bringing down sheets of hail. But it satisfies in a different way, like I'm not just doing magic for the sake of seeing my own power in action. I'm doing it to help, for a small but specific purpose.

That's why, when Olen takes a moment to inspect the other side of the boat, I pull out the knife from my sheath.

It feels like it's been a while since I used it, but it is still so familiar, fitting perfectly into the curves of my knuckles. I use it to slice a thin strip of cloth from my skirt, and then I slice another one. The pieces tear away easily, and I lay them on the sand next to each other. Then

I spit on my hand, smear what I can over the boat's carved runes, and close my eyes as I sing the short practical galdr and weave the two strips of wool over each other and then under. Over again, then under again.

The galdr is finished, but I keep weaving until both strips are completely intertwined with each other, until they're inseparable. Then I knot both ends and feel my way to stuff this new braid of cloth into an obvious hole in the side of the hull.

When I open my eyes, I see my job is done. The wood has closed the gap. It's even filled the small hole where the cloth was, and I'm amazed at how simple it all was.

I know Kaija and Mormor did spells like these to help make life a little easier, but for some reason, I always choose the hard way, saving my witching for the things that required the most power. How exhausting that turned out to be.

Olen comes back around to my side. "We'll need—"

I try to look innocent, but I can't. Never could.

He looks me up and down, searching me for signs of witching, probably looking for stones because that's what I used last time. He doesn't seem to quite know how, but I can tell he understands what's just happened. I don't mind that he knows. Actually, I kind of like it. But I also don't mind that he doesn't know how. The details are reserved for those with magic running through their blood.

"Is it uncomfortable?" he says, not taking his eyes off me. "Does it itch?"

"How—"

"I saw your sister once, going at her arm like there was a crab under there. And then I saw her another time. I think she had been doing something like what you're doing now. She had that same look."

"What look?"

"That one."

I let a smile come to my lips, and I watch him fight his.

He won't grant me a smile until he gets his answer, I can see that on his face. I want to tell him the truth. I want to tell him that the thrill of the witch moving under your skin feels like you're growing a new layer of it. That there are different types of feelings.

There's the happy witch. Like a sleeping animal after a nice meal, this version of her is contented and lazy.

There's the hungry witch: she is scratchy and relentless and won't go away until she's satiated.

Then there's the warning witch. She can sense her magic is needed, and if she's not able to reach whatever it is that needs her, she boils until the threat goes away. She won't let up, even if you try to stop the sensation by burying yourself under the deep white snow.

Mormor used to feel this kind of witching inside her a lot when we lived at the birchwood. She'd douse herself with cold water or strip naked in the dead, dark winter and run down to the river for whatever unfrozen water she could chill her bones with. I used to wonder what she was fighting and why she couldn't just do a spell to make the witch inside her happy then. *This one's a need that will never go away,* she told me, shivering and blue-lipped but content enough to sleep.

I think I understand her so much more now.

Still, I watch Olen's fingers run over the tight, tidy seams my magic created on his boat, and I can't for the life of me think of a need that never goes away.

⸝⸝⟡⸝⸝

When evening comes, we sit inside Riiga's hut, where she and her husband have invited us to sleep for all these weeks.

She's tired from her day of splitting and boning cod, and the girls are long asleep, curled into one another. But Riiga seems to have strength enough to strike up another wordy conversation with us. Olen sneaks me a glance from across the flames. He looks strangely at home here, and I wonder if I look that way. I certainly don't feel it, but I am trying. I want to settle in, but my skin is at a low simmer, and it's hard to get comfortable.

"I miss my husband when he is out fishing and trading, you know. So much to trade, so much to pay, just for living. But when he is gone, I do love the peace and quiet," Riiga says, smiling. Then she peers at me, slipping her boots off and wiggling her toes. "Tell me again why you two aren't married?"

I think I must laugh a little when she says it, because Olen has his eyebrows raised.

"Olen Bren. Olen Bren," she repeats to herself as if trying to place him. Suddenly, she turns her whole body in his direction. "You know, I keep meaning to ask you, are you a relation of Eiven Bren? Son of Holger? Oh, you're too young. You probably don't know those old men."

I look at Olen, but he doesn't move. His eyes are still and unblinking. The firelight takes advantage and reflects a little blue dance back at me. Slowly, he nods. "I'm Eiven Bren's son."

I've never heard Olen say his pappa's name before. It's thick with the juice of freshly caught fish and heavy with years of dormancy.

I suddenly feel a familiar surge of rage flow from my heart to my fingertips. That forsaken village has taken so much. No spell will ever change that fact.

"Oh." Riiga looks delighted. "And how is he? He was always flirting with us girls but then left years ago for some Norwegian woman. Beautiful, though, from what I can remember him saying."

Olen shakes his head, and I can see that words aren't going to come. I know that feeling, the desperation of not wanting to speak something into truth, the heartache of exposing your raw wound all over again. That's why Mormor and Kaija and I only spoke about the Mamma we knew when she was alive. That's why we never spoke of the fire that took her body from us, that made sure Mormor couldn't place a feather at her gravesite because there was none, and even if there had been, we didn't stick around long enough to see it.

"He died." It's me who finally speaks, and I can see the relief on my friend's face.

He looks away, and I find Riiga's eyes. They go wide with shock at first, and she lets out an involuntary *tsk*. But then she looks back and forth between me and Olen, and something softens her expression.

"Well, you're here now. And we are happy to have you. As long as you pull your weight, you can stay as long as you like."

The conversation shifts to fish, and I have nothing useful to add. I feel Olen's foot resting against mine, both of us vying for the fire's warmth, and I hear him speaking to Riiga slowly and too loud, trying make sure his Norwegian is understood.

Soon, their voices fade into the sizzle of the flames, and I know the world outside is darkening. Olen and Riiga are laughing about something now, and I realize his laugh is like a friend's hand stroking my head and twisting the ends of my hair. I can rest now. My own arms are like stones at my sides. I don't think I could lift them to scratch an itch.

The witch in me is not asleep yet. I can still feel her creeping along the skin of my wrists. It's a bubble more than a boil, the way she lets me know she's there. With my eyes finally shut, I can concentrate on her. I'm trying to figure out what she's after. Does she want to do a spell? But I can't get up right now. I can't do magic. I hear a wince from my side, and Olen tells Riiga not to worry, that he's fine.

The witch inside me wakes me up more forcefully now.

I'm needed. The tingling makes me feel it. Someone needs me. I come back to awareness begrudgingly, and my body seems to be so out of sync with my magic, it's confusing me. I can't tell if I'm asleep or awake, but I can feel the pull now.

Someone needs me, and my magic is responding.

Opening my eyes, though my body seems to resist the very small action, I look over at Olen. His hair is starting to stick to his forehead, and his face is pinched, like he's holding something back. His own eyes are closed, and he has one hand braced on his stump.

I jump up and grab his arm. He looks up at me. I must do a spell for the pain. It's been almost a full day without one, and even though it should be healed by now, it needs constant attention for a little while longer, or else the pain may be too much.

"We will be right back," I say quickly to Riiga, who waves her hand at us, and I hurry. I know Olen needs me. I can feel it running through my bloodstream.

Outside, down near the waterline, I hear the waves pushing themselves up the sand toward us. It's dark enough now that no one will see what I'm about to do, but I make Olen sink behind the boat anyway. I lift his coat, then his shirt so I can fully see the wound. I expect fresh blood to be leaking from somewhere, a hole that needs my magical hands to mend it. But the wound is healing nicely on its own. In fact, it looks as closed as it did when Tante Tilde grew new skin and attached it with the threads of her own special galdr. The scabs are falling off, revealing knots of patchwork scars and doubled-over skin, which I know means it's healing well.

"Does it hurt?" I realize I haven't asked him that yet.

He shakes his head. "Itches."

It only itches. That means it's healing.

The itching inside my own body dances a little more urgently, and so I decide to do the spell anyway. I slice my left arm with no hesitation and, with my thumb, swipe the blood that seeps out of the fresh wound. I apply the blood directly to his knotted shoulder, drawing a straight brown line down the wound. This is the rune I think will do the most good now. I suck in a breath and blow onto his skin, seeing the scars tighten and then relax in recognition of magic; then I watch skin heal over skin even more. If anything, this will take away the itch.

He looks up at me gratefully, still in awe, I think, of what I can do. But even though it's impressive, and even though I typically would have pulled him onto his feet and teased him for not being able to heal his own arm, I can't seem to do that now. The spell is done, and my friend is sitting next to me, relief settling over his expression.

But the witch inside me hasn't stopped wriggling. Something else is bothering her, and it has nothing to do with Olen.

⢀⢁⢂⢃⢄

Back in the hut, I hear the whistle of Riiga and her daughters sleeping soundly and the rustle of pelts as Olen gets comfortable next to me. So close, we're almost touching.

I wonder somehow if I have misread the witch's meaning. The tingle has shifted into stinging, and now it's starting to feel hot, like small burns. It's familiar, this type of witching running through me now—the warning kind.

I try to think back to when Olen and I first arrived. He needed daily healing spells then, for many weeks, but his arm is healing nicely, and seeing that didn't make the witch stop her scratching. It only made her more urgent.

Which means she was warning me about something else.

For a moment, I forget which side is Olen's bad arm, but then his fingers intertwine with mine. They're hot and a little clammy, which is how I know he's finally found some comfort. He runs his thumb over the raised skin of my scar, and I can feel the witch underneath searing, boiling, not giving up.

He falls asleep fast, just like that, and I don't let him go until I hear him breathing steadily, until I see his chest moving up and down as peacefully as a child's.

My throat is taut as I stand and dress for the journey.

Everything in my stomach clenches as I glance over the warm hut one last time, at the calm on my friend's face. How much that will change when he finds me gone in the morning, I'm not sure. But how much it will hurt him—that, I think I know.

The witch burns white-hot now, reminding me of who I am and where I'm meant to be. And that something isn't right.

I step out into the night, wiping the wetness from my cheek as I do, and I run.

Kaija

I thought I was prepared for this. I thought I had it all under control, but my body has been trying to tear me into two, and I suddenly don't think I can do it alone.

In between the thunder of my heart and my groans of pain, which have lasted now more than two days, I manage to bring a stack of logs inside, throw one on, and settle back. I take small sips of water as I know I should, but it hardly seems worth it, these tiny acts of necessity. If this baby is coming, she will be months early. It's all happening too fast. Childbearing for a witch is fickle indeed. But I cannot focus on the worry bubbling inside me, much stronger than magic ever has. All that seems to matter now is getting done what I know has started.

The feeling that I'm splitting open comes in waves, and while those waves were spaced out well enough before, in the dead of night now, with the cold creeping in at my back, they come faster. I'm reminded of the storm and the relentlessness of the black swells from my last week in the village. The way they just kept coming and coming, one bigger than the next, like they were going to swallow the village whole, suck it back out to sea. Part of me wishes they had. Part of me wishes I had been dragged out there to float forever on the ups and downs of its turbulent indecision rather than kneel here on my own. I would have been left to sink or swim, and as I'm a witch, I would have floated right up to the surface. Perhaps, now that I think about it, I suppose I'm much safer here. Even if things go terribly wrong, at least I won't be subject to trial by drowning.

The next thought starts out small but grows into delirium with the next wave of pain. *I'm a witch. I'm a witch. I'm a witch.* But the tearing sensation is too intense for my mind to understand what to do with it. It's only in the short time after that wave ends that I can think for just a moment. And then, just as soon, the next wave is here. I'm screaming, though I can barely hear anything. I can barely detect my own breath. I know I'm screaming because my throat is raw and my jaw is wide, and there are tears escaping, mingling with sweat as they collect into salty scratches down my face.

Another moment of reprieve. I'm spinning, unable to see straight, but I try to recover as quickly as I can. I reach down to see if I can feel anything, but I can't. When I lift my hands to look at them, I can see they're shiny with blood. Now, just as the next wave is starting to crest, I look down and see a puddle of my blood below me. I am only able to think one thing—my blood should be inside me, not on the ground— before I'm swallowed whole by another wave. It's not so much a wave this time as a knife, and I have to push a hand against the wall while I let out a roar that does nothing to stop the bleeding but is essential to my survival. When the pain subsides for a moment, I'm panting, and I can feel the life draining from my face.

But now, as this tiny moment of rest starts to slip away from me, I remember I can still do something. There are spells for childbirth. There is so much rich magic for this moment: to ease the pain, to stop excess bleeding, to ease the pain, to ease the damn pain. Another wave is on its way, and this time, my mind goes as blank as snow. Nothing but sensation can get through to me now, no matter how lucid I am in the moments in between.

In another minute, I'm gasping for breath, but the wave is over. Magic. I was thinking about magic. This is a moment meant for magic. It is a gateway between the spirit world and this one. Birth and death, together and apart, are the culmination of the occult. They are the most magical moments a person can know. That's what Mormor used to say, and bless her, she's been through both now. But, when it came to giving birth, she was unable to use her magic, and she suffered for it. Tante Tilde said the same, and Mamma even told me that Minna and I gave her trouble. Even then, that village bound its people to hopes and prayers while they watched, stone-faced and sour, making sure no one's lips moved to the ancient rhythms of galdr and that no fingers clutched amulets of amber. They chained and gagged the magic, such precious magic that could have saved so many children. So many women.

I feel a lightness in my head and a small second of nothing. It's no wonder, I think—and the next wave bursts in—that I'm in so much pain. Being a witch seems to be nothing but waves of scorching-hot pain, one after the other, crashing on a life I tried so hard to make comfortable.

I'm startled awake with the next one, suddenly aware of the urgent sensation of my body clenching. I realize I must have been asleep or passed out, and that scares me more than anything. I'm slipping. And when my shaking hands reach down to feel again for the hot liquid spilling out of me, I see it's still flowing red and viscous. And there's far too much.

I know the spell that will staunch the bleeding. I know the ritual. I know where Jon's knife is. I know the right rune. But my body is not responding to my thoughts. I cannot move. I am so filled with knowing—what I need to do, the kind of magic this baby needs right now, but my head leans back against the soft wall of the hut anyway, and my eyes flicker, then close. I'll just take a small rest first. A distant tingle reminds me that I should be fighting the urge to fall asleep, that this darkness is more than it seems, but it feels so warm and comforting, and it will only be for a moment. My head slides to the side, and I have no choice now but to let the feeling take me.

Minna

I am still running.

I have never run so much or so fast in my life. But when fatigue took over and I stopped to rest by a small spring, the witch snapped at me, making me get up and keep going.

As I approach the fell now, I start to make out the shadow of our hut through the darkness. I look around for Kaija, though I know she'll probably be asleep. I slow, realizing the incessant warnings that pulse under my skin may be for a bear or some other predator. I try to make out any shapes that are out of the ordinary, anything moving around.

Nothing.

The fell is quiet.

A tail of smoke curls up and out of the hut, which I can now see up close. My sister will be in there. I wonder if she'll be pleased to see me.

For some reason, I don't think so.

But I cannot ignore the witch's pull, not now, so I open the door and step inside.

I see Kaija there, half lying, half sitting along the wall. My first thought is that she looks peaceful, with her head leaned slightly to the side, hair black as night, just as I remember it.

But then I see the blood.

And I don't know how it's not the first thing I saw because there's a deep brown pool of it beneath her bent legs. Looking again at my sister, I see her parted lips are a pale, bloodless gray. I run to her and drop to my knees.

"Kaija," I try. Her face is limp in my hands, and when I let go, her head rolls back to where it was.

"Kaija, wake up."

She doesn't respond. Her bare knees lean to the side, dwarfed by her immense belly. She has grown so much. The last time I saw her, she wasn't even showing. Her body looked like it always did. But now, it's like she's been taken over completely. The baby has grown quickly.

I give her a shake, try calling her name again.

The witch bites at my wrist ruthlessly. I flinch, scratching at her, trying to make her leave me be. Why can't she see that I'm trying to wake my sister?

"Kaija," I try again, my voice starting to strain.

The witch bites again, only this time, she sends fire into my scarred hand, through my entire arm. I jump back, landing in a tuft of bear fur.

I catch my breath, finally understanding what the witch wants. It's what she always wants. Witching.

I stand, spin around, trying to find a stave, a stone—anything I can use. I see a box by Kaija's side, and I run over to it. My knees land in a puddle of her blood, and I allow my hand to search the box, sifting through the crumbling flower petals. Inside, I feel something hard and cold.

It's a knife. And a sharp one at that. I wrap my fingers around it, knowing what I need to do.

But what is the right rune? I don't know the right galdr either. Kaija's pale face sends sobs up and through me. Somehow, I conjure

Mormor's face, and then, strangely, Mamma's appears, too. They both arrive with a tingle that takes over everything in my body, and they're kneeling next to me, holding me. This feeling is so foreign, and yet it feels so real. I wonder if it's all me or if what's happening is some strange combination of Kaija's magic and mine. Mormor and Mamma are here with me, and it's good that they are; they're the ones who will have to remind me of the words and the ritual.

I crawl, feral and determined, over to the wall behind my sister, gripping her very sharp knife, which I know can only be from the village. I begin the jagged rune with a shaking line, carving up and down the same bone-white depression until it's deep enough. Then I scratch out two thorns, one on top of the other, that extend from above the bone line and meet it in the center and then meet again at the bottom. I drop the knife beside me.

It's not perfect, but I can feel its power already.

I reach to the ground with a free hand, and I don't have to do much because it is wet immediately, covered in blood. I didn't need to make a cut on my shoulder for this ritual; I figure Kaija's is sacrifice enough.

I smear her fresh blood onto the wall. Red soaks into the rune, and the magic comes alive even more.

I throw my arms around her then. The next moment, I am speaking words I have never heard before, and they sound like old magic as they're somehow whispered to me by Mormor or by Mamma. I can't exactly tell where they come from, but they come and they're suddenly on my own tongue. "Galath." My voice is scratched and drained, like the hollow of a tree that's dried and dead. "Malgalath." My head swims, but something is happening. I feel the itch everywhere now. "Sarathim." Kaija is heavy in my arms, and I hold her tighter. "Galath. Malgalath. Sarathim. Galath. Malgalath. Sarathim." I rock her back and forth, swallowing tears and repeating this ancient galdr that has no meaning to me but has come from somewhere deep within. I say it over and over until it's in sync with the beat of my heart, and then I realize it's Kaija's heartbeat, not mine, that I feel. And it's growing stronger.

She moans first, rolling her head from side to side.

I exhale. There's color in her lips again. She grabs my hand.

Then she's squeezing my hand so hard, I feel the bones rubbing together. And her moan turns into a deep cry that vibrates the earth below us. I look down and see no more blood spilling out of her. The spell seems to be working hard, but she has yet to open her eyes.

"I'm here," I say. I prepare for something as she grips me, but I don't know what. The whisper in my ear has changed, too. It's no longer singing the galdr. It's giving me a task.

We have stopped the bleeding, it says. *Now it's time to push.*

Who am I to fight the witching that moves me to action, the magic that runs through my blood and through my sister's?

"Kaija," I say and take her face between my hands. Her cries have subsided for the moment, and she finally opens her eyes, slowly focusing on me.

"Listen to me. You have to push now. Do you understand? It's time to push."

She says nothing but nods. Tears streak down her cheeks, and she nods again, readying herself. She is so strong. I can see it now. The blood has returned to her face, and she's tensing in preparation, breathing deeply, steadily. I understand Kaija and I are both made of witch and woman. And it will take everything we are made of to finish what we've started.

Another knuckled grip on my hand, and Kaija pushes. Her final cry is fierce but brief, and I can't believe it, but it soon makes way for another cry—this one shrill and new, coming from my arms.

The freshly blossoming sound circles the hut, finds the fire, and escapes with the remaining wisps of smoke.

Kaija

The hut is warmer than I remember it.

The baby lies in my arms, and I try to coax her to feed. She doesn't need much coaxing. She's full of energy and anticipation. My limbs—my bones—are struggling to stay upright, the exhaustion runs so deep. But her little eyes are just like Jon's, and I can't stop staring. They remind me of the sea, and of his face, and of his smile like the midnight sun.

"Your name is Jonna," I say to her. "Just like your pappa. Do you like that?"

Jonna squirms, scratches at my breast with a curled little fist. She's a hungry one. Born small, as expected for someone arriving so early into this world, she is eager to grow and has a determined cry. It's only been a few hours, but she wastes no time letting me know what she needs. I think I can already see some of my sister's will in her.

Minna hasn't slept either. She replaced my bloodied sleeping pelt with one I had left drying on the rack outside. She dutifully washed me and Jonna down as my knees and teeth chattered in the night air, then wrapped Jonna and handed her back to me before sending us right back into the warm hut.

Jonna's hunger is getting to me, too, and I try to remember the last time I ate. I can't remember much before waking up, my sister holding me, commanding me to push. A heavy tear falls onto the tiny hare fur wrapped around Jonna. She came back. My sister came back.

I don't want to dwell too much on what could have been my fate or Jonna's fate, so I don't. Instead, I stand, eyeing the bear fur on Minna's side of the hut, where, thankfully, my blood did not reach. I think I understand now that my sister isn't just reckless heat and hatred. I see she is strong. And she is one powerful witch. I am grateful she is both.

I slide Jonna's lips free and grab a long bed linen I brought with me from the village to wrap around us both. Once she is safely nestled there, tied tight and warm against my chest, I step outside.

Minna hovers over the cooking fire and fusses over a pot with her back to me. I find the basket of herbs and bring her a handful, holding my hand out like an offering.

"For the broth," I say, and she turns to take it with a small smile.

It's silent while we eat, just the hiss and whine of the fire and the baby to interrupt the wind fluttering through the birchwood. The hare meat is juicy and tender, and not for the first time, I'm amazed at how well Minna can cook. I want to ask her how she found me, how she knew I was in trouble, what it felt like. I want to ask her if she felt a pull, the way I sometimes do toward her, if she understands what she has made possible. I touch Jonna's little head, and it's soft under my hand.

The fiery leaves of the birch trees around us are muted by the darkness, and I feel protected.

"Do you—? What happened after I left? What did Tante Tilde say?" I don't know why the question occurs to me now, really, but I suddenly want to know.

Minna looks at me seriously, solemnly, and then I can see her trying to work out her response.

"Tante Tilde didn't want to burn," she says. "So she ended it on her terms."

I close my eyes. Tante Tilde, strong and safe and so like Mormor. I ache for her, though I am not surprised at her choice. "Buttercup oil, no doubt," I say. "I wonder how long she had that prepared."

A heavy silence passes between us and an even heavier wave of exhaustion. I watch my sister, seeing her afresh now that I have seen the tenderness of her heart.

"Do you remember Mamma at all?" I ask, breaking the silence once again.

"Not really."

I reach in to carefully adjust Jonna. "What about Pappa?"

"No. I don't remember Pappa at all," she says. "To me, he's just a story about a boat that never came back."

I've never heard her say anything like this before, and I feel the weight of it. She doesn't have sweet memories like I do. She only has bitter ones.

"They loved each other," I say. If he never died, I wonder what our lives would have been. Would Mamma still have burned? Would we ever have come here? I don't let these ideas escape me, but I let them simmer inside.

"What did it feel like?" Minna says.

"What?"

"When you almost—? When I found you, you were—dying." She swipes at her face.

I can't think of the best way to answer her, so I am just honest. "It felt just like sleeping."

"Were you scared?" she asks, and I remember that she may be a woman and a witch, but she is still young.

"I was. It was the most afraid I've ever been. But I wasn't afraid of dying. I was afraid to lose Jonna, afraid she would never see the beauty of this birchwood."

The firelight blinks and dances in the space between us, and I'm reminded of the night I left this place. How long ago that seems.

"Kaija, I'm so, so sorry," she says suddenly. "I was impetuous and stupid. When I cursed that village, they were strangers—they were murderers. I was red with rage after Mormor. All I could see was the fire they started under Mamma, the one they made us live with, how they tore all Mormor's happiness from her." She's looking at me through the fire between us. "I thought you might have been just saying it, that you might not really go to the village. Anyway, I didn't think the curse would hurt you. If I did, I never would have done it. I know now what magic should be. What it is. I know now what it means to do something so horrible."

I'm silent.

"I don't want your pity or even your forgiveness. I just want you to know that I'm sorry. And that I've changed. I'm—"

I move to the other side of the fire, cradling Jonna as I do. I slip my arm across Minna's shoulder and find her eyes. "It's all right now."

"No," she says. "It's not. I took away the thing you loved most, the person you loved most in the world. I took him away. I sent those people after you. They would have burned you."

To my surprise, I hear myself laugh. "No, they wouldn't."

"But you—"

"Listen. I will not lie to you." I straighten as I speak now. "I was ready to never see you again. I think I would have been happy to see you dead, honestly. It's not pretty, but it's the truth. You ripped me apart, and I was afraid I would never be whole. In fact, I didn't want to be."

Minna sits breathless, waiting for me to finish.

"But I escaped. I left that village behind, and I am the freest I've ever felt. And then you came back, my sweet, caring sister. You saved my life. You saved little Jonna. I thought I would never have anything like Jon again, and I was not wrong. This love I share with Jonna is so much more than that. Or it's just different. I cannot truly explain it. Something woke inside me as soon as I left that village. I believe it was something like what you have always had: a fierceness, a need to fight. I never had that. I always wanted things to be safe. But you helped me see that I needed to fight. That I needed strength. It made me understand I have a job to do, and that is, plainly, to live. And to love. To fight for all that life and love. For her sake."

"I'm sorry it took me so long to come back," she says, and I can only imagine what she thought when she saw me.

"You say you've changed. Well, so have I. No more running. No more wishing for something else. Now it is just me and you and Jonna and the magic of this place. Understood?" I take her hand, and I'm surprised how this small action calms me even more. "And when the spellfire burns again, you and I will toast to Mamma and Pappa—and to Tante Tilde and Mormor, who will surely be getting good and drunk up there."

⌐⊃)◁⫯⊏

The next morning is dark. I leave the baby asleep next to Minna. They look like an odd little pair, something I must get used to. But being outside without Jonna feels freeing in a way. I still feel the pull of her, her need for me and my need for her, but at least I can walk faster. I can even run. I try it out, and it's difficult but glorious.

I've got the last shreds of flower petals in my hands, and even though I'm still bone-tired, one night of sleep has given me enough energy to reach the perimeter of our little fell. I take out Jon's knife, and examine its blade, which has dulled a little since I left the village but is still quite sharp. Quickly and without ceremony, I lift my tongue and make a small slice. The cut stings, and blood fills my mouth immediately. I lean over my hands where I'm holding a cluster of the petals, letting it drip there. It's a little gruesome, seeing all this blood and feeling the throb of its source, but I've seen worse, and making a cut there is better than making a cut anywhere that would require exposing skin to the winter air. The words come easily, years of repetition behind them, though my tongue burns as I say them. "Little circle, safe from harm, protect us with this witch's charm."

I mutter it to myself several more times as I make my way around our camp. The fires Minna lit around the hut are still glowing brightly in the darkness, and I think I should throw a log or two on each to keep the animals out. It's her attempt at a protective measure, and I'm touched. Magic is a strong protector, but fire works, too. They don't always mix well together, but they can coexist, can't they? I drop the last of the petals, gold and white and streaked with red, into the snow and say the words one last time.

This little place is going to be where Jonna grows up. I wonder briefly what she'll think of it, whether she'll be like me and want something more. I vow to take her to see Riiga as often as I can. Maybe she can get to know the other children there. I vow not to make this small, desperate life her everything, so she won't have the longing in her heart like I did. I wouldn't wish that kind of longing on anyone— the kind that can't be satisfied, no matter what happens. It's reserved for the special few of us who have had something like love and then had it taken away, torn apart like a bed linen catching fire. Jonna won't know that kind of pain. To her, fire will be for cooking and keeping warm, for cozy nights when we tell stories of grand witches and even grander women. To her, fire will be life, not death. That's how it should be anyway, I suppose.

My skin tingles pleasantly. The witch inside is happy with the protective magic. She loves a good charm, doesn't she? These woods, now that I've let them, have made me a more powerful witch. I could mend a dress before, back in the village. That was easy enough. But I can fell trees and split them with my hands now, making sure they burn extra long so I don't need to collect as many. I can make the rain stop if I want to go out and see the full moon, and I can make it come down in blinding sheets if I want to hide in it. My skin is not itchy anymore, not like it was by the sea. The magic here is everywhere I need it to be. There's no hiding. Though I do miss my conversations with Tante Tilde and the touch of Jon's warm hands on my hips, I can't deny I feel more alive out here than I did there.

I take a seat on a soft bit of earth, enjoying the dark and the sensation of magic swirling around me. I don't think I've ever been so safe. I know it was Minna who cursed the village. I know she said the words with such hate in her heart. But I was the one who jumped into the flames, wasn't it? I gave her vengeance meaning. Without my choices, there wouldn't have been this thing between us to mend.

Despite that, I'm so happy we're mending it. She said she changed, and I think she was right. The old Minna was spit and blood. This one saved my life. She's more loving with her words, with her touch, with her magic. We've come a long way, these two sisters from the birch-wood. And yet we haven't gone far at all.

A sound comes from inside the hut.

Jonna must be awake. My breasts don't feel heavy yet, but now that I've heard her crying, I'm sure they soon will. Begrudgingly, I stand, brushing the leaves from my legs. I look down at the small pile of flower petals just behind me one last time.

That's when I see it.

The yellow petals have some brown in them, and I'm wondering why. If they were buttercups, I wouldn't have kept the stems. Protective charms only need the flower. I bend down and grab a dried stem. It's brittle between my fingers, and a small clump of petals comes loose, falls to the ground at my feet. This is not a buttercup. This is wormwood. It must be left over from something. But what?

Another sound comes from the hut. I realize it's not Jonna but Minna. I drop the wormwood and start to run because I suddenly remember what I've done.

↑ Minna

The first thing I sense when I wake up is the baby.

I know she's there because she breathes so fast, like there's not enough air for her. I open one eye to look at her, make sure she's safe in Kaija's arms, but Jonna is wrapped in pelts, swaddled in a blanket alone.

I sit up quickly.

I'm freezing even though the fire simmered all night and I shouldn't be. I wrap a fur around my shoulders and crawl over to the baby. Her tiny mouth is open just slightly, and her chest rises and falls sharply. Nothing seems to be wrong with her other than the speed of her breathing, but I wouldn't know what a baby is supposed to breathe like. How would I? I guess this is what they all do.

I lean away to cough, feeling it coming on like an urgent tickle.

I woke up once or twice during the night for a few of these coughing spells, but I don't think I woke anyone else up, thankfully, since I mastered letting the bear fur absorb the sound. As I lean away, I feel the mucus rising in my throat. I gasp once for air before coughing again. Nasty, this one. I think I'll do one of Mormor's spells for lung ailments. Maybe after Kaija gets back.

Once the tickle has subsided, I wonder where my sister has gone. Everything is still dark out there, and she must be exhausted. I'm still full from last night's hare soup and even feel rested. If it weren't for this annoying cough, I'd be feeling more myself than I have in ages.

Kaija's forgiveness—I didn't expect it. I definitely didn't think I deserved it. But there it was, held out to me in both her hands. The way we were before—no, much better than it was before. Before, we were young, and I was full of rage. It was like I had been practicing, all those times I wanted to control the weather, make big things happen, bring on the storms when I was feeling too much to contain it. It was all practice for the spell that would change everything.

Curse, Minna. It wasn't a spell. It wasn't a simple tidying ritual or a simple bit of magic to keep the nightmares at bay. It was a nightmare. It was an evil witch's curse.

Despite saving Kaija and Jonna, I still hate myself for doing what I did to Kaija's husband, this little pink bird's father. I hate myself for burning down the kirke, even though that's what I wanted all along. I hate myself for hurting Olen, too, and that one feels fresh because I know I hurt him twice. My self-examination is getting dark, I realize, and I want to bask in the happiness of last night. I want to feel that way always. Kaija doesn't hate me. She is alive, and we are together. And that's all the balm I need.

The little one stirs, and I feel a surge of panic when I see her eyes flutter. What do I do if she wakes up? She'll want something, need something. I look around the hut for a ball, a toy. I don't know what babies like to do, but there's nothing here anyway. Just me. I move closer again, and I'm hovering over her when she blinks all the way open. First one eye, then the other. It's so lazy, so noncommittal, I almost laugh. But she catches sight of me, I think.

"Hello, little Jonna," I say.

She moves her head back and forth, and it doesn't seem like she's upset at our little arrangement: a strange woman who's not her mamma hovering over her while her tiny arms and legs are bound in blankets.

"Let's see," I say, looking into her eyes. They're a deep sea blue. "Are you a witch, little one? Can you do a spell?" I smile to myself, and then I let that smile widen because I see I have her full attention now. She likes the sound of my voice. To my ears, it's brash and sharp, but I like that she hears something different.

I search the hut for something, anything, I can use. "I'll teach you one. If you're going to be a witch, you need to know a few things. First, always come prepared. Like I'm not prepared right now. That's bad." I keep hunting around for something. A rune stone, a stave, a flower.

"The second thing a witch should know is that her intention is powerful. She must aim carefully." I'm lifting pelts and bags and cloaks and hats, still searching. Finally, under the bear's head, where I slept, I find something. "See?" I say to the baby, who can barely see me. If I lose her interest, she could start crying, and then it would all be over.

"Now, what kind of witchy things did your mamma leave in here for us to find?" I dip a hand into the bag and pull out a drooping, dried flower with a thick brown stem. "This is wormwood," I say to Jonna. The tickle rises in my throat, and for a moment, I think it's the witch inside me excited by what I'm digging out of the bag, but then I realize it's a coughing spell coming on.

I drop the bag and lean into the ground, the furs sticking up my nose, but it's stifled and quiet, and I don't think Jonna is too bothered. I look up and find her eyes again. The tickle is still there. It's starting to feel a bit more than a tickle now. It's like the walls of my throat are constricting. I draw a breath, trying not to look concerned. Jonna stares up at me expectantly.

"Right," I say, and the words are tight. I breathe carefully, slowly. After this, it's Mormor's healing spell for me. I reach my hand into the bag again. This time, I feel powder at the bottom. I pull out a small pinch of it. My throat clenches tightly, and my hands fly to my neck, hoping it will subside. It does, briefly, and I can squeeze a breath through. But now, my panic and curiosity are building. I want to know what my sister put inside this bag. It has magic in it, I can tell, and not her usual kind either.

Wormwood is an ugly flower and isn't often used for protective spells. Dragon's blood, which is what I think the powder is, that's definitely for dark magic.

I draw a slow, intentional breath and reach into the bag for a third time. This time, my fingers close around something pointed and hard. Out it comes, with my hand caked in the bloodred powder, and at first it looks like something I should give to Jonna. It's a small stick with two runes carved roughly into it.

I look at it closely, and I draw a breath as sharply as I can. The top rune is inverted. It's a vertical line with two branches stemming from its left, reaching downward. The bottom rune is also inverted. It, too, is a vertical line, but the top and bottom points both have jagged lines coming out to the left. It's makeshift, but the intention is clear. These runes inverted in this way—they spell destruction, a sealed destiny.

I let out a scream with my next cough, and I can't keep the baby contented anymore, and I think she's screaming with me, and I'm afraid.

Because I know now that I'm going to die.

Kaija

She's going to die. She's going to die.

I'm repeating these words to myself as I run back to the hut. My feet lift high over branches and leaves, and I almost tumble head-first into one of Minna's protective fires. The short distance between my sister and me feels so much farther than it needs to be right now. I never lost sight of the hut, so why am I not there yet? Time and space stretch out in front of me, slowing me, so I can think about what I've done.

Jonna is in there. That's another thought that arrives while I lift my feet, trying not to stumble on the uneven earth. My baby is seeing the horror of what I've done. I can hear Jonna's crying now, like a wailing, like she's been betrayed. And she has, hasn't she? I can't hear Minna anymore, and that is the most worrying of all. My last step is through the door, which slams against the hut walls, reverberating behind me. She's there—Minna—hunched over the bear's head, like she wants to tell him a secret, like she's giving the dead bear her last words.

"Minna." It's all I can think to say. I see her tangles of morning hair hanging over her face, I hear my baby crying nearby, but all I can think to say is her name. And then she turns, looks at me. I stumble again, backward this time, because on her face is something I've never seen there before. Her eyes are shards of something sharp. Her neck and her hands are covered in red, and she barely has the strength to do anything other than reach in my direction. She's wild now, and she is dying.

I blink away my own fears and dive toward her, lay her back on the bearskin. I see the small black bag, which I grabbed from among Jon's things months ago, brought here, and turned into a weapon of dark magic. I see the small birchwood stave in her hand, carved with the sharp blade that once belonged to my husband. Her hand is loose around it, and her palms are stained red. Dragon's blood powder. That's what's on her neck and hands. The idea that it's not her own blood but a crushed herb should make me feel more at ease, but it doesn't. It makes me feel more afraid than ever. The dark sky outside, the dimness of this small hut, the screams of my child—it's all too much.

I'm so grateful when Minna reaches for my hand again with what little strength she has. Without that small reminder of what I need to do, I might have floated away on a cloud of my own regret and confusion and fear. But Minna's hand is warm, and it makes me think of what I wasn't able to do for Jon. I listen to my sister's sea wave of a breath, and I look into her eyes—they're cracked ice—before I start the healing charm.

I'm fumbling through the words, and I try to keep my own face bright enough so she doesn't see how much I'm losing hope. Minna's coughs are wheezes now, and then there's a sputter, and she coughs blood right into me. It splashes my face, my shirt, my hair. This is the second time I've watched someone die of this, the second time I've worn the blood of someone I love.

"Finally," I shriek, and it's because the witch inside me has woken. She sees what's going on, and she wants to help. It's just what I need because I feel my own throat closing—not with dark magic but with tears. But the witch beneath my skin propels my hands into action. I take the stave from my sister's hand and turn it so the runes are right side up. I let myself, for a small selfish moment, believe this is the way I wanted her to see it. This is the way I intended the magic to be produced, but I cannot lie to myself. I can't even lie to the witch inside me because she knows what we did. Carelessly, though, we thought this kind of witching would expel the source of evil from this place, but we didn't think about what might have to be expelled with it.

The galdr comes out of me, but it's not beautiful. It's barely audible because it's soaked in my tears. My tongue is swollen, and my throat is choked, and my nose is stuffed with regret. Minna's face is losing color now, but she's holding her eyes on mine. The last line of the incantation comes out in a wet jumble of sounds, but it's done now, and I'm blowing into her mouth, just as Mormor used to do when either of us had a cough. I'm blowing and stroking her hair and blowing harder still, trying to fill her with it.

She blinks her eyes closed and then open and then closed again, and I wonder if my magic is enough.

Mormor

When Odin traveled through Midgard alone, he was lonely, and so he created two wolves to be his companions.

Are you listening, Barnebarn? Sit down, Minna, and put that knife away. You're making us all nervous.

These two wolves were called Geri and Freki, and they crossed Midgard with Odin. Kaija, stop playing with those flowers and listen. This is a very important tale.

Now, one day, Odin realized his wolves struggled to find their own food in these vast lands, and so he went to seek the wisdom of the god Mimir. Mimir—quiet now, and listen—told him that yes, he would be happy to offer his wisdom in the form of two magical ravens. However, to access Mimir's wisdom and receive his gifts, Odin would be required to sacrifice one of his eyes.

Now, Odin considered this and finally determined that he trusted Mimir's wisdom so much, he would happily give up his eye to have it. So he cut out his eye—hush now—and was ready to accept the birds.

Finally, Mimir gave them over to the half-blind Odin: two magical ravens, both black as night. One was called Huginn and the other was

Muninn. Do you want to know what he did with these ravens, how they helped him and his wolves?

I will tell you if you sit down now, Minna. I'm waiting. Thank you.

Well, of course, the ravens helped the wolves find the meals they needed to survive. Their eyes were very good, you see. And they not only helped the wolves, but they helped Odin, too, who sent his two wise ravens out every day at dawn. They flew through the nine realms, gathering all the day's knowledge they could. Then, at dusk, they came home to Odin and told him the news.

I see it, Kaija, yes. It's beautiful. You know, your ancestors' spirits are up there. They're dancing and singing. That's why there are so many different colors.

Now, why do you think I am telling you about Odin and his wolves and ravens? You must know these stories of our gods, both of you, because they can show you the way when you need guidance. Just as Odin sought guidance from others around him—gods and even animals—you must seek guidance. And just as Odin kept his wolves around for nourishment and hunting, so must you seek help sometimes for your own nourishment and hunting. Do you understand?

All right, I'll explain it a different way—oh, that red is just breathtaking, isn't it? What magic out here tonight. Barnebarn, listen. Yes, one winter night, you will dance up there, too. Won't that be fun? But not tonight. Tonight, we will stay right here in this clearing together and watch.

Kaija, Minna, you must know this: No one is enough just on their own. Not even the god Odin was enough, so why should you be? We must lean on one another; we must rely on the gifts and sacrifices made by the ones we love. That's how we will survive. This lesson is exactly what most people have forgotten.

But you cannot forget. The two of you are witches. You will need each other if you are to survive.

Minna

It took me one full day to wake up. At least, that's what Kaija told me. She said she cried and cried and didn't sleep at all.

The old me would have reveled in my sister's regret, but not now.

I dreamed of Mormor when I was dying. I suppose it wasn't a dream, though, since I wasn't asleep but dying. It was a memory. Kaija and I were young, and Mormor was telling us we needed each other to survive.

I can't believe she told us that from the start. Why did we choose not to listen to her until now?

When I woke that day, I felt Kaija near me. I felt her magic mingling with mine before I could even feel myself breathe properly. She leaned me up and put her forehead to mine.

"Minna," she whispered then. "I can't—I'm so sorry. I forgot about—I was so angry then—"

Her words were choppy like a bird's chirps, and I remember shaking my head. I pushed her back, looked her straight in the eye. Her face. She was so filled with worry. I could see where the tears had all but carved rivers in her cheeks.

"Now we are even," I said.

That morning feels like a lifetime ago. In reality, only two months have passed.

We hugged and celebrated that night, bathing little Jonna in the moonlight. Then we both slept for what felt like an eternity. Kaija woke only to feed Jonna. I woke only to feed the rest of us. Jonna woke only to feed herself. And that's how we passed those first few weeks. Regaining strength.

Soon, even though the weather was starting to turn, snow clouds accumulating heavily over the birchwood, we became stronger.

I hunted and cooked; Kaija nursed and salted and dried and preserved everything she could before the winter. We both chopped firewood, hauled it home. It felt good to breathe the cool, thin air.

After a few weeks, I even felt strong enough to journey down to the sea and see a dear friend. I brought three fresh wolverine furs and some dried elk meat from my most recent hunts, and I stayed for a week. Olen was there, rowing his boat to shore with Riiga. He actually ran up the beach to wrap me in a tight hug. Dropped his oar and ran.

It feels different having a friend who's only a couple of days away from here. Like I'm not just destined for darkness and despair but for laughter and maybe some lightly flaked cod once in a while.

As Kaija and I walk now, the warm hut disappears behind us. I have the bear wrapped around me twice, and yet somehow the cold still stings at me. But it stings in a way that reminds me I'm alive. I'm alive, and it feels magical. I'm strangely light, like some heavy weight has molted from my shoulders and exposed something new, something soft and reborn, underneath.

Kaija holds Jonna next to me, and we're almost there. She keeps checking inside her cloak to make sure the baby is all right, that she's still asleep. And she keeps stealing looks at me, too. We walk in step, and our steps are certain because we've walked this route a thousand times.

The birchwoods are silent, and I can see my breath in front of me. The moon is a sliver, barely there, and yet we're lit up by the brilliant sky above. Once we reach the clearing, we'll see it in all its glory.

And what a reward it is.

The spellfire is the brightest I've ever seen it. It's dominated by green tonight, though a mystical blue trails after the green in a piercing blaze. We take a seat in the snow, and then, shivering, we lie back. The fur cushions my head, and I start to warm up. Kaija rocks back and forth and hums to Jonna.

I'm reminded of Mormor's lessons when we were girls, when we would listen but get distracted by things children get distracted by. I would wonder if Mamma lived up there in the spellfire just like Mormor said she did, dancing with the gods and our ancestors.

"A toast," I say, sitting up and pulling the wine from my cloak.

I hear my sister laugh, and I'm not sure why, but it reminds me of Olen. I think I will invite him here to stay for a while, once the winter is over. It will feel right to have the people I care about all together around our little cooking fire.

The idea of it settles my heart, and my body sinks into this new calm.

"To Mormor and Tilde and Mamma and Pappa and Jon and everyone else we love," I say, and I take a drink. "Keep dancing until we get there."

I pass the flask to Kaija, and she sips, too. "But don't expect us anytime too soon." At the sound of Kaija's voice, Jonna cackles, and my sister and I exchange a quick look because it's such a witchy sound.

I wonder if I'll have anything to teach little Jonna when she's old enough to sit still and listen, old enough to gape at these heavenly colors with her own awe, old enough to be her own witch.

But I already know I will.

I think I've known for some time what my lessons will be. I will teach her about power and restraint and sacrifice and sharing.

She will have to know it all. To understand, she'll have to know her mother's story, her mormor's story, her oldemor's story, and those of all her ancestors. She'll need to know the stories of the gods, of the nine realms, of the magic that lives beneath her own skin. But Kaija will tell her that much; I know she will.

Suddenly, I feel something skitter along the scar on my hand. I look down at my side, and there, on the green-glowing snow reflecting the spellfire, is the witch's cloth I lost more than a year ago. Its fresh linen has somehow escaped the darkness of this past year, and it sits next to me, clean as the day I cut it, patient and unassuming. I lift it and tuck it into the little bundle wrapped tightly to my sister's chest. I can't see the baby's face—she's all fur—but she squirms at the feel of my mitten on her skin.

That's when I realize I'll have to tell Jonna my story, too, even the parts I won't want to because they're dark and it will hurt that she knows. But I must tell her the stories that have brought us here.

These stories are the only ones that matter. They are the stories she'll need if she's to survive.

They are the stories she'll need if she is to live.

Author's Note

Dear reader,

Truthfully, the story of two sister witches tumbled around in my mind before I understood where these women needed to be situated in time and space. Then, I learned just how sinister the witch trials in northern Norway were in the seventeenth century, and I became completely entranced. There was so much about these witch trials that horrified me and begged me to dig deeper.

In Finnmark, the northernmost region of Norway, nestled cozily up into the in the Arctic Circle, 137 people were accused of Trolldom (witchcraft) in a span of less than one hundred years. Of those accused, 92 were killed, either by execution or by dying while in custody. This may not sound like a high number. After all, roughly 12,000 people were executed across Europe during the witch hunt years. But in a region with a population of only about 3,200 at the time, this would have been an incredibly high ratio of people accused and executed for witchcraft.

Some years, more than 10 people were killed in a "chain" of accusations. Once one woman was accused, it was common for that accusation to lead to other accusations in the village and neighboring villages, although Sami men and women often were accused randomly and not as part of a chain of accusations, and Norwegian men were largely left out of the accusations altogether. Horribly, a few Sami men did not even make it to their sentencing because they were murdered while in legal custody. Some of the indigenous traditions that Sami men and women practiced, like the use of rune drums, for instance, were considered to be some form of sorcery or witchcraft by the Norwegian authorities at the time, which likely meant that any Sami people living amidst Norwegian communities had to take care to shun or at least hide many traditional beliefs and practices, lest they be accused and killed for it. Terrible bigotry is at fault in these cases of Sami accusations and murders, and these stand out as distinct in some ways from the killings of Norwegian women accused of witchcraft.

There are plenty of theories today about what could have caused such an uproar over witchcraft during this period. Some blame ergot, a fungal contamination of wheat and barley that caused hallucinations. Others claim that the harsh environment of the arctic and the dependence on weather caused people to blame witches for their misfortunes. Others blame religion and power and good old-fashioned misogyny. Most likely, it is a combination of all these factors.

So much of Europe was plagued by witch trials, many of which are well covered in history books and fictional stories. If you want to go back in time and start analyzing the *why*, I would point you to a fifteenth-century treatise on witchcraft, *Malleus Maleficarum* or *The Witch Hammer,* written by a Catholic inquisitor. This treatise explained who were most likely to be witches (women), how to find witches, and what lawmakers and communities should do when they were caught. This was, of course, the text that explained that women were more susceptible to the temptations of the devil because they were the weaker sex—a claim that formed (or perhaps only confirmed) the foundation of the misogyny that pervaded the witch trials throughout Europe, including Norway. This text wasn't necessarily referenced in the witch trials of Finnmark, but many of the concepts were certainly consistent, which makes it tough to argue that this text did not play a role.

Bringing us closer to the setting of this particular story, in 1617, Christian IV of Denmark and Norway issued a royal ordinance condemning witchcraft, which intensified the witch trials in this region.

From 1600 to 1692, witchcraft panic swept eastern Finnmark, largely in the towns of Vardø and Vadsø but in other surrounding villages as well. Basically, this decree criminalized witchcraft, and the result was witch pandemonium in Scandinavian communities.

A quick word on sexism, torture, and absurdity: 78 percent of those accused and 81 percent of those killed in this region during this one-hundred-year span were unsurprisingly women. Accused women would often denounce friends, neighbors, and acquaintances as witches. Why? The most conceivable explanation that I have seen is, of course, torture. Women accused of witchcraft were arrested and usually tortured, forced into making outrageous claims that they had made some kind of pact with the devil. These women were tortured into admitting that they'd lain with the devil or turned into ravens to fly to an evil mountain to drink beer and celebrate the devil. It got weird but was taken as truth. For an in-depth analysis of the actual court records that remain, I highly recommend reading any of the research and books by Liv Helene Willumsen, an incredible scholar who has written widely on this topic.

So there's a little historical context for you. My intention is not to leave you with despair. I actually think exploring histories like this one sheds light on struggles of power that are still prevalent today in various ways. And bringing in a little magic—which, in my opinion, gives power to the otherwise powerless—flips the narrative on its head, making us question who has power and what they should do with it when they're allowed to wield it at will.

The story of Kaija and Minna is not fact but fiction. We can never truly know what people from the past thought or felt, but we can guess. And it's the guessing that is sometimes fascinating enough to write a story about.

Thank you so, so much for reading.

Chelsea

Reading Group Guide

1. What are some differences in Kaija's and Minna's magic at the beginning of the novel? What do these differences say about themselves and their relationship with each other?

2. Minna casts a dark curse on the village Kaija is traveling to because of her anger. Do you think her actions are justified considering what was done to her family? Why or why not?

3. Mormor tells Kaija that "Not even magic can temper pain in our hearts." Describe the ways in which this idea manifests throughout the story. How do both Minna and Kaija learn this lesson?

4. Minna sees an ominous vision of her sister burning at the stake. What emotions does this stir up in her? Given her animosity toward her sister, were you surprised at the actions she took throughout the rest of the novel? Why or why not?

5. Kaija is met with nothing but coldness from the townsfolk when she marries Jon. Why were they skeptical of her? If you were Kaija, how would you have handled being treated as an outsider in your new home?

6. Minna is quick to trust Olen and show him her powers. For some-
    one who knows the hatred that people hold toward witches, why
    do you think she did this? What does this moment between them
    change in Minna for the rest of the story?

7. Kaija discovers that Minna's curse is behind all the deaths in the
    village, including her husband's. Though she's angry, in time she
    finds a way to forgive her. How did this make you feel? Do you
    think Minna deserves to be forgiven for her actions? More broadly,
    what role does the theme of forgiveness play throughout the novel?

8. What role does religion play in this story? How is the witchcraft
    of Minna and Kaija at odds with the Christianity of the village?

9. As Minna's heart begins to open, Kaija's heart begins to grow
    fierce. Think of all the ways that Minna and Kaija's positions have
    switched by the end of the novel. Is this the way you thought both
    of their stories would go?

10. Minna and Kaija call the powers inside them their "inner witch."
    Why do you think they speak as if their powers are separate enti-
    ties? What do you think your own inner witch would be like?

11. Minna and Kaija end their story in the same place they began it:
    in the birchwood. What is different now about their home in the
    trees? Did the end of their story satisfy you?

A Conversation with the Author

Your novel takes place in such a unique historical moment and setting: Norway in the seventeenth century. What inspired you to write this story in this specific time and place?

The story of these two sisters whose lives were defined by their mother being burned at the stake came to me separate from time and place, in a way. Or at least, that was how it seemed. But I knew these sisters needed to live somewhere isolated, somewhere life was difficult. After doing a little digging about witch hunts in Europe, I learned just how intense the witch trials and executions in northern Norway were, especially for women, of course. I have Norwegian family heritage, so maybe in part that helped, but that remote, arctic setting felt like the only location this story could take place.

There are so many theories about why the Finnmark witch hunts were so intense, but one is that the isolated landscape and harshness of the environment meant that there were lots of natural disasters—storms and capsized boats and lean seasons—that seemed to require explanation. Witches were the perfect scapegoat, I suppose. Anyway, the zoomed-in look at human cruelty that happens in this story had to take place in the northernmost stretches of the European continent during a time when nature dictated that survival for anyone was not necessarily a given. To me, it seemed like the only possibility.

The magic within the narrative draws heavily upon Nordic myths and legends. What was your research process like, and how did you decide what magical elements to incorporate into Minna and Kaija's story?

Oh, I became completely obsessed with Nordic folk magic, diving into some really in-depth videos and books. The thing is, people have been doing folk magic forever, basically, because it's essentially been used as remedies for illnesses and childbirth and other challenges of being a human forever. Paganism is chock-full of folk magic, and Scandinavian history is chock-full of paganism. I knew I wanted magic that was closely tied to the earth and the elements—partly because I'm just naturally into that stuff but also because it fit the time and the place.

Some of the magic, especially the way the sisters used their runes and a few of the spells, was inspired by modern witchcraft and Wiccan-type practices, again because I'm into runes and alternative ways of seeing the world and because they're the kind of practices that are irresistible to me as a writer. They're so tangible and symbolic. I filled in some of the gaps with good old invention as well because, while I wanted to pay due respect to folk magic, I needed *magic* magic to happen in the story.

Oh, and weirdly, some of the magic the sisters use in the story came from a few of the actual written witch trial accounts from seventeenth-century Finnmark. There were certainly some strange depictions of what people thought witchcraft entailed in those accounts, especially in some of the "confessions" those accused of witchcraft gave (given under duress and torture, mind you). Sex with the devil, drinking beer with the devil, doing other weird stuff with the devil, and then turning into a bird and carrying out his evil here on earth—stuff like that. But there were some small "spells" that a few of the accused mentioned that I thought were more realistic feeling, and I did incorporate some of that into the magic Minna and Kaija used.

Did you find any parallels between Minna and Kaija's world and our own reality while you were writing? Was there anything that surprised you?

Loads. Being outcast, physically or socially, from a majority group is a huge parallel. Good old-fashioned sexism, blaming others for things that have gone wrong, the desire to fit in, the desire to burn it all to the ground, the pain of losing a loved one to violence, herd-mentality (even when the mentality is completely absurd)—those are just some of the themes that I think came up for me. I am curious to know what parallels others discover as they read through.

Witch trials seem so distant for us I think. They seem particularly strange maybe because of the incredibly weird associations: *Oh, my cow died unexpectedly, and I am mad at you; therefore you are a witch.* And maybe, too, because of the undemocratic and downright unfair "trials" these victims faced. (Don't even get me started on the water ordeal!) But if you take out the references to the devil and the belief in magical occurrences, really it's just bigotry and power dynamics at play. The influence of power on what's deemed right and wrong, and on who wins and loses, is incredibly relevant today.

Also, I hate that the term "witch hunt" has weirdly been turned on its head in our modern society and has lost some of its meaning. The people who were persecuted in the witch trials were very often executed. Killed. Murdered. I personally feel disturbed that we've extracted this phrase from its origins.

Why do you think Minna and Kaija's story is important to tell, and what do you hope readers will get out of the novel?

One thing I was really interested in exploring was the lasting impact of our actions. If cruelty uproots your family, if violence is part of your history, then what are the implications for your future? I think each sister explores this concept in different ways, just as people today explore their lives in different ways depending on their family or cultural histories. But people do not live in a vacuum. Not even Minna did. Her actions, though they may be reactionary, still have an impact, just like all of ours. I think the modern-day solution to this might be therapy and not, you know, deadly magic, but I do think reflecting on our actions is critical.

Another important part of the story, I think, is the impact of power. Clerics and religious leaders used power throughout Europe during this period to essentially bully pagan practices out of cultures. Now, this is super nuanced and dependent on the situation and people involved in all cases, and this is my own interpretation of historical events, but I think it points to something crucial: power is hard to see when it's doing its thing. And it can be incredibly destructive, be painful, and have lasting effects when it goes ignored and unquestioned for any period of time.

I hope readers will close this book feeling satisfied for Kaija and Minna, if not happy for them. There is a lot of moral gray area explored in this story, so it may not be a straightforward feeling, but maybe there's a message in there about choosing to be together instead of apart and holding ourselves accountable for our actions.

Or, if not all that, for those who have sisters, maybe just give her a hug!

What does your writing process look like? Are there any ways you like to find inspiration?

My writing process is eclectic. It honestly depends on what I am writing and what stage I am in. The first draft of this book was brought to you with the help of a hot and un-air-conditioned June, homemade chocolate (for some reason I thought this would be healthier...), and eight-hour power-writing days.

Edits were slower and more methodical. Historical and other

research happened a little beforehand but a lot during the revising process, once I really know what the story was. This is when the specifics begin to snap into place like puzzle pieces and I finally had that satisfied feeling.

Inspiration for me, honestly, comes from two things. First, I'm a naturally observant person, always have been. I'm kind of obsessed with what other people are thinking and feeling all the time. I've unintentionally been studying humans my whole life, which gives me lots of material for inventing them on the page. Second, I read and watch things. I become inspired by a surprising story structure or a beautifully written passage. And I love a good character relationship.

What are you reading these days?

Currently, I am reading *The Lighthouse Witches* by C. J. Cooke. It's dark and creepy, and there are characters (sisters!) of all ages that I'm connecting with. I'm also reading *The Unseen* by Roy Jacobsen, which is a book I picked up while traveling in Norway. It's a historical story that follows a family on a remote island and is the first of a series. It's simple and beautiful and clever. I highly recommend both books.

Acknowledgments

This story grew from a desire to write about sisters who happened to be witches. In the end, it has become so much more than that, and there are some people who have to be thanked.

First, thank you to the incredible positive force that is my editor, Jenna Jankowski, who discovered me on Twitter of all places and then expertly helped me sculpt this story into one that sparkled. Special shout-out to my dazzlingly astute production editor, Jessica Thelander, and the talented Stephanie Gafron and Lisa Marie Pompilio. I am in awe of your visual powers. Thank you also to Cristina Arreola, marketer extraordinaire, and the whole Sourcebooks family, who championed this book and worked so hard to get it out into the world. And thank you to my lovely and supportive agent, Nicole Cunningham, for having my back through it all.

Here's to Brynn Vollmer, Courtney Iversen, and Samantha Santamaria, the inspiration for the fictional sister relationship in this book (and for inspiring most things I do, really). No, I didn't base the characters on any of you. (Or did I?) Courtney gets special recognition for listening to my plot problems on long walks, reading this story first in its raw form, and making me blush with her praise. ("It was like reading a real book!")

Thank you to my dad, who introduced me to the magical world of books and stories and libraries. And thanks to my mom, for saving all the koala stories I wrote as a seven-year-old, reminding me about my lifelong dream, and being my biggest fan before a single word was ever written. And to the rest of my amazing family—I have so much gratitude for your support and for your joy about this story becoming a Book. I love you all.

I also want to make sure I thank my dear friends Kelly Kellermann and Jen Stier, who both took me seriously as a writer even before I did, and whose wisdom and bookish opinions I admire.

And of course, to Ryan, who threw sticks for the dog and brought me meals while I sweated out drafts and fretted about edits: You have cheered me on, lovingly noodled ideas with me, and kept me going through it all. Don't think I haven't noticed. I have, and I'll be grateful forever. I love you. Here's to our next chapter.

About the Author

Chelsea Iversen has been reading and writing stories since before she knew what verbs were. She loves tea and trees and travel and reads her runes at every full moon. Chelsea lives with her husband and pup in Colorado. This is her debut novel.